COCAINE CATASTROPHE

Some stepson of Satan has set me up! Camellion thought, as the Mexican captain waved the bag of cocaine in his face. The Death Merchant saw that five of the narcs had holstered their weapons. Only Squinty Eyes, with the sub-gun, and Baggy Britches, holding the Condor automatic, had him covered.

"Is it all right if I smoke?" the Death Merchant asked.

"He's clean," Squinty Eyes said. "They're only cigars —cheap ones."

Take six deep puffs to light the cigar, then count normally to seventeen. . . . A split second before he reached seventeen, the Death Merchant tossed the cigar across the room. It exploded before it hit the floor.

The concussion was so strong the window rattled. Camellion twisted a machine gun from one of the startled narcs. The Death Merchant's stream of 9-millimeter projectiles exploded suit, shirt, undershirt, and flesh, slug-smashing Squinty Eyes to his back on the coffee table.

The Mexican captain was next in line to be scratched from life. The captain probably didn't feel it when flesh and teeth flew from his face and a giant gush of red jumped from the hole in his throat. He jerked like a rag doll and fell sideways against Baggy Britches, who slid to the floor leaving a large smear of blood on the door.

Who said Mexico couldn't be fun? the Death Merchant thought as he counted three down and four to go. . . .

The Death Merchant Series:

#26 in the incredible adventures of the

DEATH MERCHANT
THE MEXICAN HIT

by Joseph Rosenberger

PINNACLE BOOKS   LOS ANGELES

DEATH MERCHANT #26: THE MEXICAN HIT

Copyright © 1978 by Joseph Rosenberger

An original Pinnacle Books edition, published for the first time anywhere.

ISBN: 0-523-40118-3

First printing, January 1978

Cover illustration by Dean Cate

Printed in the United States of America

PINNACLE BOOKS, INC.
One Century Plaza
2029 Century Park East
Los Angeles, California 90067

This book is dedicated to
C.L.K.,
who recently retired from the Pickle Factory,
and to
Carl Campanella, who gave help when help was
needed

Terror is nothing else than justice,
prompt, secure, and inflexible. . . .
Terror without virtue is fatal!
Virtue without terror is powerless!
> Robespierre
> February 5, 1794

The unrealist always involves himself
with complicated solutions to the
problem of terrorism. The realist,
going straight to the heart of the
matter, knows that there is only
one cure for terrorism—kill any
terrorist by *any* means possible.
> Richard J. Camellion
> July 6, 1974

Chapter One

The three days that Richard Camellion had spent in Magdalena had not been boring, notwithstanding the fact that, in keeping with his cover as a tourist from England, he had been forced to act as though he were a complete stranger to *Los Estados Unidos Mexicanos*—the Mexican United States—its customs and its people. This pose had required that he ask any number of ridiculous questions in broken, phrase-book Spanish and take innumerable photographs with his Mamiya 35mm camera.

He had, however, accomplished his primary objective: he had made contact with Salvador Bunuel and Emilio Moncada, the two DEA informants. Neither man had reported anything of value. Camellion had not been surprised. Since last year, when the Mexican army had struck at the narcotics network in Magdalena, the traffic in drugs in northern Mexico had become extremely secretive.

Nor had monotony marred the flight from Magdalena to Mexico City. For one thing, "Justin Alfred Lawrence" had been too busy being alert to succumb to boredom. For another, this was a nice time of the year to visit Mexico City. During January, the average low was a comfortable forty-two degrees. A third reason was that the Death Merchant, in spite of his "at-home" familiarity with Mexico, continued to be fascinated with the nation. The physical contrasts of the country were overwhelming. Geographically, what was true in one place became false a few miles away, a few hundred feet higher or lower, because rainfall, soil and elevation created variations in flora, fauna, and men, making everything suddenly new and different.

There were the people—another study in contrasts. Mexico is a *mestizo* nation, a people of mixed blood whose character is composed of two contradictory elements: tradition and revolution. Tradition enters into the smallest everyday things of life. The bloodshed of revolutions has made the Mexican value independence, stability, and continuity. Yet the Mexican is a paradox, an inconsistency to even himself. For example, he may be devoutly Catholic, or he may be bitterly anticlerical. Or he may be, as many Mexicans are, both Catholic *and* anticlerical!

1

Riding in a cab from the airport to the Maria Isabel-Sheraton, where a small suite of rooms had been reserved, Camellion reflected on the areas of uniformity and agreement that existed in Mexican society. He admired the Mexicans for being a strong family people—a closed unit against the world. Women, for the most part, led lives that were cloistered and protected. But unlike American women, Mexican women permitted their husbands to completely dominate them—all evident in the *casa chica*, or "little house," the separate extramarital establishment for the husband's pleasure. Yet the *casa chica*—common in all levels of society—was so deeply rooted in the mores of society that the custom did not impair the sanctity of the home.

Mexican children were always reared in a tight cocoon of discipline and affection, usually with agreeable results; the Death Merchant was fond of saying that all the world's children should be required to be Mexican until the age of sixteen.

I suppose stoicism—either military or political—is the highest Mexican virtue. And their fascination with the macabre, with the circumstances and trappings of death, is unusual! The Death Merchant reasoned that this preoccupation with Old Rattle Bones was a logical development from the executions of the Spanish Inquisition, which had functioned in Mexico until the early nineteenth century, and from the human sacrifices of Indian Mexico.

Amazing! concluded Camellion. *One of Mexico's most popular holidays is the Day of the Dead, when deceased forebears are honored ceremoniously and children are given candy skulls to eat. Considering my nickname, I should feel right at home, and I do! As the Mexicans say, "Como Mexico no hay dos!" I agree! There is no other country like Mexico!*

Camellion checked in at the Maria Isabel-Sheraton and unpacked his British-made Carry-All flight bag. The two-room suite—bedroom and a sitting room—was adequate. He didn't intend to do any entertaining. The only thing that irked him was that, without firearms, he felt half-naked and vulnerable.

He left the bedroom, walked to one of the windows in the sitting room, and looked out over the Avenida Juarez, one of Mexico City's main thoroughfares. Directly across from the hotel was picturesque Alameda Park. Camellion didn't foresee any immediate problems. Today was Friday, the

20th. He was right on schedule. Tomorrow afternoon, like any interested *turista*, he would visit the National Natural History Museum, at the northwestern section of Chapultepec Park. In the Maya-Toltec section he would just happen to meet Rossana del Moreno, who worked for Polar Cold, Inc., the American company located in Mexico City and owned by the Central Intelligence Agency.

Senorita del Moreno would not know him—*But I will definitely recognize her from having studied her photographs, taken at all angles. I'll decide when to meet Moore and Eubanks after going over the situation with her. Either I find and kill The Parrot, or the mission will fail.*

Richard consulted his wristwatch; it too had been manufactured in Great Britain. 1:53 P.M.—midway in the hours when Mexicans took the midday meal. He went to the bathroom, washed his face and hands, took several vitamin pills, then went back into the bedroom. Making sure that the two cigars were in place, he slipped into his sports coat, left the suite of rooms, took an elevator from the fourth floor to the lobby, and strode into the hotel's dining room, which was not overly crowded. He ordered a small steak, a large salad of *tomate-jitomate* and *nopal*, and, for desert, *ananas*, or pineapple, mixed with *zapote*, a soft green-skinned fruit with black pulp. The *zapote* tree is the source of chicle, from which chewing gum is made.

Camellion had time to burn. He ate leisurely, ordering a third cup of *epazote*, an herb tea, and lingering over it.

It was almost 3:30 by the time Camellion returned to his rooms. He had just closed the door and was fastening the chain guard in place when three men stepped out of the bedroom, all three pointing Obregon .45 pistols at him. Two men who had been hiding behind the sofa lounge stood erect and stared at him. One held a Spanish 9mm Super Star autoloader; his partner pointed a Mendoza submachine gun at Camellion, who automatically raised his arms above his head, the surprise on his face genuine.

Walking toward him from the bedroom, one of the men said in perfect English, "Senor Justin Lawrence, I am Capitan Alfaro Siqueiros of the Mexican Federal Police, from the *Departamento de Narcotico*. I arrest you in the name of the Federal Republic of Mexico. The charge is smuggling of cocaine."

Some stepson of Satan has set me up! Camellion thought,

3

but very politely he said in Spanish, "Capitan, I think that you have made a serious mistake."

"I do not think so, Senor Lawrence," Captain Siqueiros said courteously. The middle-aged Federales narcotics officer, with the big brush of a mustache, kept his .45 pointed directly at Camellion's stomach. "Stand still while we search you. I would advise you not to make any sudden moves."

Camellion did as he was told, very much aware that Mexican cops didn't give a damn about anything as silly as "civil rights." Both the Federales and the Rurales—the country policemen—had a tendency to shoot first and mumble "*Perdoneme*" later.

Richard didn't move a muscle as the two men who had been behind the couch patted him from head to shoe-soles. They were good: they patted the inside of his legs, felt around his ankles, and probed the inside of his armpits.

One of the men nodded to Captain Siqueiros just as two more Mexican narcs came in from the direction of the bathroom. One of these narcs was carrying a small brown paper packet, which was still wet and dripping water. In his baggy suit, the narc with the water-repellent package reminded the Death Merchant of a clown in a cheap Mexican movie. A triumphant look on his swarthy face, the man handed the package to Captain Siqueiros.

"*Cocaina!*" said the narc in the baggy suit. He looked from Siqueiros to Camellion.

Captain Siqueiros stared at the Death Merchant, his dark eyes accusing.

"*Como se llama esto?*" he said, and shook the bag of cocaine in Camellion's face. "We found this in the flush tank in the bathroom."

"What do you want me to call that?" Camellion repeated the question. "I say, your chap just said it was cocaine. However, I didn't put the bag there." The Death Merchant sighed. "I believe the Americans have an expression when illegal goods have been planted on a victim. I think they call it being 'framed.'"

Captain Alfaro Siqueiros and the other narcs smiled sinisterly.

"Senor Lawrence, our prisons are full of men and women who have been, as the *norteamericanos* say, 'framed.' Lower your arms and sit down, but I warn you—no tricks."

Siqueiros handed the bag of nose candy to one of the other narcs, who looked as if he needed to spend an hour in a barber's chair. The Death Merchant sat down in the nearest chair, a high-back, handwoven willow deal close to the door between the bedroom and the sitting room. All the while he measured distances and took careful note of the positions of the seven men.

Captain Siqueiros, who had found Camellion's expertly forged British passport in the bedroom, sat down on the couch, took the passport from his pocket, and began to study it, glancing at Camellion as he compared the small photograph in the book with the man sitting before him.

The agent with the submachine gun moved to Camellion's left. When he stopped, in the doorway between the bedroom and the sitting room, the muzzle of the submachine gun was only four feet from Camellion's head. Another man sat down next to Siqueiros on the sofa. There was another narc in front of the door that opened to the hallway. A fifth Mexican Fed leaned against the wall to the Death Merchant's right, while the cop with the baggy suit sat on one end of the long, Spanish-type cocktail table, his 9mm Condor *pistole* unwavering from Camellion. The seventh man stood by the window, arms folded.

Baggy Pants leered at Camellion. "Englishman, I would advise you to cooperate with us. Your sentence will be shorter if you do. You might get off with as little as ten years. Tell us where you got the cocaine. Were you to deliver it to anyone here in Mexico City?"

"Are you working with the Twenty-third of September League?" the agent by the hall door asked. "We'll find out, sooner or later."

The voice of the squint-eyed man with the Mendoza submachine gun warned ominously, "If you don't tell us now, you'll talk after we take you to headquarters. We have many ways to loosen the tongues of *Communista bastardos* like you . . . many ways."

"*Si,*" laughed the man by the window, the Mex Fed with the ragmop of hair. "*Esos Communistas! Siempre estan juntos porque son pajaros de la misma pluma!*"

The Death Merchant, remaining silent, thought of what the man had just said. *Well, 'birds of a feather might stick together'—but this bird is about to fly from the nest!*

Camellion saw that five of the narcs had holstered their weapons. Only Squinty Eyes, with the sub-gun, and Baggy Britches, holding the Condor autoloader, had him covered.

"Senor Lawrence, would you care to phone the British

5

Embassy?" Captain Siqueiros suddenly asked. His voice was mild, but wasted neither useless inflection nor unnecessary words. "You have my permission to use the phone in this room." He winked broadly and shrugged his broad shoulders. "Go ahead, *mi amigo*. Phone your ambassador."

He's a pretty sharp cookie! Camellion realized he was cornered, that Siqueiros suspected the British passport was a fake. It wouldn't be difficult for him to prove that it was! Almost smiling at the absurdity of it all, Richard decided it was time to show some smarts of his own.

Deliberately, Camellion sighed loudly, then looked forlornly at Siqueiros. "Is it true what he said?" He glanced at Baggy Pants, then snapped his eyes back to the leader of the Mexican squad. "I'll get a lighter sentence if I cooperate fully?"

"Yes, but only if you tell us the full truth," responded Siqueiros. His voice was even, but his eyes remained dark with doubt and suspicion.

Again Camellion exhaled loudly. "Is it all right if I smoke?" He pointed to the cigars in his handkerchief pocket. "A cigar relaxes me and I can think better."

Siqueiros' eyes shot up to the man with the machine gun.

"He's clean," Squinty Eyes said. "They're only cigars. Cheap ones at that."

"Very well. Smoke if you want," Siqueiros said. He closed the passport, put it in the inside pocket of his coat, leaned back, and crossed his legs. "You're an *Americano* and the *cocaina* is payment for weapons delivered to the Twenty-third of September League. Am I not correct?"

Camellion, who had taken a cigar from the left breast pocket of his sports coat, bit off one end. "I'm from Chicago," he said, faking hesitancy and making the proper "trapped" expression fall over his face. He paused deliberately and put the cigar in his mouth, confident that he had anticipated correctly because Squint Eyes had already cradled the sub-gun in his right arm and was reaching into the left pocket of his suit coat. Now the man pulled out a lighter, leaned down, snapped it on, and touched the flame to the end of the Death Merchant's cigar.

Take six deep puffs to light the cigar, then count normally to seventeen! Camellion took the sixth puff, removed the cigar from his mouth, exhaled smoke and muttered *"Gracias"* to Squint Eyes, who stepped back and started to drop the lighter back into his coat pocket—*fourteen, fifteen, six-*

6

teen . . . A split second before he reached seventeen, the Death Merchant dropped the cigar to the floor, to his left, and leaned forward.

Seventeen! The cigar exploded with a terrific *bang*, with all the force of a super-giant firecracker, the concussion so strong that the window actually rattled.

A thousandth of a second later, Pedro Niebla, the chili-pepper Fed with the machine gun, was trying to reason out how any human being could possibly move with such incredible speed. The Death Merchant had leaped to his feet, spun around, and was twisting the machine gun from Niebla's right hand. *Madre Dios!* Niebla gasped in terrible pain from the knee that came up and smashed into the pubis, the bones forming the front of the pelvis located at the bottom of the abdomen. A grenade, filled with a billion needles, exploded in his loins, and a roaring filled his ears. He was aware that the *Americano* had possession of the machine gun, but the pain prevented him from resisting Camellion, whose lightning attack had come as a complete surprise to all the Mexicans. For several seconds, astonishment held them immobile; then they swung into action. Yet those few precious seconds had given the Death Merchant the advantage. When trouble came, it was where and how fast you put the first bullet that counted most.

With the Mendoza sub-gun in his hands, Camellion threw himself forward, darted to his right, and dropped very low as Luis Calavera's Condor automatic cracked and a 9mm slug missed Richard's left shoulder by less than three inches. *Move! Keep moving!* Baggy Pants didn't get a chance to fire the second time. Camellion jumped three feet off the floor, kicked sideways with his right leg, swung the machine gun down to his left and fired.

He had used a Karate *Yoko Geri Keage* side-snap kick on Federico Esmercurio, the Mexican leaning against the wall— the heel of his foot smashing into the man's stomach. Esmercurio, his Star automatic half-drawn, gagged in intense pain, doubled over, and forgot all about trying to shoot the *Americano.*

So did Baggy Pants—forever. The Death Merchant's stream of 9-millimeter projectiles exploded suit, shirt, under-shirt, and flesh, slug-smashing Calavera to his back on the coffee table. He lay lifeless as a brick, his dead eyes staring at the cream-colored ceiling.

One of the 9mm Mendoza slugs had torn all the way

7

through Calavera's body and hissed to the left of Felipe Becerric, the narc standing by the window. In the process of drawing his Obregon .45, Becerric jerked himself to the right, lost his balance and fell heavily to the floor as the Death Merchant dropped flat to avoid two slugs tossed at him by a frantic Hernando Zumara, the Fed by the hall door, and Captain Siqueiros. Both slugs missed by almost a foot. Camellion swung the submachine gun up and around in a wide semicircle, starting with the door. Four 9mm pieces of copper-gilded lead ripped into Zumara just as the narc again fired his .357 Combat Magnum, a beautiful weapon with pearl handles. The bullet tore through the cloth of Camellion's right pants leg, several inches below the knee, then nipped into the rug. Richard couldn't have been happier. A single 158-grain Magnum bullet can split an engine block at twenty yards. Had the powerful projectile struck his leg, it would have torn it off.

Butchered, his chest a mess of bloody cloth, torn flesh, and shattered bones, Zumara sagged against the door and slid to the floor, leaving a large smear of blood and gore on the door, in which there were three holes. A fourth piece of lead was half buried in the door.

Captain Siqueiros was next in line to be scratched from life. A terrified look on his face, he was raising his .45 when one of the Death Merchant's 9mm slugs punctured his Adam's apple. Another smashed him in the upper lip. A third bullet tore through his right cheek. Stone-dead in the twinkling of an eye, Alfaro Siqueiros didn't feel it when flesh and teeth flew from his face, and a giant gush of red jumped from the hole in his throat. He jerked like a rag doll and fell sideways against Juan Redes, who in blind panic was trying to draw his Obregon autoloader and, at the same time, crawl over the back of the couch. He didn't succeed in doing either. There was another short burst from Camellion's sub-gun.

"OHhh!" Redes uttered a short cry of pain from the bullet that broke his hip and buried itself in the mush of his intestines. His head, with its jungle growth of hair, fell forward, and he never knew about the other four slugs that stomped up his left side, broke a rib, and smashed through his lungs and heart.

The Death Merchant didn't see Redes fall. He moved to one side a microsecond before Felipe Becerric, down on the floor across the room, pulled the trigger of his Obregon.

Richard could have sworn that the bullet passed so close to his left temple that he felt its heat. But he didn't have time to ponder the question. Detecting slight movement behind him, he pushed himself toward the hall door on the balls of his feet. As he shot forward, he fired a short burst at Becerric, then spun around and dropped down, just in time to keep from being killed by Federico Esmercurio, who had somehow, in spite of the agony in his stomach, gotten off a shot with his Star automatic. The 9mm almost made a bloody part through Camellion's hair; yet a near-hit might as well miss by a yard—or a mile! Camellion had not missed Felipe Becerric, who lay across the room on his face, as still as the rug.

Esmercurio was far, far too slow in his efforts to get off a second shot—too slow, too full of pain, and too clumsy.

"*Hasta luego*, Hot Tamale," Camellion said, and exploded Esmercurio's face and head with a six-round blast. There was a loud *plop* and the Mex Fed's skull came apart like a jigsaw puzzle hit by a hand grenade!

Yet years of experience had taught the Death Merchant that only fools don't sop their bread in the gravy while it's still hot. He hadn't forgotten Squint Eyes, who was down on both knees, his face contorted with pain. There he was, pulling a blue-black Obregon .45 from underneath his coat!

"You're going to hell, Chili Pepper!" Camellion said as he swung the machine gun, pulled the trigger, and instantly felt like an idiot! A dull click told him that the magazine of the Mendoza was empty—*or maybe I'm going to hell!* He jumped wide to the right, a loud boom, a tug on his right shoulder, and a thud informing him that Pedro Niebla had fired, that the bullet had almost smacked him in the shoulder, and that it had struck the door.

Good God Gerty! What a gold-plated mess this is! The Death Merchant threw the now useless submachine gun with all his might, and made a dive for the Combat Magnum dropped by Hernando Zumara.

The end of the sub-gun's magazine struck Pedro Niebla on the side of the neck, the leather sling strap smacking him across the face. The empty weapon fell to the floor, and once more Niebla raised his automatic. In that extra-thin slice of a second, as his arm came up, he saw the .357 Magnum in Camellion's right hand, the yawning gape of its big muzzle belching flame. Niebla died too fast to feel pain. The powerful .357 bullet smashed him in the center of the chest, bored

9

all the way through his body and tore into the doorframe. Niebla spun around and crashed to the floor.

The Death Merchant, feeling as unwelcome as a virgin in Sodom or Gomorrah, jammed the Magnum into his belt, went over over to the corpse of Zumara and searched the body, finding a flat plastic case containing a dozen .357 Magnum cartridges. He next picked up the Star automatic that had belonged to Federco Esmercurio, dropped it into his coat pocket, then searched the dead Mexican police officer. He found two clips for the Star in a leather holder on Esmercurio's belt, dropped them into his pocket, and hurried over to the corpse of Captain Siqueiros, which was lying sideways on the couch, took two .45 clips from the dead man's belt, picked up Siqueiros' Obregon from the rug, and checked it. The automatic contained four shells, three in the magazine and one in the firing chamber.

It's time to get out of here! And go where? The entire time schedule had fallen apart. He had memorized all the necessary addresses, the nearest of which was Drive Rio De La Loza 1473—*only a few miles from here. But first I must get out of the hotel.*

Another worry was the backup force of the dead Federales in the suite. Or were the seven dead men in the sitting room the total force that had come to arrest him? Either way, the Mexican civil police had to be on the way up to the fourth floor. The racket of the gunfire must have been heard all the way to the ground floor.

Camellion removed the four shells from the Obregon, shoved in a full magazine, and cocked the automatic. With the .45 still in his hand, he opened the door and looked out. Up and down the hall, doors were open and men and women stared at him in fear. When they saw him holding the pistol, they drew back and closed the doors.

Speculating on how he had been framed and who might have done it, Richard ran down the hall. *No. Don't use an elevator. If it stalls or if they throw off the power, you'll be literally boxed in.* He soon found what he wanted: the door with the sign over it, the red letters spelling out *Salida*—Exit!

Camellion opened the door and moved out onto the landing of the service stairs. The steps led down to another landing, from which another set of stairs angled to the platform on the next lower level, and so on until the ground floor was reached. His self-preservation mechanism alert to the sudden appearance of anyone, he hurried down the stairs, careful to keep close to the wall and not to let his heels strike down hard on the serrated surface of each step. He had passed the third floor and was on his way to the second when he heard a door slam and a thump-thump-thumping below him.

Feet pounding on the steps—and more than one pair!

Camellion rushed back to the bottom of the first flight of stairs on the third floor, crouched down, took the Spanish Star *pistole* from his coat pocket, and waited by the three-foot-high concrete wall, to the top of which was attached the steel railing that served as a banister.

Within a few moments the footsteps were very loud and he could hear talking, one man panting, "All that firing! No doubt they're all dead by now."

And so are you! When Camellion judged the men were halfway up the second flight of steps, between the second and third floors, he stood up, moved to his right onto the landing, turned around and pointed both the Star and the Obregon downward. Seeing that the six men coming up the steps were members of the regular *policia,* he pulled the triggers. His first two bullets slammed into the first two men, who crashed backward into the two cops behind them. As the four men went down on the steps in a tumble of arms and legs, the Death Merchant punched the tickets of the last two cops on the stairs. They had jumped back in surprise and confusion, not comprehending what was happening. By the time they realized that they were face to face with the enemy, it was far too late. A .45 bullet tore through the dark brown uniform of one man, catching him high in the chest, while a 9mm projectile popped the cop with the Astra machine gun in the stomach. Both men fell backward, the sub-gun also falling to the landing at the bottom of the stairs.

The two Mexicans in the middle of the steps, half-buried by the first two men Camellion had scratched, tried to draw their weapons and at the same time disengage themselves from the two dead men. They might as well have tried to win a maracas-playing contest with a rattlesnake. One man got a 9mm Star slug through his left temple. The other became dead meat when a .45 projectile tore through the hollow of his throat.

With the echo of the shots stinging his eardrums and ringing up and down the stairwell, the Death Merchant threw caution to the winds, pounded down the steps, leaped

11

over the first four bodies, and landed on the metal platform. He switched on the safeties of the two automatics, dropped the weapons into his coat pockets, picked up the submachine gun and checked it, satisfied when he found that it had a full magazine.

Camellion raced down the next flight of steps to the ground level. He paused by a door that opened to a short hallway behind the large, semicircular counter used by the desk clerks at the Maria Isabel-Sheraton.

QUESTION: How do you hide a 28.7-inch-long submachine gun?

ANSWER: You don't! *And I don't have the time to linger!*

Holding the Spanish chatterbox behind his back with one hand, he opened the door with the other, stepped out into the hall and moved straight toward the main desk. He saw at once that, as a result of the gunfire in the stairwell, people were evacuating the large lobby; yet there were still some well-dressed men and women milling around, those whose curiosity had gotten the better of them. Others simply did not know what was going on. They soon found out when one of the desk clerks, who was leaving the area, saw Camellion rushing from the hallway and yelled a warning at one of the three members of the Guardia Civil—the regular Mexican police—who were standing not far from the beautiful water fountain in the center of the lobby. The clerk and several other hotel employees near him dropped to the floor and covered their heads with their hands. The three policemen, Mondagon carbines in their hands, stared around, uncertain for the moment as to whom, or to what, the clerk was warning them about! Their uncertainty ended when they saw the Death Merchant vault over the desk and land lightly on the blue marble floor of the lobby. And when they saw the submachine gun, they were positive that here was the enemy—coming straight toward them!

"He's the one!" yelled one of the cops and tried to fire his carbine. They were the last words of his life. Hunched over, Camellion raked the three policemen with a line of slugs that slammed them to the floor, the loud, irritating chatter of the Spanish Astra reverberating throughout the lobby. One cop groaned, managed to push himself up a foot from the floor; then he fell flat on his face and lay still, as dead as the other two.

However, four Mexican detectives who had just run into the lobby from the street were very much alive and filled

12

with blue-hot hatred for the man who had just gunned down three of their *compadres*. Shaking in rage, Sergeant Juan Fermepi jerked up his Mendoza submachine gun; the other three detectives reached for their shoulder-holstered Obregon .45s.

The Death Merchant dove for the side of the huge circular fountain only a wisp of a moment before Fermepi fired. One 9mm Nobeloy-gilded bullet zipped through Camellion's left pants leg, missing his ankle by an inch. Another tore through the tail of the sports coat flying out behind him. The rest of the full-metal-jacketed projectiles tore into the registration desk, except two that hit one of the revolving colored lights beside the fountain and exploded it into junk.

Fermepi assumed Camellion would try to crawl halfway around the side of the large fountain and fire from the opposite end. Accordingly, he rushed forward and, while keeping an eye on the side behind which Camellion had jumped, concentrated most of his attention on the other end of the fountain. The only thing that Fermepi had not counted on was Camellion's experience and uncanny intuition. A born survivor, the Death Merchant guessed Fermepi's incorrect deduction and staked his life that the Mexican would not expect him to fire through the huge spray of multicolored water.

The Mexican detective caught only a very brief glimpse of Camellion rearing up thirty feet away. Then he was dead from the chain of 9mm projectiles that erased his face and exploded his chest.

Diego Alegre and Rafael Landivar managed to get off a quick shot each, but both .45 slugs missed. Then they too were dead, cut down by Camellion's machine-gun fire. Vincente Inmolecto, the fourth cop, tried to jump behind a potted banana tree. Only four feet from the tree he caught three slugs with one hand outstretched and, seemingly, reaching for a tiny banana as he dropped and the eternal blackness bloomed in his brain.

The Death Merchant charged around the side of the fountain and headed for the main entrance of the hotel.

I hope there are still a few miracles left in the world!

Chapter Two

The run-down, two-story house had once been the center of a large hacienda. Then agrarian land reform, begun after the start of World War I, had broken up the large estates and reinstated *ejido*, the principle of common land ownership. All over Mexico land had been divided into plots for farming by individuals; other land was farmed communally. Non-*ejido* lands could be individually owned, but the amount could not exceed 247 acres.

Now the colonial-style house, designed around a patio, clearly revealed the ravages of the years. The latticed iron-work around the second-floor balconies was red with rust, the tiled roof, finished with the traditional crenellations, faded to a very pale pink. The archways around the long rectangular patio were cracked; the stucco, over the bricks, had fallen off in large patches.

Diego Tuchilan, the owner, could not have cared less about the condition of the house, although he could have afforded repairs. Tuchilan's main interest in life was making money; and because he loved to watch the pesos pile up in the hidden safe he had in the house, he found it not at all unpatriotic to let notorious revolutionaries, wanted dead or alive by the Mexican government, use his place as a hideout and storage-station for drugs and firearms. It was an arrangement that worked very well, since no one suspected that Senor Tuchilan would help the same communist revolutionaries he was so prone to curse in the village square of Xochimilco. Senora Tuchilan, imbued with the concept that the husband was lord and master, remained silent and pretended not to notice the strange faces that often appeared at the farm in the middle of the night.

As a precautionary measure, a secret room had been dug twenty feet beneath the patio, the entrance beginning in the vegetable cellar some fifty feet away. An escape tunnel led from the meeting and storage room to the shed—a hundred feet east of the house—used to store henequen, the hard reddish fibers derived from agave leaves and used in the production of binder twine.

Twilight had settled over the farm, with only a hint of red-orange sun showing through the palmettos west of the house. A single shaded bulb, hanging from the low ceiling on two pieces of twisted electric cord, burned over the table, at which sat Hector Mudejar and Alvar Gomara, who were drinking mezcal, and Juanita Maria Sojeda, sipping black coffee.

In one corner of the room sat Paul Torres Escutia, eating red beans and enchiladas filled with pork, his plate resting on a long crate, its sides stenciled, "M3A1. Submachine Guns. Caliber .45. Ithaca Gun Company, Ithaca, New York. United States Army. Property of the Government of the United States."

Juanita Sojeda let her eyes drift to the fat Escutia, a worried expression on her oval face. "You are sure that the radio said he escaped?"

"Of course I'm sure!" Scowling, Escutia spoke and chewed at the same time, a habit that the well-bred Juanita Sojeda despised. "The last anyone saw of the *Americano* was when he grabbed a car in front of the hotel, pushed out the driver and drove off. He shot four police cars full of holes before he roared off."

Escutia paused, took a huge bite of enchilada, then resumed speaking, both cheeks bulging. "The official police report is that the massacre was the work of a lone terrorist who is a member of the League."

"Basura!" Alvar Gomara said bitterly. "Garbage! That's all those lying *Federales* are. But what can you expect of a government that calls itself a 'Democracy' but doesn't have democracy? Now all of Mexico will think it was us who gunned down those slime." Squeezing his glass in anger, he turned in the direction of Escutia, who was wiping his mouth with the back of his hand. "What else did the newscast say? How many police were killed?"

Escutia reached for a bottle of tequila that was also on the crate of submachine guns. "Just the usual, 'An arrest is expected any moment.' I don't think they'll ever catch him. He's too good! He killed twenty of them." Escutia raised a hand and pointed a finger at Gomara. "Bam, bam, bam! Just like that."

"We have failed," Juanita Sojeda said in a flat voice. "And the fact that this American narcotics agent could kill twenty of the *Policia* and escape"—her eyes became very hard—"proves he is an extremely dangerous individual and a direct threat to our cause. Who he is doesn't really matter. It's the next shipment, our meeting with the *Americano*

15

gangsters, that counts at this point. Once the transaction is made, we'll have enough arms and ammunition for an entire army. Then, the Revolution!"

A slim woman, only 29 years old, Juanita glanced first at Gomara and then at Hector Mudejar, who sat hunched over at the other end of the table. Deep in thought, Gomara stared reflectively at the mezcal in his glass. He was like that: a moody but deadly introvert who hated capitalism and religion and was constantly planning the destruction of both. In another age, he might have been a mystic.

Smoking a cigarette, Hector Mudejar twisted his mouth and studied Juanita Sojeda. Not only did he respect her, he was afraid of this woman young enough to be his daughter. He respected her because she was extremely intelligent, very imaginative, and a Creole—a person of pure Spanish descent born in Mexico. Mudejar often asked himself why a daughter of wealthy parents—her father was an industrialist—would give up a life of security and wealth to become a hunted *Revolucionario?* Ideals? Dedication to a cause? There had to be another reason, perhaps one that even Juanita herself did not understand.

Mudejar's thoughtful eyes raked over Juanita, whose short black hair framed a thin but pretty face. She wasn't tall; yet her body was well-shaped, her breasts firm and hard. And always there was that thrusting animal vitality under her creamy skin.

The FRAP revolutionary leader feared her because once, when he made a pass at her, she turned on him in instant hate and pressed an icepick against his throat with such force that the point drew blood. *"If you ever touch me again, I'll kill you!"* she'd said. Mudejar also feared her because, as a graduate psychologist, he knew she was utterly ruthless, never giving anyone the slightest advantage. Pragmatic enough to work with the Devil—if Satan could get the job done—Juanita Sojeda dedicated herself to keeping the Mexican Federal police off balance and reaping the benefits from bombings and burnings, kidnapings and assassinations. Himself highly intelligent, Mudejar had pinpointed Juanita's weakness: she was not fascinated by the apparatus of power. In this respect she was like Che Guevara in his fight against Yanqui Imperialism: she was a pure idealist who, once the revolution was won, would be lost even to herself. Mudejar doubted if Juanita herself realized it, but it was not the anticipation of eventual victory that furnished

16

her energy and drive. It was the fight itself. Like Che Guevara, Juanita Maria Sojeda had to have a *Cause*.

"Well, Hector, what are you staring at?" Juanita demanded icily, her eyes flashing. "I suggest you put your animal instincts into the closet and consider the business at hand." With a nod of her head she indicated the scores of brown boxes stacked neatly at one end of the room, on top of, and between, wooden crates of American arms and ammunition. There were also three crates of hand grenades.

"We have six hundred and forty kilos of heroin sitting there," she said, speaking with that utter sobriety which very often masks immense apocalyptic visions. "That heroin represents hundreds of American automatic weapons, even heavy machine guns and anti-tank weapons. The American crime syndicate is just as anxious to get its hands on the drugs as we are on the weapons. They are so anxious that they are even willing to come across the border to make the trade. But now that the U.S. Drug Enforcement Administration has agents snooping around down here we—"

Juanita flinched, as if in pain, and stared in disgust at Paul Escutia when he belched loudly, but did not even have the manners to say *perdon*.

"We have made the deal with the American gangsters, and there is not really a problem," Hector Mudejar said. "All we must do is set the date of the transfer."

"The date doesn't concern me," Juanita said quickly. "It's our own police and this Yankee agent."

"Come, come, Maria. I think you are letting fear overcome your logic. The Federales and the agents of the *Departamento de Narcotico* are concentrating all their efforts on Magdalena, in the northwest, and in and around Culiacan in the central east. Why should they suspect that we would use the Barranca del Cobre in our operations? That section of the mountains is so wild and primitive that not even the Zapotec Indians go there. The Canyon of Copper is perfect for the transfer, just perfect."

"The Canyon of Copper is even deeper than the Grand Canyon in the United States," Alvar Gomara joined in. "There are no patrols on the floor of the valley. There's nothing in the area. The Federales of the Interior Service do not even patrol the Sierra Madre Western Mountains. Of course, there will be a small risk in our getting from Mexico City to Huatabampo, and from Huatabampo to the Barranca del Cobre."

Juanita Sojeda frowned. "The distance from Huatabampo to Copper Canyon is a hundred and sixty kilometers," she reminded her fellow conspirators. "The yacht of the Americanos will be in the middle of the Gulf of California, so the distance is closer to two hundred kilometers! And you call it a 'small risk'! *Ridiculo!*"

"No! The plan is not ridiculous," Paul Escutia spoke up. He got to his feet and moved toward the table, holding the bottle of tequila in one hand. In spite of the two electric fans at each end of the room, perspiration flowed freely down his triple chins. "In Huatabampo we will pose as *capitalinos* from Mexico City; our papers will be in order. It will only be natural that we should go fishing in the *Golfo de California*. We will be far enough from the coast so that no one will see us make contact with the American yacht. All of us will fly to the Copper Canyon in a helicopter which will be assembled on the yacht. I think you worry too much, Senorita. We will carry out the operation at night and the nearest Mexican Air Force base is outside Chihuahua, several hundred miles east of the mountains."

Escutia placed the bottle of tequila on the table, pulled out a chair and eased his blubbery body down next to Alvar Gomara.

Before Juanita Maria Sojeda could reply, Gomara looked at her, grinned, and said, "And if you're afraid that the American Mafia will double-cross us—ah, no! They are men of no honor and are ruthless, but still very good businessmen. They wouldn't dream of killing the goose that lays golden eggs." He laughed sinisterly, and looked at the stacked heroin. "Or in this case, the revolutionaries who lay such fine 'Mexican Brown'!"

Slender, dark-complexioned, and with a thick mustache, Gomara's overall appearance was that of an old-time Mexican *bandito* who might have ridden with Emiliano Zapata or Pancho Villa—but only because of his clothes. On his way to the farm, he had worn typical Mexican peasant garb—sarape, high boots, and the indispensable sombrero. He still wore the boots and embroidered shirt. But he had removed the sarape and the *chamarra*, his short, handwoven jacket. The sombrero hung on the concrete-block wall.

"It's not the American crime syndicate that worries me," Juanita said, then pushed back her chair and stood up. "The American criminals need us as much as we need them. We

18

control the majority of the drug traffic, and the Mafia accepts that as a fact of life."

She sat down on a crate of M16 rifles after first making sure there were no wooden splinters that would rip her green slacks.

"It is possible that I am being overly cautious. Nevertheless, I'm still uncomfortable about our posing as tourists from Mexico City. I don't like the part of the plan which calls for us to fly from the *Sea Hawk* to Copper Canyon. A two-way trip is much too dangerous. Besides leaving the first shipment of arms in the canyon—No! I don't like it!"

Hector Mudejar cleared his throat, which felt very dry. It disturbed him that he and Gomara needed the support of Juanita Sojeda and her Mexican Students' Freedom Society. Worse, she and her silly students hated the Soviet Union as much as they hated the United States. *We will never—after the Revolution succeeds—become a Soviet captive like Cuba!* was one of her favorite warnings.

"So, you are worried about our being intercepted by Mexican Air Force planes," Mudejar broke the short silence. "We have been assured by the American gangsters that two American ex-soldiers will be along, men who will know how to operate the small heat-seeking Russian missiles. Come to think of it, I wonder where those *Americanos* got the missiles. No doubt on the international black market on guns. However, the missiles are not our concern." Mudejar smiled broadly at the sullen-faced Juanita Sojeda. "Yes, the entire plan does contain large elements of risks and unforeseen developments. But I ask you, Maria: Can you suggest a better way to make the transfer?"

Paul Escutia tilted the bottle of tequila to his thick lips. Alvar Gomara lighted a cigarette, pushed a hand underneath his shirt and scratched his chest.

Juanita Maria Sojeda stared at Hector Mudejar, who was a monolith of a man—6 foot 5 inches, 270 pounds, every ounce pure muscle. Everything about him seemed larger than life. His features were thick and fleshy, as if sculpted from day-old bread dough. His eyes were clear and intelligent. It was his nose that attracted attention, a nose that was large and curved sharply at the end, a nose that resembled a beak.

A sudden thought crossed Juanita's mind: letting a man his size make love to her—it would be like being stabbed with a

19

gigantic spear! She grimaced inwardly. Letting any man make love to her filled her with a sickening revulsion.

Maria's cold eyes gave Mudejar an unsettling feeling, as though he were an insect pinned to a dissecting board. He was about to speak when Paul Éscutia said, "We can be sure of some things. For example, the first shipment of weapons will be safe in the canyon. No one ever goes there, and the crates will be buried." He turned his dog eyes on Juanita. "We can't expect the *Americano bandoleros* to deliver all the weapons in one shipment."

"I never said I did!" Juanita replied, her manner more abrasive than usual. She snapped out a glare at Escutia, whom she considered a pig, then turned and moved toward the coffee pot on the two-burner hot plate. "I agree that we must implement a plan to bring the remainder of the shipments into Mexico," she continued, "and the operation can't involve Juarez, Nogales, and other Mexican-American border towns. At the moment, I'm not concerned about the rest of the shipments."

She picked up the old-fashioned enamel coffeepot, walked back to the table and filled her cup, listening to the two fans and the humming of the ventilation system, the outside vents of which were hidden in the bottom of the unused water fountain in the center of the patio. Cigarette smoke and other odors were drawn up through the center of the column in the middle of the fountain and trapped in chemical filters that were replaced every month. Fresh air was pumped in via another pipe hidden in the center of the ornamental column.

"Nor should you really worry about anything else," Hector Mudejar spoke in a tone he knew revealed nothing of his own feelings about Juanita Maria Sojeda. All over Mexico, student revolutionaries respected and looked to her for leadership. And it was the daring students who threw the grenades and executed the bank robberies. The old-guard revolutionaries were more cautious. Watching Maria take the coffee pot back to the hot plate, he knew that it was better to reason with her than to use verbal force.

"While we are waiting for the rest of the weapons, we can acquire more heroin from the farmers," he said, "and distribute the weapons we already have to such key cities as Guadalajara, Acapulco, Veracruz, and Chihuahua. The distribution will be a difficult task—it will take months."

Alvar Gamara, watching Juanita take the coffee pot back

20

to the hot plate, said frankly, "It's that American narcotics agent who escaped from the Isabel-Sheraton. He's the cause of your worry, isn't he?"

Paul Escutia made a motion with his hand. "He is of no importance. He is only one hombre who was very lucky this afternoon. The next time the police will kill him."

Juanita Sojeda spoke as she returned to the table. "All of us are being too smug. We're assuming too much success and not looking at the possibilities of failure." She sat down and looked from man to man. "How can we be positive that there isn't an informer within our own ranks? We can't be! We can't really be sure of anything, except that the usefulness of our man in Magdalena is over. We will have to kill him before the Americans get to him and force him to talk."

"Nonsense!" laughed Gomara, who wasn't as clever, nor as diplomatic, as Hector "Perico" Mudejar. "There is no indication that any of our people are informing to either the *Americano* DEA or our own country's narcotics people. As for the *Americano* agent knowing who tipped off our people, who planted the heroin in his room, you're assuming too much. The *Americano* agent could have had other contacts than the two in Magdalena. But if he didn't, then it is possible that he might deduce it was either Bunuel or Moncada." Nodding as he laughed, he said, "The man we should kill is Bunuel. Maybe the *Americanos* will think it was he who informed, and for that reason had to be silenced."

"I agree fully," said Paul Escutia, looking at Juanita as she sat down. He tilted back his chair so that it rested entirely on its two rear legs, and clasped his hands behind his head. "The only thing that *Americano* agent has proved is that the U.S. narcotics people have begun an operation and are working in Mexico independently of the *Departamento de Narcotico*."

"We knew that when the man calling himself 'Lawrence' met our agent in Magdalena," Juanita said, annoyance in her voice.

Hector Mudejar interrupted her with a curt wave of a huge hand.

"We can't stand still," he said somewhat roughly. "We must move forward. At this late date, it would be very difficult to change our plans with the American Mafia—almost impossible."

Escutia caught the eye of Mudejar. "We certainly can't

change our plans because of one man." He turned his head and frowned at Juanita Sojeda. "I refuse to." He sounded gruff to the point of rudeness.

"We shall go ahead as planned," Juanita Sojeda said, moving a hand across her eyes and speaking as though the final decision was her sole responsibility. She glanced at Mudejar. "We'll remain here for three days, then proceed north. But I want the three of you to know that I think we should postpone the entire operation for at least a month. I've been outvoted, it seems, so—"

"That's right," Escutia said curtly. "You have. I'll start for Guadalajara in the morning."

"Day after tomorrow, I'll take a bus for Durango," Alvar Gomara said. "We'll have more than enough time to meet in Huatabampo."

"Be very careful in Guadalajara," warned Juanita Sojeda stiffly. "The Federales are very thick in Guadalajara."

Again she thought of the man who had called himself "Justin Alfred Lawrence."

For some reason she could not get the shadowy figure out of her mind. How could any man be so "lucky" as to kill twenty narcotics agents?

The man was *inhumano!*

Chapter Three

The apartment house at Drive Rio De La Loza 1473 was very modern in design, in contrast to the Catholic Church, a few blocks away, and other nearby buildings, which were of Spanish Renaissance architecture. Using a number seven lock pick to let himself into Rossana del Moreno's apartment on the sixth floor, Richard Camellion felt instinctively that the young woman would be every bit as modern as the building in which she lived. He already knew that she was very unusual, or she wouldn't be the private secretary of Leland Moore and Eldridge Eubanks, the two CE agents who operated Polar Cold, Inc., a CIA "front" company which sold air-conditioning equipment to Mexican businessmen all over Mexico. The work of Moore and Eubanks was far more dangerous and involved than counterintelligence gathering. Counterespionage operations always involved the activities of foreign intelligence services. In Mexico City—a hub of international intrigue and an exile haven for Latin Americans of various political convictions—CE business meant keeping track of known Soviet KGB and Cuban DGI agents. The CIA had lent Polar Cold to the Drug Enforcement Administration for this particular DEA operation.

Now, half an hour after meeting Rossana del Moreno, the Death Merchant was certain he had been right the first time. Senorita del Moreno was not only very much in the latter part of the twentieth century, she was also very cool when she thought the chips were down.

After letting himself into her apartment, Camellion had waited in the bedroom for her to come home. Finally, when she had walked into the bedroom, he had put a hand over her mouth to keep her from crying out in surprise or screaming in terror, while he identified himself. He need not have worried. She had instantly tried to shatter the bones of his left instep with her sharp heel. At the same time she attempted to back thumb-stab him in the eye and smash him in the gut with an elbow.

A short time later, after he had convinced her who he was, she proved that she had not been brainwashed by Mexican morality for females only by changing into an Oriental silk print lounger, with a sashed top that had

23

"barely-there" capped sleeves and a deeply V'd neckline. The matching Oriental pants—white bamboo print on jade green—were just as sheer as the top. While the top clearly outlined the nipples of her ample breasts, the thinner-than-tissue paper pants revealed a tantalizingly dark area at the bottom of her loins, a deeply shaded wedge between her thighs. Yes. . . . Rossana del Moreno was even more emancipated than many American girls. And from the way she walked, she apparently didn't care if Camellion knew it. It was an optical orgy to watch her as she walked away, when she left the kitchen and went into the living room to call Leland Moore.

A few minutes later, carrying an ashtray, she came back into the small kitchen and sat down at the table where Camellion was eating left-over chicken and *chiles en nogada* —green peppers filled with pork loin, almonds, citron, crushed apples, tomatoes, and brown sugar—and drinking *bedida de cacao,* a chocolate-flavored cola drink.

"I assumed you contacted either Moore or Eubanks," Camellion said. He knew she had or she would have said at once that she hadn't.

Rossana put her elbows on the table, holding the lower part of her right arm up, a cigarette between her fingers. Camellion noticed that her silver-painted nails were very long.

"Moore said that he would be here within a few hours," she said in excellent English, with almost no accent. "He didn't say so—he couldn't over the phone—but I can tell you that first he'll pick up Eldridge. They'll bring the clothes and the box that the Embassy smuggled to us a week ago."

"What about a passport?"

"Yes, a Canadian passport. Being Canadian, you won't need a Mexican visa."

The Death Merchant tapped his lips with a napkin and smiled.

"I assume that the Canadian passport is a contingency process. A forged passport on a moment's notice is very good work."

"Not really," she said. "We always have a few on hand, just in case they are needed." Her long lashes fluttered. She closed her mouth, then her lips parted, as though she might be deciding whether to say what she was thinking.

Camellion decided that she had made up her mind to tell him when she said, "Don't be surprised to find that Moore and Eldridge are upset. We heard the news of your trouble at the hotel before we left the office, and they feel that the entire operation has suffered a serious setback."

"Those two hot dogs think I blew it! Is that what you're saying?"

"That is what I am saying." She tapped ash into the ashtray.

Camellion placed the napkin on the table, pushed back the chair and stood up, amusement flowing over his lean, tanned face. He picked up the plate and fork.

"I suppose those two jokers expected me to let myself get locked up and worked over by the Mexican narcs!" he snickered, on his way to the garbage disposal built in the wall. "For two CEs, Moore and Eldridge ought to know that when one swims with sharks, one either gets swallowed or becomes a bigger shark and kills the rest of the pack."

He scraped chicken bones from the plate into the garbage disposal, then walked to the left and put the plate and fork in the dishwasher. With a twisted smile on his face, he turned and faced Rossana, who was watching him with a solemn expression in her cinnamon eyes.

"What amazes me is how you managed to escape from the hotel and succeeded in coming here," she said. "Are you sure no one saw you come into the apartment?"

"I'm positive," Camellion said and sat down again at the table. "Getting into the apartment was, in some respects, the most dangerous part of all. Picking the lock only took a few minutes, but if anyone had seen me, I would have had to run for it. The real danger was that, if I had been seen, the police would connect me with you, and you with Polar Cold. And that would have been a severe setback. But time was against me and I had no choice but to come here."

Smiling ironically, Rossana took a final puff on her cigarette.

"That's another reason why Moore and Eldridge are probably more angry at this moment than they were this afternoon: because they feel that you endangered their cover." She crushed her cigarette in the ashtray and brushed strands of raven-black hair from her forehead. "You haven't told me how you were able to get here. The radio said that the last anyone saw of you was when you drove off in a police car."

"It's not all that important," said the Death Merchant, toying with a glass half-filled with *bedida de cacao*. Ac-

25

tually, the escape had been compounded of nerve, know-how, and luck. He had driven away from the hotel very fast, gone a block, turned the corner and then slowed to a normal rate of speed. He had driven another long block before turning and driving three more blocks. He then turned west and finally parked in the middle of an alley. He reversed his sports coat, got out, walked down the alley, turned, and caught a bus. Four blocks later, he left the bus, found a clothing store, and bought a dark hat and a lightweight topcoat, grateful that his luck was holding.

After he had left the *almacen*, wearing the new hat and topcoat, he walked another block and hailed a taxi. The cab had driven him to within two blocks of Rossana del Moreno's apartment house.

"Here's part of the answer," Camellion' explained. He stood up, unbuttoned his coat, and held it open.

"Oh, I see!" Rossana said in a small voice. "The coat is reversible—a blue check pattern on the outside and cream on the inside." She gave a slight laugh. "Or vice versa. And with two handkerchief pockets."

"No, *mio querido*. It's the same pocket but with different handkerchiefs pinned on each side," Camellion said. He shifted the Star automatic in his belt and sat down. He had left the Combat Magnum and the Obregon .45 in the police cruiser.

He looked at the clock over the sink—six o'clock on the nose.

"Have Huff and Korse arrived in town yet?" he asked.

"Yesterday afternoon," Rossana said. "They phoned, but haven't been around to the office. I guess now they might wait until either Moore or Eubanks contacts them."

Leland Moore and Eldridge Eubanks arrived at 7:45, each man carrying a suitcase, Moore telling Camellion, "This is all the man from the Embassy gave us. He said that there are also two SIG automatics and five boxes of cartridges in one case, and a twenty-two Ruger with a silencer."

If the two men were angry, they certainly didn't show it. They removed their hats and topcoats, placed them across a chair, and sat down on the longest section of a corner-set sofa lounge.

"We were surprised to hear about the shoot-out at the hotel," Eubanks said, his voice friendly. "Then we tried to figure out what moves you might make."

He rubbed his hands together, peered at Camellion through his glasses, then smiled up at Rossana, who placed a large ashtray on the cocktail table which was a copper-studded brass chest. Rossana then sat down on the short section of the sofa and crossed her legs.

"I don't mind telling you that we were surprised when Rossana phoned and said her brother Carlos was in town," Leland Moore commented. "She has three brothers, but none of them are named Carlos. In case you're interested, 'Carlos' is your C-N in our reports."

" 'Carlos' is as good a cipher-name as any," Camellion shrugged.

"The fact that you got here safely is all that matters," Eubanks said, scratching his chin. "At first we were afraid that your rash action might destroy the Polar Cold cover. Fortunately that did not happen."

"It's all academic," Moore said matter-of-factly, taking a thin but long cigar from the inside pocket of his jacket, "although your being wanted for murder by the Federales does pose some difficulty." He gave Camellion a serious look and removed the cellophane wrapper from the cigar.

Relaxed in an armchair, directly across from the cocktail chest, the Death Merchant mentally dissected the two company counterespionage agents. He was aware that Rossana del Moreno, to his left, was watching his every move.

The tall Leland Moore, around forty years old, had a willowy build, a strong chin, and eyebrows perpetually peaked in a natural expression of disdain. His wavy brown hair was carefully combed. Camellion concluded that Moore's predatory eyes matched his eyebrows.

Of average height, Eldridge Eubanks was in his late thirties and had prematurely gray, curly brown hair. A carefully trimmed mustache seemed pasted to his upper lip. Behind his silver-rimmed glasses, his eyes were quick and intelligent. But to Camellion, Eubanks seemed out of place as a deep-cover agent. He appeared to be more the tweedy sort, in the best traditions of the old OSS. Eubanks reminded the Death Merchant of the kind of career men one often met in Washington, D.C., during the early days of the Central Intelligence Agency—men who were the finished products of the right families and the right schools, who wished to serve their country and fight world communism without getting their hands dirty. But appearances do not mean much in the violent world of counterespionage—Moore and Eubanks had to be good or they would not be operating a deep-cover front net. Nonetheless, Camellion always liked to test the reactions of the men and women with whom he worked.

He leaned back in the chair, put the outside of his right ankle on his left knee, and stared demandingly at Eldridge Eubanks.

"I'd like to know what you meant by my 'rash action'?" he said coldly. "I was in custody of seven Mexican narcs, who had arrested me on a charge of smuggling cocaine. Did you expect me to go in with them and end up serving a ten-year rap in some stinking Federal prison? Suppose you tell me what either of *you* would have done. And in case either of you are interested, my name is Richard Camellion."

Leland Moore blew out a cloud of smoke, looked sideways at Eldridge Eubanks who was wiping his glasses with a handkerchief, and said with a half-laugh, "Well, they said the guy they were going to send down here to this peso-paradise to boss the operation would come on stronger than gang busters! By God, they were right!"

While Rossana del Moreno looked as if she might be holding her breath, Eldridge Eubanks merely glanced at the Death Merchant and continued to wipe his glasses.

"Camellion, we've been told that you're clever enough to work problems in Hindu trigonometry while juggling a dozen billiard balls on ice skates, and we've been given to understand that we must follow your orders," Eubanks finally said, with a hint of pit-dog ruthlessness that belied his Yale blueblood appearance. "However, you had better get something straight. Whip-cracking tactics won't work with us."

"You haven't answered my question!"

Leland Moore's reply was quick and firm. "We can't tell you what we might have done, had we been in your place at the Maria Isabel-Sheraton. I wasn't there. Neither was El. We might have reacted differently. We'll never know. I'll still second what El just said. Don't come on heavy with us. We're not impressed. Understand?"

"If I didn't, none of you would be working with me in this operation." The Death Merchant smiled slightly, his tone humorous. The smile widening to a broad grin, he slumped down in the chair, put his elbows on the metal arms, and rested his chin on his folded hands. He enjoyed the sudden look of surprise on the faces of the two CEs and Rossana del Moreno.

28

"Well now!" Moore began nodding slowly, like a man who knows how to take a joke just played on him.

Eubanks put on his glasses. "A personal psychological evaluation! Not bad, Camellion, not bad at all. I like that, and I like the way you operate."

"I would have done the same thing," Moore said good-naturedly and tapped ash from his cigar. He nodded toward Rossana. "Speaking of the mess you were in at the hotel, she would have tried some of her Kung Fu tricks. I've been teaching her and she's pretty good at it."

"I already tried it with him. He was much too fast," Rossana said with a tiny nervous laugh. She then explained to Moore and Eubanks how Camellion had surprised her in the bedroom. "I still don't know how he countered my moves," she said, looking admiringly at him. "It all happened too fast."

Moore's hawk-like eyes shot to the Death Merchant. "I assume you're interested in Kung Fu, Karate, and the other martial arts," he said, sounding not only curious but anxious. "Did you know that the father of Zen Buddhism was also the originator of Kung Fu?"

"Yes—Bodhidharma, an Indian monk who arrived in China around A.D. five hundred and twenty after crossing the Himalayas on foot," Camellion said. "Bodhidharma developed Shaolin Temple boxing. It was also called *Chun Kuo ch'uan,* which means 'Chinese Fist,' and *Ch'uan shu* and *Ch'uan fa.* As these systems of fighting began to spread throughout China, they became known collectively as *Kung Fu.* Translated *Kung* means 'Master' and *Fu* means 'man.' Kung Fu therefore means 'master of man.' "

"But in the sense that it's 'master of self,' " Moore said quickly, "since people who practiced Kung Fu were attempting to better themselves through a self-improvement program." He laughed. "On the other hand, Kung Fu often settled matters once and for all."

"I would suggest that's what we do," Camellion said. "Settle the deal in which we are involved. I know some of the factors facing us, but I'd appreciate if you gave me a complete briefing."

"Good thinking. How much do you know?" Eldridge Eubanks said.

"I know that one of the staple imports into the U.S. is drugs," Camellion said. "Marijuana used to come in by the kilo. Now it's by the ton. Since the disruption of poppy farming in Turkey, ninety percent of the heroin coming into the U.S. is the distinctively brown variety known either as Mexican Brown or Mexican Mud. I know too that Tucson, Arizona, is a first-class smuggling center and dispersal point for junk coming in from chili-land. The drugs ride up from Mexico by car or vegetable truck on the Pan-American Highway, which runs through Tucson south to Culiacan, the 'Marseilles' of Mexico. Drugs also come through the cactus desert in pickups or by jeep. They're even brought across the Papago Indian Reservation by mule train. But for the most part they sneak through a network of ravines in private planes, which can fly undetected the fifty air miles separating Tucson from the Mexican border. In brief, that's the stateside situation regarding drugs from down here."

Both Moore and Eubanks nodded in satisfaction.

"And I understand that the narcotics being grown in Mexico are connected with Mexican revolutionaries who are cutting in on the dope trade," Camellion said. "The revolutionaries have banded together to finance the revolution by selling drugs to buy guns."

Leland Moore looked thoughtfully for a moment at his cigar, then at Camellion. "There is an indirect trade of dope for money, or dope for guns. We don't think you could say it's one for one. We'll know more when we talk to Huff and Korse. Huff phoned me at home this evening"—Moore glanced at Rossana—"right after you called. He said he and Korse would come to the office tomorrow morning."

Eldridge Eubanks said, "There is one thing you must understand. Here in Mexico the whole economy is based on drugs. It's a business, with everybody getting a piece of the action—the police, government officials, everybody."

"It is drugs which are responsible for a large part of an old Mexican custom—the *mordida,* or the 'bite,'" Rossana del Moreno said bitterly, spreading one arm across the back of the couch. "It's the graft demanded by Mexican officials. The practice is so common and accepted that lucrative border assignments are routinely rotated by Mexican custom officials. It's a disgrace."

"She's right," Eubanks said. "Criminals of all types, but mostly smugglers, pay the *mordida* and consider the bite an ordinary business expense."

"Camellion, let me start at the beginning and put the entire picture before you," Moore said, and put his cigar in an ashtray. He started by saying that for years the flow of narcotics north into the U.S. balanced a long history of American goods smuggled into Mexico to avoid stiff tariffs. The Mexican government ignored the smuggling in either direction, considering both In and Out routes good business. After all, channels that brought contraband into Mexico were usually the same ones that carried drugs out.

"What I'm saying is that narcotics once constituted an unofficial industry in Mexico. While the government pretended it didn't exist, it still got its cut—or *mordida*. But within the last few years, firearms have changed a lot of government minds in Mexico City. I guess you know that a Mexican citizen can't own a gun of any caliber. This means that a pistol that sells for a hundred and fifty dollars in the States is worth six to seven hundred bucks down here. Automatic weapons are more precious than gold. For instance, an AR–15 can be bought in most State-side sporting good stores for around three hundred bucks. Here in Mexico, the same automatic rifle is worth an ounce of Mexican Brown, which will bring almost two grand in Arizona. Get the drift of the profit involved?"

The Death Merchant moved his head slowly up and down. "I recall reading an evaluation report in D.C. a few weeks ago. Part of it said that after a shoot-out south of Guadalajara, Federales discovered the revolutionaries had sixteen M16 rifles that had been stolen from a U.S. Armory in Fresno, California."

"You're getting the picture," Leland Moore said. He met Camellion's gaze levelly. "It used to be that the stolen weapons were swapped with traffickers in the Sierras—guns for dope. The middlemen then sold the weapons to the revolutionaries, who got the money for purchase by sticking up banks or kidnaping prominent people. Finally the revolutionaries wised up and eliminated the middle people. Now they deal directly with the gun runners. Individual operators are mixed up in the gun runnings, but eighty percent of it is controlled by organized crime—the damned Mafia."

Richard Camellion went straight to the core of the mess. "The revolutionaries are trading drugs for weapons so they can start *La Revolucion*. The government is trying to kill all the revolutionaries in an attempt to prevent a national uprising."

"Now you've buttoned it down." Eldridge Eubanks' voice was heavy with irony. He sighed heavily and shifted his body

31

on the sofa. "Heroin is responsible for a lot of blood and violence. Almost every day revolutionaries turned *narcotraficantes* are murdering Federales and Mexican soldiers. It's not unusual for peasants to become snipers and put a bullet through a soldier or member of the Federales, whom the farmers consider 'bandits with permission.' You see, it's the farmers, the *campesinos*, who grow the opium poppy, mostly in fields hidden in the Sierra Madre Oriental Mountains in eastern Mexico. Some poppies are grown in the Sierra Madre Occidental—West—Mountains, but only in the south. The rest of the Sierra Madre West is too rugged."

"It is the *campesinos* who are caught in the middle," explained Rossana del Moreno, letting her mouth turn down in distaste. "The campesinos are poorer than mice. They scratch out a bare living growing corn and beans while they live in a medieval relationship to their *caciques*, the powerful landowners and political bosses who rule with an iron hand." She spread her other arm on the top of the sofa and leaned back, her movement pushing out her nipples against the silk of her sashed top and displaying her breasts in stark outline. "The *campesinos* see no harm in growing the bright red heroin poppy. They're only paid a few pesos per flower and are only trying to better their miserable existence. It's a perversion of justice that they are being slaughtered by the army soldiers."

"Yes, but the government is also killing a lot of revolutionaries," pointed out Leland Moore, "and a lot of students, both non-revolutionary and revolutionary *narcotraficantes*, especially in Guadalajara."

"Culiacan is the center of the narcotics traffic in Mexico," Eubanks said, pious-faced. He loosened his tie, unbuttoned his collar, and turned to Rossana. "Sweets, be a good girl and make some coffee—*por favor*."

"*Por cierto*," Rossana smiled. She got up and walked from the living room, Camellion and the two counterespionage agents watching her until she disappeared into the kitchen. Moore winked knowingly at the Death Merchant, jerked his head toward the kitchen, then opened his mouth and jerked his tongue in and out, much to the obvious annoyance of Eubanks, who leaned toward Camellion.

"Magdalena de Kino used to be one of the main drug centers," he said, "but not any more."

"Is that the same Magdalena in the state of Sonora?"

Camellion inquired. "If it is, where does the 'de Kino' come in?"

"It's been Magdalena de Kino since the remains of Father Kino were discovered under an old church that was razed near the town square. He was a venerated Jesuit missionary," Eubanks explained. "About a year ago the Mexican Army surrounded Magdalena de Kino and struck just before dawn, in an effort to capture Hector, 'The Parrot' Mudejar. They raided his headquarters, but 'Perico' was too smart for them. He had somehow escaped during the night. All they found were two hundred stolen television sets, two trucks of pornography, and half a ton of mary jane."

Camellion glanced briefly toward the kitchen, then turned back to Eubanks, who had taken a pack of American L&M Long Lights from his coat and was tapping one end of a cigarette against the back of his hand.

"It's Mudejar and his FRAP—the *Fuerzas Revolucionarias Armadas del Pueblo*—who have combined forces with Alvar Gomara, the Socialist, and his *Fuerzas Armadas de Liberacion Nacional*," the Death Merchant said. "That's what I was told in D.C. Or has there been a change?"

Leland Moore answered for Eubanks, who was lighting the L&M.

"Gomara's Armed Forces of National Liberation is not as large as The Parrot's People's Revolutionary Armed Forces commie group. Even combined, FRAP and FALN don't have the numbers of the Mexican Student's League, which is controlled by Juanita Maria Sojeda. Several years ago, the three groups coalesced under the banner of the Twenty-third of September Communist League. It was Sojeda who chose the date in the title. It's a date commemorating a useless attack in 1965 on a military barracks in the state of Chihuahua by *campesinos*."

For a moment, Camellion glanced around the room. He saw that Rossana had closed the drapes tightly over the windows across the room. Only two lamps burned, one at each end of the L-shaped sofa. He shifted his gaze to Moore and Eubanks.

"Don't make the mistake of thinking that Juanita Sojeda and her students are only adult delinquents, like the Weather People in the United States," Eubanks warned. He let a thin trickle of smoke curl from his nose, and Camellion wondered why he held his cigarette between thumb and middle finger. "The Weather People are just annoying pests who

33

plant a bomb now and then, but always warn people away in advance. They don't have the nerve to plan an assassination. The commie students down here, drawn from the Mexican university system, are a different breed. They've murdered at least a hundred Federales and assassinated scores of officials. When they plant bombs, they don't warn society in advance. Believe me, Juanita Sojeda is one dangerous bull bitch. She's a dedicated fanatic of the most violent kind."

"Bull bitch?" The Death Merchant's eyebrows arched questioningly.

"Sojeda is a lesbian," Moore said in disgust. "She's as queer as a four-buck bill printed in Eskimo."

With a kind of gentle laugh, Eldridge Eubanks flicked ashes from his cigarette. "This business down here is worse than the religious war in Northern Ireland. Talk to a Mexican government official and he'll use terms like command zones, interdiction areas, and operational aerial reconnaissance units."

His puckish mouth remained half open and he fingered the knot of his loosened club tie at the open collar of his white shirt. "The students claim that the Federales have killed almost a thousand of them. The students have just vanished. You see, the Mexican Feds have their own 'Death Squads,' similar to the ones the Uruguayan police employed against the Tupamaros."

"And that's only a part of the situation down here," Moore said slowly. "It's not generally known in the United States, but Mexico is rapidly turning into an out-and-out police state. We've estimated that there are more than two thousand political prisoners rotting in jail. Right now the Mexican government's prime targets are the states of Sinaloa, Durango, and Chihuahua to the north and Guerrero to the south. They're slaughtering peasants left and right."

"Well, in a way you can't truly blame the Mexican Feds and the soldiers," commented Eubanks. "Take for example the Mexican highway police. Those poor bastards aren't even safe on the public roads. A few weeks ago, there was a wreck outside Mexico City. The highway police were flagging every passing motorist to go slow. A man and a woman passed, and when the cops tried to flag them, the woman pulled a submachine gun and began firing. Four patrolmen were killed. On the other hand, the *campesinos* swear that the police and the soldiers fan out into the rural areas, arrest people by the score, and frame them by planting marijuana in their houses. The students who are communists claim that it's all a part of a government campaign to terrorize the populace and keep down an incipient antigovernment movement."

"We don't think it was the Federales who planted the cocaine in your room," Moore said firmly. "They would have no reason to single you out. Mexican relations with Great Britain are friendly."

"Do you have any evidence that the KGB is helping the Twenty-third of September League?" queried the Death Merchant.

"No, we haven't." Eubanks crushed out his cigarette. "The Soviet Union—"

"Wait a minute, I want to finish," Moore interrupted. He glanced at Eubanks, then back to Camellion, his eyes narrowing. "There are always those x-factors and the unforeseen unknowns. As we see it, your first stop was in Magdalena de Kino, so it was either Salvador Bunuel or Emilio Moncada who tipped off the Mexican narcs or the Twenty-third Nine-month League people here in Mexico City. Either the Feds or some of the commies then planted the junk in your room at the hotel."

"I don't intend to do anything about it, not at present," Camellion said. "We must develop a lead to neutralize The Parrot, Gomara, and their dyke *camarada*. We'll do that through your cover 'spots.'"

"Our Polar Cold cover cells?" Moore's voice was harsh. He stared at Camellion with open coolness. "I hope the brass in D.C. explained that our cover spots in Mexico City were established for CE work only."

"What about the KGB?" Camellion was calm but forceful. "How do the Russians fit into the puzzle?"

"We haven't found any evidence that the Soviet Union is helping the Twenty-third Nine-month League," Eubanks said. "The Ruskies don't have to. The League is doing all right on its own. You know how cautious the KGB is. The 'Sword and Shield' never gets involved as long as a situation is developing in a manner favorable to Russian overall strategy. But you damn well bet that the Soviets have a black cover agent buried in the League. We do. Why shouldn't the Russians?"

The Death Merchant kept his intense interest to himself, watching Moore, in whom he detected more than a touch of displeasure—*ever since I mentioned Polar Cold's 'spots.'*

35

Moore got up from the sofa and sat down, facing Camellion, on one end of the copper-studded brass chest, his sharp eyes darting to the Death Merchant.

"How much information did the DD/P give you about the cells in Mexico City?" he demanded. Without giving Camellion a chance to answer, Moore went on. "We can use the spots. That is not a problem. But neither El nor I were ordered to give you the names of any spot members. Don't even bother to ask. Even Rossana doesn't know their identities."

Moore got to his feet and looked toward the kitchen, at Rossana del Moreno, who was approaching the living room carrying a tray heavy with a gold-and-black beverage server, cups and saucers, and cream and sugar bowls to match. Moore walked toward her.

"Did I hear my name mentioned?" Rossana smiled and let Moore take the tray from her. She glanced at Camellion, smiled again, and sat down once more on the short section of the sofa.

Eubanks shoved the ashtray to one side and Moore put the tray in the center of the chest. Bending over, he reached for a cup, and glanced furtively at the Death Merchant, who was giving him all the time in the world and silently admiring him for being so dedicated to duty.

The heavy silence continued. While Moore poured coffee, Eldridge Eubanks snatched an L&M from his pack, lit it quickly, looked at the Death Merchant, and said with calculated evenness, "Each cell is self-contained. The members of one spot don't know the members of another cell. However, this security measure will not prevent us from using the cells in any operation you might plan."

Moore looked at Camellion. "Cream or sugar or both?"

"Black. Leave it on the chest." Camellion got up, moved the armchair closer to the chest, and sat back down, thinking that Leland Moore was a good man to have around. *He has an intuitively suspicious mind. His own trouble is that he shows it. I've learned enough; I'd better put him at ease.*

"I don't need to know names," he said in a moderate tone. "In fact, I don't want to know. All that concerns me is putting the biggest dent possible in the drug traffic moving north and the gun traffic flowing south." His icy stare held on Leland Moore. "Do you have that pasted to your brain, Leland?"

36

Without looking at the Death Merchant, Moore raised his eyebrows with some surprise and bobbed his head in ready agreement, relief showing visibly on his face.

Rossana Moreno cleared her throat. "El, put a dash of brandy in mine."

Nodding, Eubanks reached into his inside coat pocket, took out a silver flask and handed it to Moore, who removed the cap and poured a couple of shots into a cup. Then he held out the flask to the Death Merchant. Camellion shook his head.

"The only way to crush the double-traffic is to blow away Mudejar, Gomara, and Sojeda," Moore said with lowered voice. "To that unholy three we can add another human scum—a tub of Latin lard named Paul Torres Escutia."

He recapped the flask, handed it back to Eldridge Eubanks, and continued to talk as he poured coffee from the beverage server into the cup containing brandy.

"Escutia was head of the People's Party and had a guerrilla movement going in central Mexico, around the Concepcion del Oro region. Whenever the army would move in on him, Escutia and his band would retreat into the Sierra Madre East. The last time, about a year ago, the Mexican army dropped in on him with paratroopers. They wiped out nearly his entire band. Those who surrendered were executed on the spot. Only Escutia and a few of his men escaped. He then linked up with the Twenty-third Ninemonth League."

Moore placed a spoon on the saucer, picked up the cup and saucer, then turned and stabbed a strong look directly at the Death Merchant.

"Now here's the good news. It's possible we can kill all four of them either tomorrow afternoon or tomorrow night. The time is up to you. We don't have anything to say about the place, which is a farm three miles south of Xochimilco."

"We haven't told you yet about Efran Rebaderos," Eldridge Eubanks said, his voice taking on a brittle edge. Having paused between sips of brandy, he continued to eye Camellion expectantly. Moore, standing as still as a statue, frowned, as if disappointed that Camellion was not registering surprise.

Without the barest flicker of emotion, Camellion edged forward in his chair and picked up one of the cups from its saucer. Moore turned, walked over to Rossana, and handed her the cup and saucer in his hand.

37

"Xochimilco is seven point two miles southwest of Mexico City," Camellion said in a monotone, nodding thoughtfully. He looked calmly at Eubanks, who was recapping the flask; then Camellion's eyes searched Leland Moore, who was resuming his place on the sofa.

"Let's have it," Camellion said. "Start at the beginning."

Occasionally taking a sip of coffee—*she made it plenty strong!*—Camellion listened attentively as Eubanks explained that Efran Rebaderos was a Mexican-American working for both the U.S. Drug Enforcement Administration and the U.S. Treasury's Bureau of Alcohol, Tobacco, and Firearms. Seven years ago Rebaderos—*Emerald-4*—had been "developed" by the CIA and planted in Mexico with instructions to infiltrate the Mexican communist party. *Emerald-4* had made slow but steady progress, until finally he had become one of the lieutenants of Alvar Gomara.

"E-4 got word to his contact—in one of our cells—this morning," Eubanks reported. "The contact got word to me this afternoon after I had left the office and had gone home."

Eubanks next told the Death Merchant that E-4 had reported that the three leaders of the Twenty-third of September Communist League and Paul Escutia were planning a master operation, and were meeting at the farm of Diego Tuchilan to iron out the details.

"There isn't any reason why we can't sneak up on the farm and kill the four of them," Moore added carefully, his steady gaze on the Death Merchant. "I grant that the operation will be dangerous, but in my opinion it's necessary. We can't afford the opportunity to scratch all four. To ignore the farm would be extremely poor maneuvering."

The Death Merchant ignored the implication and turned his attention to Eldridge Eubanks. "Is E-4 reliable? Is he completely trustworthy?" He added slyly, "Or could the commies be trying to draw out you deep-net CE boys?"

Eubanks shuffled uneasily on the sofa, uncrossing his legs.

"I would trust Rebaderos with my life," he said peevishly. "You don't know his record, Camellion. I do."

"So do I," Moore chimed in, agitated. He leaned forward and placed his cup and saucer on the chest. "If Washington had given you a thorough briefing, you'd know that Emerald is our man, not the other side's."

Camellion let Moore's comments pass. "Then E-4 knows your identities!" he smiled, looking from one man to the other. "If that's the case, it's god-terrible covering!"

"No he doesn't!" Moore said sharply. "Rebaderos doesn't even know we exist. He never will. We only meant that his record down here is excellent. Time after time we've received vital information from him, and D.C. is positive that none of it was a plant—disinformation." His voice became more irritated and impatient. "There isn't any point going into it. You'll have to take our word for it that E–4 is our boy."

Camellion put down his cup and saucer. "Huff and Korse are posing as 'sales executives' from the States, right?" he said. Seeing that Eubanks had taken out the flask again, he wondered just how much the man drank.

"That's right. They'll report to the office the first thing in the morning," Eubanks said and uncapped the flask.

"They know you're the case-man in this deal," Moore said in a more friendly voice. "They'll agree to anything we—to any plan you decide to use. Their main job is to get a first-hand report from me and El and to discuss new ways to get informers."

Eubanks tilted the flask, took a quick swallow, then looked over at Camellion. "It will be a simple matter for us to meet at my house tomorrow evening and proceed from there," he suggested hopefully. "I have a house on the outskirts of Chapultepec, a suburb west of Mexico City."

"Another thing in our favor is that there aren't any Federales around Xochimilco," Moore said. "In fact, the entire area in the Federal District, south of Mexico City, is relatively free of police. And those we are around will be asleep."

The Death Merchant deliberated. "We'll need automatic weapons, preferably with noise suppressors. Another thing, did E–4 say how many communists would be at the farm?"

"A couple of dozen," Moore said hesitantly, "and they'll have guards posted. Like I said, the operation will be dangerous. We have plenty of weapons—grenades, smoke, gas, anything you want."

Rossana broke into the conversation, saying in a low but pleasant voice, "You will have to stay here tonight. To leave without a disguise would be asking for death."

Standing in the kitchen doorway, Camellion glanced up at the wall clock as he watched Rossana put cups and saucers into the dishwasher—10:35 P.M. His mind skipped back to some of the information he had read in her dossier. Her father had immigrated to Mexico from Portugal in 1947 and settled in Mazatlan. In 1950 he married an American prostitute living in Villa Union. She had been killed in an automobile accident shortly after Rossana was born in 1951.

Camellion deliberately uttered a low laugh, smiling when Rossana regarded him with a puzzled expression on her face.

"You are amused?" she said and walked toward him. "At something I have done?"

"I was only thinking that Moore and Eubanks would have a double heart attack each if they knew that I know the names of all forty-six cell members," he said, then laughed again. "Ah, the joke is on them."

"Oh!" Rossana's eyes became round with surprise. "I didn't know the spots had that many members."

"You do now, and I shouldn't have told you," Camellion said gruffly. "Don't let them know I told you. Promise?"

"Yes, I promise." She reached up, unloosened his tie, and unbuttoned his collar. "There! Now you will be more comfortable."

"*Bien, gracias,*" Richard said, and placed his hands over hers, which were still on his collar. "There is only one more thing I need. A blanket and a pillow for the sofa."

"The sofa will be far less comfortable than a bed," she whispered, moving closer to him. He inhaled her perfume and noticed how slim and curvy her neck was.

"Hmmmmm, then you have a spare bed?" he asked with a straight face, all the while knowing he wasn't fooling her with his mock innocence.

"I have a king-size bed and there is ample room," she breathed, looking up into his eyes. "After all, what good is a king-size bed without a king?"

With a wisp of a smile, she slowly pulled her hands from under his, gave him another sensuous look, and went into the hall between the kitchen and the living room. Camellion followed, pausing to watch her move toward the bedroom.

Halfway down the hall, she turned and looked at him, frowning.

"Aren't you coming, *Amado?*"

"I guess I am," sighed Camellion and followed her into the bedroom.

Chapter Four

The day had been blessed with a butterfly morning and a wild-flower afternoon. After sunset the twilight had faded into a mellow moonbeam night seasoned with a soft breeze that waved the palms and rippled the tall *hoz* grass, at the top of the rise, in which the eight men lay. Each was dressed in navy blue coveralls, wore a Halloween false-face mask, and was weighed down with ammo pouches.

Leland Moore was stretched out prone to the left of Richard Camellion. Eldridge Eubanks was on his belly to the Death Merchant's right. Next to Eubanks was Cletus Huff, the United States Treasury's BATF agent, who talked with a dirt farmer's drawl and retained the sun-faded look of Kansas, the state in which he had been born and reared. Harley Korse was only a few feet from Huff. A big-boned man who was 40 but looked 50, the U.S. Drug Enforcement Administration officer had a gaunt, weary face, as if years of trouble had eroded his youth prematurely. There were three Mexicans next to Korse, lying side by side. Two were in their thirties; the third was almost sixty. Another member of the Polar Cold cover-net was a quarter of a mile away with Rossana del Moreno, in the van parked between two hills covered with dwarf evergreens and thorny shrubs.

"I don't see a damn soul," Leland Moore whispered. Like the Death Merchant, Moore was staring at the farm through Star-Tron light-intensifying night-vision binoculars.

"I don't either, but you can bet they're there," Camellion said. "It isn't ghosts who are playing that *mariachi* music on the record player."

Camellion continued to study the layout of the farm. A few hundred feet to the northwest were scattered pine and oaks and cactus-like euphorbia. Beyond, to the north, was the deteriorated *palacio* of the hacienda. A hundred feet east of the house was a rock wall. Crumbling all along its length, it too had become a victim of time and neglect. East of the wall was a large wooden barn, tottering, weatherworn, and baked brittle by the sun, as was the long, open shed filled with henequen fibers. The other outbuildings, an empty tractor shed and an empty corncrib, would not have made good kindling. Beyond the farm, to the north, were dark fields.

There were more fields and hilly rock rises of land to the west and to the east.

The Death Merchant did some analyzing: he and the others had come in from the south because the south approach had been the closest, offering the path of least resistance. There were some facts: the world over, one and one had to equal two. Men were different in their habits, in their political and religious beliefs, and in their overall philosophy of life, but some things were constant the world over—like common sense and self-preservation. And security.

If I were in charge of security up yonder, I would have men high in the barn and on the second floor of the house, guards who could observe all approaches to the house.

Camellion lowered the Star-Tron binoculars and looked up at the midnight sky. Damn the full moon. There was some hope—scattered clouds, the thick, heavy residue of thunderheads that had broken up.

Eldridge Eubanks put down his S-T binoculars, rose up on his elbows and looked at Camellion across the short space. "Why are we waiting?" he whispered intensely. "The only way to get to the house is to go forward. We sure as hell can't fly!"

Lying next to Eubanks, Cletus Huff pushed himself up and said impatiently, "A total frontal assault is kind of stupid—no offense to you, Camellion. I think we should attack from both the front and the rear. We shouldn't stay bunched together."

"We are going to make a two-pronged attack," the Death Merchant said. "We're only using this position to recon the target."

Camellion looked again at the sky, then swung to Leland Moore.

"Tell me, are you married? Do you have a family?"

"Yes, my wife and two boys," Moore replied, his voice puzzled. He was going to ask what his family had to do with the attack on the farm, but Camellion turned to Eubanks and the other two U.S. government agents and asked the same questions.

Eubanks was just as mystified at Moore. "Married or single? What's the difference?"

"Eldridge, pass the word to the three Mexicans," the Death Merchant whispered. "Have them go around to the west and come in to the rear of the house. They can contact you by walkie talkie when they're in position and ready to attack.

Tell them that it would be wise to have one man advance while the other two watch the rear of the barn and the back of the house through the Star-Tron scopes on their rifles."

Eubanks moved back on his hands and knees and crawled over to Porfirio Leyendas. For several minutes the two men whispered back and forth in Spanish; then Leyendas and the other two Mexicans moved out.

The Death Merchant and the four other men waited, Camellion pondering the information sent by Emerald–4. There was a hidden below-ground meeting room. But E–4 didn't know where it was. Although he was a trusted aide of Alvar Gomara, the revolutionary leader had never given him, nor any of the other men, the location of the room, and E–4 had known better than to ask and run the risk of arousing suspicion about his motives. All E–4 knew was that the entrance to the hidden room was in a cellar that was under the northeast corner of the house.

It took the three Mexicans almost forty-five minutes to get into position to attack from the fields to the north of the house.

"Porfirio said he's all set to move in," Eubanks told Camellion, his hand over the mouthpiece of the walkie talkie. Behind the Halloween mask, Eubanks' eyes reflected portions of moonlight. "Should I tell him to proceed?"

The Death Merchant looked up at the quiet sky and saw that a long island of cloud was approaching the scarred face of the moon. He estimated that once the cloud totally covered the moon, a ten-minute period of darkness would follow.

"Tell Porfirio to wait until the moon is hidden," Camellion said. "Tell him I'll move forward toward the front at the same time."

As Eubanks relayed the instructions to the three Mexicans, Moore touched Camellion lightly on the shoulder. Richard rolled over on his right side and looked at the perplexed company man. "What's your problem?"

"When you move out, what are the rest of us supposed to do?" Moore cracked dryly. "Sit back and watch?"

"All four of you had damn well better watch—the top portion of the barn and the second story of the house!" Camellion warned in a low voice. It was obvious to the Death Merchant that neither Moore nor any of the other U.S. agents were familiar with this type of black operation. *If we did it their way, we'd all get blown away! Now I have*

43

to worry about keeping them alive for their wives and brats.

Camellion again looked up at the sky. The edge of the cloud was only five minutes away from the moon.

Placing the Star-Tron binoculars into the case hanging from a strap on his shoulder, the Death Merchant said, "Moore, I want you and Eubanks to keep an eye on the barn while I go forward." He raised his voice so that the other three men could hear. "Huff and Korse can watch the front of the house. Your job will be to keep the enemy pinned down if I'm spotted."

Camellion rolled over on his other side and stabbed Eubanks and the two other U.S. Feds with his eyes. "Did the three of you get that? I'm putting my life in your hands. Let me down and I'm dead. *Comprender?*"

The three men nodded like obedient children. Harley Korse put an inhaler under his mask, stuck it into one nostril and began to sniff. It seemed to Camellion that Korse had been sniffing ever since he had arrived from the States.

"Smart thinking on your part, Camellion," drawled Cletus Huff. "I suppose you want us to move up as soon as you secure a position close to the house and can give us cover?"

"You got it down pat," Camellion said. He checked to make sure the flaps of his hip holsters were secure, then pulled the special .22 Ruger pistol from the Berns-Martin holster fastened to the center of his chest. A seven-inch-long Sionics silencer was attached to the barrel of the Ruger; its butt lacked a magazine. Camellion remedied the situation by pulling a foot-long magazine from a canvas ammo bag attached to his belt and shoving it into the butt of the Ruger. He then pulled back the slide and cocked the weapon, placing a .22 cartridge into the firing chamber.

The cartridges were also special. While they were still high velocity rim-fire brass-case cartridges, each bullet was a Half-Jacketed Flat Point, the soft lead being swaged to final shape and dimension inside a thin copper cup that extended only partially up the length of the bearing surface. Contained in the lead core of each bullet were five grains of Fentolite. One could drop any of the cartridges without danger, even on its lead nose; the shock would not be sufficient to detonate the Fentolite. But when one of the .22 long rifle bullets traveled at 1,369 f.p.s. and struck an object with 149 foot-pounds of kinetic energy, the force was more than enough to explode the shock-sensitive Fentolite, and each bullet became a midget grenade.

44

The night was silent, except for the noise of various tropical insects and the brassy sound of the *mariachi* music drifting from the run-down palacio.

The cloud began to move across the face of the moon.

"All of you get set," Camellion ordered. He pulled on the rifle strap across his chest, making sure the M16 was secure on his back. He glanced around him and saw that the four men had raised their M16s and were sighting in through the Star-Tron scopes attached to the top of the automatic rifles, which had also been fitted with long Sionics silencers.

The moon disappeared and darkness dropped over the countryside. The Death Merchant moved down the slant of the rise. Keeping as low as he could, he ran in a zigzag pattern through the foot-high hoz grass and headed for the end of the low but thick wall. He was halfway to the wall when an automatic rifle began its vicious coughing to his right— *It has to be from the barn! Sounds like a CETME!*—and he heard the zip-zip-zip of high velocity slugs slicing into the grass all around him.

He felt a tug along his left hip, but the bullet had not touched the skin. Then two savage pulls on both sides of his right leg, one on the outside, by the ankle, the other on the inside, by his thigh. There were pulls across both shoulders. He felt the air by his right cheek disturbed. A bullet ripped downward through the long bill of his field cap and twisted the cap to the left, proving that the firing was coming from the upper level of the barn.

Now another automatic rifle opened fire, then a third one— both from the rear of the large house ahead. Porfirio Leyendas had been spotted!

The Death Merchant did have a choice: he could either fall to the grass, keep down and hope that none of the projectiles found him, or he could keep going and try to reach the wall, the end of which was at an angle that made it impossible for anyone from the barn to fire down on him.

A die-hard fatalist, Camellion kept moving in a wild, swerving course, 7.62mm CETME projectiles cutting all around him. *What the hell are Moore and Eubanks doing?* He didn't expect to hear any firing because the M16s were silenced. *But can't those two boobs hit the side of a barn?*

Suddenly there was a faint scream of pain from the direction of the barn, and the *kar-kar-kar-kar* of the CETME stopped. The echoes of its firing were dying in the distance as automatic weapons started to roar from the front of the

45

house and Camellion made a dive for the end of the wall, projectiles cutting the night air all around him. A dozen or more zinged into the side of the wall and sent up a shower of stone chips as Camellion snuggled up to the end, made himself small, and took stock of his highly precarious position.

He heard glass shatter and dozens of richochets from the front of the house and realized that Huff and Korse, and maybe Moore and Eubanks, too, were dosing the faded stucco with streams of 5.56 millimeter slugs.

I should have my head examined! Camellion didn't like working with family men. Married men made good paper pushers and were ideal for desk jobs, but out in the field their wives and crumb-snatchers became dangerous distractions.

The sporadic firing from the house continued, but none of the projectiles were hitting the wall. Either the enemy thought he was dead, or else were concerned with the firing coming from the rise. The roar of automatic weapons also continued from the rear of the house.

Camellion looked around the end of the wall. Ahead were pine and oaks and a scattering of euphorbia. Thirty feet in front of the wide porch was a large oak, and to the left of the oak was a ten-foot-long raised flowerbed, filled with weeds, red begonias, and golden marigolds.

I can't remain here and get the job done! Richard took the walkie-talkie from its holder on his belt, switched it on and held the device close to his mouth. "Moore?"

"Yes?"

"Listen carefully. I want the four of you to concentrate your fire on the top story. That will hold them down long enough for me to get in close enough to use grenades. Remember: fire at the top floor only. I don't want any of your slugs tickling my back. Got it?"

"Got it," Moore's voice came back. "Give me a few minutes to brief the others."

"Keep in mind—the top floor only."

"Don't worry. We won't hit you—over and out."

Richard put the walkie talkie back into its case, counted to sixty, then carefully looked around the left corner of the wall. M16 A-R projectiles were tearing into the top story of the house. There was the high whine of ricochets from the stucco. Pieces of glass fell from the windows. A large piece of pottery, suspended on a macrame hanger, exploded as a

46

5.56mm bullet hit. The front of the house was being chopped to pieces; nonetheless, an automatic rifle and a submachine gun were firing from the windows of the bottom floor.

Camellion pulled his head back and pulled a SIG P210 automatic from the left holster on his hip, switched off the safety catch, and for a moment looked at the Swiss auto-loader. It was a high-quality pistol seldom found in military inventories, one notable feature being that the slide was carried inside the frame, rather than moving on the more common external milled surfaces.

Holding the SIG in one hand and the Ruger in the other, the Death Merchant jumped up and started a crooked run toward one of the rugged oaks. M16 slugs were cutting through the top branches of all the trees, the hatchet job sending chopped leaves floating to the ground. The A–R and the sub-gun were still roaring from several windows on the ground floor, but before the gunners could swing down on him, Camellion reached his goal: the oak tree—thirty feet closer to the porch.

Flattened against the side of the tree, he felt his own M16 digging into his back and heard enemy slugs thudding into the bark on either side of him. He holstered the SIG and the Ruger, thinking that the revolutionaries inside the house certainly could see the tree. The friendly cloud had passed, and once more the night was so bright that one could almost read by the light of the full moon.

Camellion listened as he removed a fragmentation grenade from one of his chest straps. He detected that more firing was now coming from the rear than from the front of the house. Two M16s and the deeper roar of at least three enemy sub-guns—*They sound like cartucho Largos!*

He pulled the ring from the grenade and flipped it, with a backward motion, toward the porch. He was taking the second grenade from the strap when the first exploded with a crashing roar. Richard waited for a moment, listening to shrapnel PING against the stucco and break the jagged pieces of glass that still remained in the windows. A man cried out from the ground floor.

More high-velicity projectiles hit the front and both sides of the oak. He pulled the pin of the second grenade, counted "ONE, TWO, THREE!" and tossed it up and backward. The grenade exploded in midair three seconds later, shrapnel stabbing into the trees and shooting through some of the

47

windows of the top floor. There was a short shriek and a man cried, *"Mi faz!"*

I hope you don't have a face left! Camellion thought. He spun to his right and, keeping low, made a wild dash to the raised flower-bed. He dived to the side of the bricks and lay in a horizontal position as a stream of submachine gun slugs butchered weeds, begonias, and marigolds. All the while, the record player inside the house kept screaming *mariachi* music, no one having shut it off.

Lying as he was on his left side, the Death Merchant now had a better chance to place the grenades where he wanted them. His first grenade demolished half the roof over the porch and tore out one of the window casements upstairs. Giant splinters, broken boards, and pieces of tile rained down over the area. With a loud crash most of the porch roof caved in.

Half a brick had struck the tile on top of the flowerbed wall and had rolled off onto Camellion's back. Part of a two-by-four had glanced off his back. But he wasn't hurt. He held the second grenade for three seconds before he threw it. It exploded a few feet from the stucco of the second floor, and when the smoke and flame cleared there was a four foot hole in the bricks. The two guerrillas inside the room were knocked to the floor, stunned. They weren't put on the road to recovery by the third grenade's exploding only ten feet from where the second grenade had detonated.

Breathing hard with tension, Camellion pulled the .22 Ruger and charged toward the house, his long legs impelling him forward. He was safe from the submachine gunners on the first floor, a large section of the roof having fallen in front of three windows to the left of the door. A figure appeared by the side of the fourth window at the same instant that Camellion reached the porch, the commie gangster trying to raise the Largo sub-gun in his hands. He never got the chance to level down and pull the trigger. The Death Merchant, jumping up on the porch, snapped off a shot with the Ruger. There was a mild POP as the bullet sped through the silencer, hit the man in the chest, then exploded with the sound of a shotgun being fired. Pieces of colored shirt, hunks of flesh and sternum bone flew outward from the corpse, which was falling backward.

Camellion tore to the side of the front door, dropped to one knee and removed another grenade from his strap. He pulled the ring with his teeth, flipped the grenade through the fourth window and flattened himself against the wall at the same time that a submachine gun roared and a dozen slugs punched holes in the front door, some of them barely missing Harley Korse and Leland Moore, who were racing toward the house with Eldridge Eubanks and Cletus Huff.

The grenade exploded inside the room, the concussion shaking the front wall of the house. An 8″ x 8″ beam crashed down from the shattered ceiling, one heavy end striking the brick floor only a few feet in front of Camellion. But the grenade had done its work. The machine gun stopped firing. The record player became silent. On his feet now, Camellion put a couple of explosive .22 bullets into the lock, stepped back, pushed open the door with one foot, then spun around and went to the fourth window—all to the loud tune of a machine gun that began tossing slugs through the doorway.

The whole damn business was a risk, but so was living. He leaned through the window and saw that the commie bandolero with the Star machine gun was crouched at the end of a hall that opened to the spacious room. The man dropped the Star and threw up his arms when a .22 explosive bullet exploded his skull and splattered his brain against the dirty yellow wall.

Killing a man was easy. It was staying alive that was difficult! Drawing the SIG autoloader, Camellion instinctively thumbed off the safety catch and started to crawl through the window. He threw his body forward when, through the drifting smoke, he saw a woman lean around one end of an old-time player piano. For a mini-moment she hesitated and stared in astonishment at the lean killing machine wearing a Santa Claus mask that had been blackened with camouflage face paint—*Dios!* Very quickly then she triggered off a shot with a Campo Giro automatic. Another figure —a man naked to the waist—stepped into the doorway of the room to Camellion's right and raised a Mondagon carbine.

The Death Merchant, who ducked to one side as the woman fired, swung up his own weapons, moved his arms into a "V" and pulled the triggers, aiming strictly by instinct. The woman's 9mm bullet missed him by half a foot. His 9mm SIG projectile struck her a few inches below the navel. The .22 slug from the silenced Ruger sliced into the man's groin, exploded, tore off his penis and testicles, and exposed a section of ropy gray colon. Tottering, he still tried to raise

49

the rifle. He flopped like a headless chicken when the second .22 exploded in his chest. As for Eva Cardenaz, her mouth flew open. She stared in shock at Camellion, groaned loudly, doubled over, and fell sideways across the record player, which rested on a table. With a crash, corpse, record player, and table fell to the floor.

Camellion swerved to the wall on the west side of the room, and took stock of his position. A dead man lay in front of the outside door—the man he had shot through the window. Another corpse was sprawled face down in the doorway of the room to the east. Across the room, to the north, was the end of a hall—and another body. The grenade the Death Merchant had tossed through the window had knocked furniture around and shattered an overstuffed chair. The floor was thick with cotton, torn cloth, and twisted springs.

Richard turned his gaze upward. Not far from the mouth of the hallway were stairs that curved upward to the long, open-sided landing of the second floor; a carved wooden railing, with a lot of knobs and decorations, fronted the open length of space.

To Camellion's left, six feet from where he crouched, was the doorway of the room to the west, the very same room from which had come the vicious streams of submachine gunfire.

Un huh! So where are those two boys now? Either they left by another door, or else they're still in there, playing it safe!

He removed another grenade from his chest strap. He was pulling the pin when he heard the blast from a grenade toward the rear of the house, toward the outside end of the hallway. The explosion was followed by a scream and the roaring of either four or five machine guns. The noise was terrific. The explosion of the grenade that Camellion tossed into the west room was even more thunderous. A split second later, Camellion was going in right behind the blast, the PLINK of recently fallen shrapnel ringing in his ears. The explosion had terminated the life of one guerrilla. He lay on his back, a look of utter horror on his face, the broken leg of a wooden plant stand protruding from his chest.

Julio Asonada, the second chili bean in the room, was stunned but unhurt. He had been waiting behind a massive couch covered with horsehide, and now he staggered to his feet and made an effort to use the Parinco machine gun on the dark-suited invader wearing a Santa Claus false face. The next thing Asonada felt was a horrible agony burning in his chest, waves of pain that numbed his mind to the extent he didn't know he was dying from the 9mm SIG bullet that the Death Merchant had put into his chest. He fell across the back of the couch, drops of blood dripping down onto the horsehide-covered cushions.

The Death Merchant—now he heard gunfire from the opposite room—turned around and dodged to his right just in time to avoid a line of .45 slugs. He almost didn't succeed. One hot piece of copper-gilded lead zipped through the left sleeve of his navy blue coveralls. If the bullet had been an inch and a half farther over, it would have ripped through the trapezius muscle and torn off his arm.

Stumbling slightly over an overturned ladder-back chair, Camellion swung up both the Ruger and the SIG and fired four times. A .22 Ruger bullet bored through the red shirt of the heavyset, button-eyed man with the .45 M3 grease gun and exploded in his stomach. He dropped the grease gun and fell against a thin chili-pepper who, with his long hair, neatly-trimmed beard and pencil-mustache, reminded the Death Merchant of a seventeenth-century poet. Then the man reminded Camellion of an ordinary bloody corpse. A 9mm SIG slug had shot through his teeth, bored out the back of his head, and had struck a third Mexican gunman in the lower lobe of his right ear. The man screamed in terror, dropped his Condor automatic, and spun around from the impact of a .22 Ruger bullet that exploded in his left shoulder, tearing off an arm and releasing a deluge of blood from the left axillary artery. Behind him, the fourth Mexican revolutionary attempted to rush toward the front door. Camellion solved all his problems by stabbing the man in the side of the neck with a 9mm bullet, the impact snapping his head to one side. Choking on the blood bubbling in his throat, the dying dummy dropped to the floor, which was already slippery with fresh blood from the corpse lacking an arm.

The Death Merchant heard a machine gun firing in the hall. In the distance, toward the rear of this section of the house, another sub-gun answered in reply. Camellion ran to the side of the doorway closest to the porch. He holstered the SIG and the Ruger, removed the M16 from his back, switched the automatic rifle to semiautomatic firing and clicked off the safety. He couldn't have picked a more opportune time to look around the side of the door.

Two men and a woman were moving on the open balcony of the second floor, the woman carrying a pistol and leading one man, who had his hand over his eyes. The second man had his hands filled with an American Colt CAR–15. A fourth man was coming down the stairs. He was carrying an Armalite AR–18 and dividing his attention between the mouth of the hall and the door of the room harboring Camellion, who switched his M16 to full automatic fire, then raised the A–R at the same moment that two other revolutionaries backed out of the hallway and the gunman coming down the stairs spotted the Death Merchant.

"Santa Claus" in black face was the last thing the 23–9–League commie saw before three 5.56 millimeter projectiles cut apart his midsection and pitched him backward on the stairs.

Camellion calculated the lag-time. He figured he could waste the two long-haired dudes backing out of the hallway before they and the three terrorists on the balcony could organize their senses enough to return his fire. A few grenades could then topple the balcony and he could ice-out the two men and the woman.

He was only half-right. His stream of M16 projectiles hosed into the two long-haired jokers as they were swinging around toward him, the 5.56mm slugs butchering them, flooding them right out of this world into the nothingness of infinity.

Richard was ducking back to the security of the wall as three M16s roared from the front door and a woman screamed. He poked his head around in time to see a man pitch over the balcony railing and crash to the floor of the room below. He had been riddled to the extent that it would have taken a neuro-surgeon and a Swiss watchmaker to put him together.

The woman, dressed in shorts and halter, fell across the railing, blood dripping down from a dozen holes in her body. The man who had had his hand over his eyes was crumpled on the floor of the balcony.

Moore and Eldridge and the other two Feds! Camellion thought.

He yelled out, *"I'm in here!"*

"Out here!" a voice—Harley Korse's—called back from the opposite room.

Hearing a scraping sound behind him, Camellion swung around and saw that someone was tugging at a section of roof that had fallen in front of the window. Whoever it was pulled the boards to one side, then stuck his head through the window. He wore a "Dick Tracy" false face—Cletus Huff.

"Why don't you be more careful?" warned Camellion. "I could have been one of the hot tamales!"

"Ho! I looked between the boards and saw it was you!" Huff said cheerfully and crawled in through the window.

On his way to the other room, the Death Merchant didn't argue; yet he was still annoyed with Huff. Instead of saying "yes" or "no," the ATF agent always responded with "ho!" —a habit that also irked the dour-faced Harley Korse, who spoke when he had something direct to say.

Camellion had also detected—by observation and by being sensitive to other people's moods—that Korse disliked and felt superior to Huff for other reasons. Korse was a conservative and a non-smoker, fastidious about his clothes and appearance. A chain-smoker, Huff more often than not finished an entire Pall Mall without removing it from the center of his mouth. If he thought about it, he might brush ashes from his coat.

"Orphan Annie," "Moon Mullins," and "Peanuts"—Eubanks, Korse, and Moore were poking around the bodies in the next room. None of them had received as much as a scratch in the battle.

"We did it," said Moore, who had pushed his "Peanuts" mask up to his forehead and was wiping sweat from his face. "We've won."

"Not yet we haven't," the Death Merchant corrected. "We still have to check the upstairs, and we can expect almost anything in the cellar. Don't count your lives before you know for sure you're going to hang onto them."

Camellion turned and looked at "Snoopy" and "Jiggs," who were coming down the hall. "Maggie," the third Mexican of Camellion's force, followed.

"You're to be congratulated on a job well done. The three of you acted like professionals," Camellion said to "Jiggs," the first man, who was carefully stepping around the corpses of revolutionaries.

"How many of the scum did you get?" Eldridge Eubanks asked, then shoved a full magazine into his M16.

"Jiggs" nodded toward Camellion. "Gracias, Senor," replied Luis Jalisco in a low, serious voice. "Two of us are members in the *Guardia Civil,* and"—he suppressed the name on the tip of his tongue—"the third man was a *soldado* for many years."

"Damn it! You're divulging classified information about the Polar network!" Moore said between clenched teeth. "Never reveal to anyone the work you do. I've warned you about that before."

"I didn't reveal any names," Jalisco said, unperturbed. "There are thousands of men in the civil police and a lot of ex-soldiers around."

"*Tengo sed,*" one of the other Mexicans said, wiping the front of his neck. "*Hace calor.*"

Moore rattled off a stream of Spanish to "Maggie." The man nodded, then turned and walked back down the hall, holding his M16 in a ready-for-action position.

"What's going on?" asked Cletus Huff, the only man present who did not speak Spanish. "Where is he going?"

"He said he was thirsty because the weather is hot." Moore acted annoyed. "I told him to hurry up and find the kitchen and get a drink."

"Hot? It's only forty-five outside!" exclaimed Huff.

"That's what I told him," Moore said. "I told him it was only tension." He peered curiously at Huff. "There's nothing personal in this, Huff. Don't take offense. But why did the Treasury Department send you down here to Mexico? You don't even speak the language."

"I think it's rather silly myself," Huff agreed, sounding as though he considered his assignment a big joke. "The BATF is undermanned and Congress won't appropriate funds for more personnel. We have more work than we can do. New York, Chicago, L.A., Detroit—name any city. It's an armed camp, and half the guns are stolen. I came down here because I was the only man available."

It's like sending an Eskimo to dig for oil in the middle of the Atlantic Ocean! Camellion thought dismally.

The eight men checked the three rooms upstairs. In the last room they found an elderly man dressed in typical farmer's clothes—white cotton shirt and pants, *huaraces* on his feet. The sandals looked new. The old man, lying on his back with his eyes closed, had been shot in the chest. The brown bag of bones next to him, dressed in a faded blue dress, was also a corpse. Her *rebozo*—shawl—lay on the floor.

"It must be Senor and Senora Tuchilan," Moore said, staring down at the two bodies covered with plaster dust.

"The commies must have neutralized them to keep them from telling what they knew."

"They deserved to die," Jose Anahuac, one of the Mexicans, said. "They helped the *Communistas* and were traitors to the nation."

The men looked around the small bedroom. The faded yellow walls were filled with bullet holes, the plaster cracked, much of it lying on the floor. Somehow a statue of the Virgin of the Conquistadores, resting on an old dresser, had not been touched. Neither had a small wooden stool on which rested a glass bowl filled with chunks of what resembled gray-green buttons.

"Peyote buttons," Harley Korse muttered, then glanced disdainfully at the two corpses on the bed. "Maybe they died with visions of heaven."

"More probably hell," Luis Jalisco said.

Eldridge Eubanks turned to the Death Merchant, who had come back from looking out the shot-out window. "Say, Camellion. I think we ought to check the house on the other side of the patio."

He didn't know what to say when the Death Merchant merely shook his head.

"E–4 said that the east side of the house wasn't being used," Moore pointed out. "The rest of the bandits could be over there anyhow. They're not here or they would have opened fire on us when we charged in."

He turned and followed the Death Merchant, who was leaving the room. The rest of the men followed Moore.

They left the house by way of the rear door, crept across the patio, and moved up alongside the house toward the northeast corner.

"Emerald–4 said the doors to the cellar were on the outside," whispered Eubanks nervously. "Those must be the doors up ahead." In the lead, Camellion stopped when he reached the side of one door, which slanted down from the side of the house. He put out his arm and blocked Eubanks, who had moved out from behind him and was trying to get in front of the double doors, which opened by pulling them up and then letting them fall back to either side.

"Don't stand in front of those doors, you fool," hissed Camellion, and pulled Eubanks back. "High-powered slugs would tear through that dry wood as though it were tissue paper."

Leland Moore eased up beside the Death Merchant. "Christ,

Camellion! You can see for yourself that the hasp is closed and that there's a lock through it." The CIA spook was half-angry. "No one could have entered the cellar, then closed the doors and put on a lock. You're being too goddamn cautious!"

"We don't have all night, either," intoned Eubanks. "The Rurales in Xochimilco will get up enough nerve to come out here and investigate the explosions when they think there's no danger."

"And you are not being cautious enough—none of you," half-laughed the Death Merchant—an eerie chuckle that made Moore and the other six men vaguely uncomfortable. "Or you'd realize that the clever way to do it would be to have someone on the outside secure the hasp after the others were on the inside."

"So what the hell do we do?" Moore asked, his voice husky with impatience.

Camellion turned and addressed the men, speaking in a quiet voice. "All of you move back to the southeast corner of the house, and I'll show you how."

As the group began to move to the front corner, the Death Merchant placed two grenades on the ground by the side of the doors' brick foundation. Quickly he ran to the corner of the house, seventy-five feet to the south. He motioned to the men to stand in front of the house, and he joined them, his eyes probing the shaded area by the northeast corner of the house. The grenades were untouched by moonlight, but he could still see the dark form of the cellar doors.

"Here we gooooo!" he said like a circus barker. He leaned forward, raised the M16 to his shoulder and pulled the trigger. The A-R roared and spit out a stream of slugs.

There was a flash of red flame and two terrific explosions, so close together they might have been one. Rubble and debris rained down—huge splinters of wood, sharp chunks of broken bricks and stones from the lower foundation. The concussion almost knocked Camellion to the ground.

"All right, **guys**. Spread and be ready to fire, but don't get in front of the entrance," Camellion said. His eyes were ringing, his own voice a hollow echo within his head.

He stalked ahead, the M16 ready to be fired. The rest of the men formed a line to his left as they advanced.

The locked doors had been replaced by a jagged, smoking hole in the ground. Even the top of the stone steps had been exploded into rubble and powder. Camellion cocked his head and motioned to the others, indicating he wanted complete silence. He listened, almost positive he had heard movements in the darkness below. After he motioned for the men to move back, he picked up a rounded chunk of brick and flipped it into the hole, twisting his mouth in satisfaction as he heard it plop down the lower stone steps.

"Granada!" They all heard the word *"Grenade"* shouted below—the voice of a man in panic. The shout was followed by the racket of automatic weapons and the deeper booming of pistols. The Death Merchant, who had flattened himself against the side of the house, could picture the dozens of projectiles zipping through the demolished entrance. He could hear some of the slugs, too, smashing against the stone sides of the entrance and zinging off.

"Oh my . . . Some people don't know when to quit!" sighed Camellion, who pulled the pin from his last grenade and easily sent it flying into the hole, spinning it so that it would roll into the cellar.

The explosion was deafening!

Thick dust boiled up from the blackness below.

The Death Merchant and his men waited. Presently they heard a voice call out weakly in Spanish: *"Rendir! Rendir! Entregar! Vamos a hacer escala en rendir!"*

"Then come up with your hands up!" Camellion shouted. *"Leave your weapons behind. Any false moves and we'll throw in another grenade."*

Within a few minutes, three men and two women stood in front of the cellar entrance, their arms raised toward the moon, their eyes mirrors of fear and hatred. Their arms and faces were as dirty and dusty as their clothes.

Camellion and his men closed in around the five terrorists, who faced them defiantly, trying to hide their fears. They hadn't expected an attack and were demoralized.

"How many more of you are waiting in the cellar to ambush us?" Camellion asked, his voice a chilling warning. Very suddenly the M16 in his hands chattered off a very short burst, the unexpected blast surprising his own men as much as it astonished the trapped revolutionaries whose number had now been reduced by one.

"Well I'll be damned!" muttered Eldridge Eubanks in a shaky voice. He stared at Camellion, then looked down at the terrorist Richard had gut-shot. The corpse lay on its back, mouth open, eyes wide and fixed.

Camellion shrugged. "He started to lower his arms," he said chattily. "That was a no-no."

The two men and the two women prisoners gaped incredulously at the tall man in the Santa Claus mask. Here was a man who killed at the blink of an eye, *a buque de guerra*—a man of war—who was as ruthless as they were.

Slim and rather pretty, Lilia Chapardez began to tremble. Her arms were raised so high her shoulders had begun to ache. The three other prisoners, frozen with fear, stood still.

"How many others are down in the cellar?" Camellion repeated.

"All dead! They're all dead from the explosion," mumbled Amado Asbeje. A thickset man, with most of his front teeth missing, he had the hound-dog look of a person unjustly hurt. "There isn't any trap. We—"

Again the M16 in Camellion's hands snarled. Three 5.56mm slugs hit Asbeje in the chest, knocking him to the ground.

"Lies are not acceptable!" Camellion raged contemptuously. Pretending to be dominated by fury, he shouted at the three remaining prisoners, who were transfixed within his eerie stare. "I want the full truth, or I'll kill every one of you and give you over to the tender mercy of Hell!"

Richard ignored his own people, who were disturbed at what they believed to be true behavior on his part. Why bother? Why should he tell them the true reason for his supposed outburst and his very real ruthlessness? Because time was running out. Because, if the second man had not been telling the truth—*I think he was*—the three still alive would think twice about continuing the lie. Murder? A Communist couldn't be "murdered" any more than a bedbug could be "murdered"!

Very slowly Camellion raised the automatic rifle, swinging the barrel to one of the women.

"*No, Senor! No!*" screamed Isabel Manelto. "Amado spoke the truth. The others in the cellar are dead. The grenade killed them."

Misty with fear-tears, her eyes were a silent plea for life.

Camellion regarded the young woman with contempt. She was dressed in blue slacks, a gray turtleneck sweater, and short black boots. Her dark hair was piled on top of her head.

"She is not lying," Lazaro Apotes said quickly, his voice

cracking with nervousness. "I swear she is not. I swear it in the name of the Creator and on the head of my dead mother."

More Indian than mestizo, Apotes couldn't tear his eyes from the black muzzle of the M16 which had swung to his belly. He waited for a bullet to stab into his body. But none came.

Harley Korse broke into the questioning, his voice low and threatening. "We know that there is an entrance to a passage in the cellar, and we know that the tunnel leads to a secret room."

His Spanish was terrible, but he managed to sound half as maniacal as the Death Merchant had. "We want to know how many are in that room with Mudejar, Gomara, and that bitch Sojeda!"

"If they're not hiding in the room, where are they?" Leland Moore joined in.

Lazaro Apotes' lower jaw slackened. Isabel Manelto and Lilia Chapardez glanced nervously at each other. Both women had the ashen look of people who make the discovery that something totally alien is eating at their sanity and self-control.

"But El Perico and the other leaders left yesterday afternoon!" Apotes' voice was a croak. "The room is empty."

"Well, I gave you a chance," Korse said with a tone of finality. "I guess 'Santa' will have to put a slug in your gut."

Right on cue, Camellion acted as if he were about to pull the trigger of the M16.

Overcome with fear of death, Apotes screamed, "NO, Senor! It's the truth! I can prove it. I'll take you to the room and show you. It's empty!"

He lowered his arms, partially covered his face and stepped back a few feet, as if bracing himself inwardly for his execution. Tiny flashes of relief flooded his consciousness when he found he was still alive. Then he remembered Camellion's order about raised arms. His hands shot up above his head.

The Death Merchant wanted to laugh—*I had better tell him to put down his arms before he pulls himself apart!*

"*Compadre,* no matter how hard you try, you will never be able to touch the moon," he mocked. "All of you lower your arms, but keep your hands where we can see them."

The three captives relaxed their arms and folded their hands in front of them. Words jumped out of Lilia Chapardez's mouth. "Senor, we didn't even know that the underground room existed until Commander Sojeda told us about it yesterday. We three have never been in the room, but some of the others went in and took a look. They said the room was empty."

The Death Merchant fired off a question. "It's all very convenient, but why should Juanita Sojeda tell you about the room just before she and the others left? What was her purpose? What was her plan?" He stepped closer to Lilia Chapardez and ever so gently pressed the muzzle of the A–R against her stomach. She began to shake; tears flowed down her cheeks.

"I-I don't know!" she sobbed, and made a great effort to control her voice. "Commander Sojeda just told us in conversation. The room is not part of any 'plan,' none that I know of."

Eldridge Eubanks looked hard at the three captured guerrillas.

"Why did Juanita Sojeda and the other leaders leave the farm?" Eubanks demanded, his voice taking on a speed and haste of assertion.

"And where did they go?" Camellion grated, poking Lilia Chapardez.

"I swear I don't know," the woman sobbed, twisting her hands in front of her. "I heard her talking to some of the other members of our force, and I remember her mentioning an apartment where she once holed up in Mexico City."

"I'll just bet you remember the address, too!" Camellion laughed.

For a moment Chapardez stared at the man in the Santa's false face, trying to fathom his meaning. Was he making fun of her, toying with her, before he cut her down?

"Yes, I do. I have a good memory," she replied haltingly. "The address is San Juan de Latran 47744. I remember it so well because I have an aunt living at 48522. It is the truth, senor. Why should I lie? I don't want to die."

"I know another location," Isabel Manelto interrupted in a desperate effort to prove she wanted to cooperate. "I overheard Alvar Gomara and Paul Escutia discussing a sugar mill on the outskirts of Zacoalco, not far from Lake Chapala. I, too, am telling you the truth."

Her mouth slack, she looked pleadingly at the Death Merchant, convinced that he was the most dangerous of all the captors. She and Manelto and Apotes watched with mounting apprehension as Eubanks thundered, his eyes blazing poison, "Answer my question. Why did your leaders leave this farm? I want to know right now, or I'll do some killing of my own."

"We don't know," Lazaro Apotes answered the question. "They never confide in us. We were told—I mean the entire force—to leave tomorrow . . . two and three at a time."

Leland Moore moved over to Camellion and, in English, whispered in his ear. "Listen, Mr. C. The way the top people cleared out, something's not right in Denmark. There could be a trap waiting for us in the tunnel or in that room—I'm not convinced there isn't one."

Camellion turned his head slightly while Harley Korse whispered in his other ear. "That bitch is lying about that San Juan de Latran address—or else it's a setup!"

"Don't worry about it," Richard said. "I've been through all this before." He speared Lazaro Apotes and the two women with a poisonous stare.

"It's high time that all of you started talking about the trap waiting down there for us. Where and what kind? In the tunnel or in the room itself?"

The same tone of definite menace, and an implicit "or else" in his voice!

"I don't know anything about a trap," Lazaro Apotes replied weakly.

"If anything's down there we don't—we weren't told about it," Isabel Manelto said in a small voice. "Your shooting us won't change anything. We can't tell you what we don't know."

Lilia Chapardez quickly added, her voice cracking, "But there are two tunnels. There's one from the cellar to the room. Another tunnel goes from the room to the henequen shed over there." She jerked her head to the east.

"I thought you said you had never been down there?" Camellion said lightly. Shouldering his rifle, he pulled out the .22 Ruger.

Chapardez's eyes jumped to the weapon.

"I haven't been," she choked. "One of the men who was in the room told us. Maximo Lerdo. He's not in the cellar. I guess you killed him."

"The escape tunnel," Leland Moore muttered. "Just like we figured."

The Death Merchant looked directly at Lilia Chapardez. "I hope for your sake you're telling the truth. If Death is

61

waiting for us down there, the three of you will be the first to feel his bony embrace."

A few minutes later, Lazaro Apotes stood with his wrists handcuffed behind his back. Steel cuffs also imprisoned Lilia Chapardez's hands behind her back. Isabel Manelto's hands were cuffed in front of her.

"The two of you are going in first," Camellion said, and motioned with the Ruger to Apotes and Chapardez. His strong fingers found Isabel Manelto's left arm. "You're staying with me, honey lamb. You other two—*move!*"

While Leland Moore and the three Mexican members of the Polar Cold deep-cover net waited by the side of the house, Camellion and the others moved down into the cellar. Apotes and Chapardez were the first to half-stumble down the half-wrecked steps, the beam of Eldridge Eubanks' flashlight showing them the way.

Once in the cellar, Camellion and his men had proof that the three captives had spoken the truth. The grenade had wrecked the small cellar. Five bodies lay in the rubble—four men and a woman. The woman must have weighed 300 pounds. She had not been attractive in life, and in death she was hideous—her mouth frozen in a twisted smile, her eyes open but turned up so far it appeared she was staring into her own eye sockets.

By the sweeping beams of their flashlights, Camellion and his people saw that concussion had scattered boxes and other junk and had knocked fruit jars to the stone floor. Broken glass and spilled home-canned fruit and vegetables were everywhere, wet and sticky. A few of the corpses had even been splattered with jam and jelly. All around was a stink—the smell of dust, stale air, drying blood, and the sweet odor of spilled food.

"Some of the jars are still intact," Cletus Huff said. He played the beam of his light on a jar on the floor. "Looks like berries."

The Death Merchant flashed his light full on Isabel Manelto's pale face. "Where were you and the others when the grenade went off? None of you are even scratched."

She blinked against the brightness of the beam. Camellion lowered the light from her face.

"We were in the mouth of the tunnel," she said soberly. "It's over there behind shelves hinged to the stones."

Camellion saw Harley Korse's beam move over the far wall and stop at a low narrow entrance.

"Here it is," Korse said triumphantly.

"One of you hold a light on the prisoners," Camellion said.

When Huff complied, Camellion switched off his own flash, stuffed it in his pocket, took out a key and unlocked one of the steel cuffs from Isabel Manelto's left wrist. He then snapped the open cuff around Lazaro Apotes' left wrist, after pulling Isabel's left arm behind her back. And since both of Apotes' arms were behind his back, it was a partnership in steel that made walking very awkward for the two terrorists.

"Get over to the tunnel and start moving," Camellion said brusquely. He handed his flashlight to a badly frightened Isabel Manelto, who took it with her right hand.

"But moving down the tunnel like this will be so difficult," she protested feebly. "If any explosives were set in there, we'll be killed. . . ."

"All of you can die right now if you prefer," Camellion said with mock solemnity. "As for moving slowly, that's the idea. We'll be twenty feet behind the three of you. Now get in there or die."

The three terrorists moved toward the black mouth of the tunnel, Isabel Manelto tugging against Lazaro Apotes, who had begun to sob.

Chapter Five

The van was the type used by companies to deliver packages, the kind one could stand up in; nevertheless, the vehicle was crowded because it contained ten people and bulky radar equipment.

Ten minutes after the van had left the vicinity of the farm, Leland Moore had detected fast-moving vehicles on the radar, police cars several miles up ahead, and had given the warning. Rossana had swung the van off the road and had driven at an angle straight across the uneven scrub-land, commenting that driving without lights was not exactly to her liking. Finally she had parked in the middle of a group of low hills, a quarter of a mile from the dirt road. Two of the Mexicans had jumped out, climbed one of the mounds, and waited for the police cars and jeeps to go by in the distance.

Now the van was on the road again, and the Rurales were far behind. Rossana would by-pass Xochimilco. She would keep on the dirt road for another mile, then turn off onto the asphalt road that, three miles ahead, would intersect the main highway which twisted into the southern outskirts of Mexico City. She would keep to the outskirts and drive to Chapultepec, where everyone would spend the night at Eldridge Eubanks' house.

"We were lucky that the Federal police didn't have a station around Xochimilco," Harley Korse said. "From what I've heard the country policemen back there couldn't catch a cold."

Sitting on a bench bolted to the wall, Korse leaned against the Death Merchant as Rossana slowed the van to negotiate a curve. Camellion, watching the road ahead, sat on the edge of the bench, behind the raised bucket seat of the driver.

"This night's operation was a calculated risk," Leland Moore said with heavy petulance. "I don't know who told you about the Rurales, but whoever it was told you wrong. The Mexican country cops aren't as efficient as the Federal police, but once you engage them in a fight they don't know when to quit, and you have pure hell on your hands."

Korse's eyes darted toward the center of the van, toward Moore, who was sitting behind the radar set. The drug con-

64

trol agent had detected the note of antipathy in Moore's voice, but he couldn't see the CIA man's face. The interior of the van was too dark. Previously Moore's face had been outlined in the greenish-white glow from the screen. However, once the van had lost the Rurales, Moore had switched off the radar set.

Eldridge Eubanks said, "I think we're all missing the heart of the matter: the fact that we failed to find The Parrot and the other League executives. We risked our lives in what was nothing more than a huge exercise in futility. We're no better off now than we were yesterday."

"I am wondering if it was only fate that caused Mudejar and the others to leave so suddenly, before we could corner them?" Jose Anahuac said thoughtfully in English, without any accent. As he moved his hand, the end of his cigarette glowed in the dark. He laughed sinisterly. "Or am I being too suspicious and exhibiting paranoid symptoms?"

Camellion, Korse and Huff did not know Anahuac's profession. They knew only that he was a member of the Polar Cold network. But from the way he enunciated his words, they suspected that he was an educated man.

"What do you mean?" Luis Jalisco asked.

"He is intimating that The Parrot and his people may have been warned," explained Eldridge Eubanks in a monotone.

"No one could have tipped off *El Perico*," Moore pronounced imperiously, as if he were making an announcement. "No one knew of our plan, only the ten of us. Not one person in this van is a traitor."

For a moment Moore forgot that the rear of the van was dark. He turned to his right and glanced quizzically at Anahuac, who was sitting between Cletus Huff and Porfirio Leyendas.

"I didn't say that there was a double agent among us," was Anahuac's rebuttal. "But it seems to me that we shouldn't ignore all the strange coincidences. We can, but I prefer not to."

"Emerald-4 must have suspected what we intended to do?" Porfirio Leyendas interrupted, almost involuntarily. Like Luis Jalisco, he spoke English with a thick accent.

"E-4 has proved his reliability ten times over," Moore snapped, insulted by Leyendas' suggestion that Efran Rebaderos might be playing both ends against the middle.

"Ho! But what that other man said makes one sort of wonder," mused Cletus Huff, leaning heavily against Jose

Anahuac as Rossana jerked the van to avoid a rut in the road. "Yet a lot of it doesn't add up in the opposite direction. If Gomara, The Parrot, and the other leaders knew we were coming after them, why didn't they leave a trap, say like fifty sticks of dynamite in the tunnels—or a few pounds of plastic stuff in the room? Damned odd that the room and the two tunnels were clean. If The Parrot knew we were coming, why did he pass up the perfect opportunity to blow us away? It doesn't make sense!"

"Maybe they didn't have time to set up any kind of elaborate explosive trap?" offered Jose Leyenda. "Or there's the possibility that they lacked timing mechanisms or triggering devices."

"I don't agree," Huff said firmly. "The commies had more than enough time to rig up *something* for us. The prisoners said that Hector Mudejar and the other three bigwigs flew the coop yesterday afternoon. The captives we had didn't lie. An idiot could tell that. So if the regular members of the League knew we were going to hit them, why didn't they set up an ambush? All they had were guards posted—like sitting ducks. To me that proves that at least the regular members of the commie force had no previous knowledge about us."

"We'll never be able to ask them any more questions," Porfirio Leyendas said slowly. "Those three never knew what hit them."

Luis Jalisco's short laugh was eerie in the darkness. Then he said, "The way we're talking, the next thing you know someone will be saying it was a shame we had to execute the three bastards."

"I think it was," Harley Korse said crossly. "Personally, I dislike killing helpless people, even communist terrorists."

"You should not feel sorry for those three murderers," Jose Leyendas's low voice was one constant snicker. "After all, we did leave them in a ready-made crypt!"

Leland Moore and Cletus Huff laughed, but the rest of the men remained silent. It was a silence that remained. To repair the embarrassing break in the line of communications, Eldridge Eubanks finally called out in a loud voice, "Mr. C! All this time you haven't said a word. What is your opinion?"

Thinking that some people talk simply because they think sound is more manageable than silence, the Death Merchant turned and looked toward the rear of the van.

"I have been thinking that Korse hasn't done much to

make muddy waters clear," Camellion responded lazily. "He doesn't cater to the necessity of executing commie terrorists, but he hasn't said a word about Americans who come down to Mexico thinking the Mexican cops don't have enough sense to come in out of a downpour. Then when they get caught trying to smuggle narcotics and tossed into prison, they start crying how they're being 'mistreated.' And the damned do-gooders back home start screaming, 'Free our poor innocent children.' I'd stand those smuggling sons of bitches up against a wall and shoot them!"

Camellion turned and looked directly at Korse. "But tell me, wouldn't those men and women be kind of 'helpless' when they were stood up against a wall?"

First giving a belly laugh, Cletus Huff drawled, "Well, he's got you there, Harley. Whether you execute terrorists or college kids carrying coke or an ounce of H, what's the difference?"

From the dim light coming through the front of the van, Huff and the others could see that Korse's face was fixed in controlled rage. *Hell, Korse didn't belong in the BATF. He should have been a missionary,* his fellow agent thought.

"Huff, it's a waste of time to talk to you," Korse said sarcastically. "As liberal as you are, I suppose you would free all the Americans in Mexican jails, even if they were convicted of trying to smuggle narcotics."

"Gentlemen, gentlemen! Enough of this bickering," Eldridge Eubanks said soothingly. "We would do better to discuss our next moves. The Communist League is planning some kind of immense operation, and we're not any closer to stopping it than we were yesterday. We don't have a single thing to go on!"

"I'll buy that," Leland Moore agreed. "It makes more sense than squabbling over a bunch of smugglers!"

"We have several avenues of approach to the problem," Camellion said with a note of hidden triumph. "The sugar mill around Lake Chapala, and the address on San Juan de Letran Avenue."

As far as I'm concerned this whole set-up sounds phony. Too many things don't add up. . . .

Chapter Six

Earlier that morning, Rossana had sighed and said, "I think you have self-destructive impulses that are forcing you to take ridiculous chances. You know as well as I do, if you go poking around that apartment on San Juan de Latran Avenue, you'll end up lifeless."

"I'll pray on the way," the Death Merchant had said. "Anyhow, I don't intend to die today. It's too sunny and nice. Let's go, doll."

The car moved through the mid-morning traffic of the wide Paseo de la Reforma, the largest of Mexico City's boulevards. In appearance the car was as much a fake as the two persons in the front seat: Rossana del Moreno, who was driving, and Richard Camellion, who sat relaxed beside her. A faded green and white, the '66 Plymouth Fury looked as if it were only a few kilometers away from the junkyard. The bumpers had lost their chrome, and parts of the body were corroded. But underneath the hood was a souped-up engine that made it possible for the Plymouth to outrace any police car.

No man would have given Rossana a second glance. Camellion's incredible talent with the pastes and solvents and other materials from his makeup kit had added forty years to the young woman's face. With her gray wig, sunken cheeks and pale thin lips, Rossana appeared to be a woman in her sixties. She didn't mind her facial appearance, but she was not at all happy about the tight binding across her breasts, so necessary to give her a flat-chested look.

Richard had not used plastic putty and makeup sticks to change his own features. Since an instant "change-back" might become a necessity, he had used a special Cytex rubber face mask which had been molded originally from the features of a Mexican who had worked for years as a hand at Camellion's *Memento Mori* ranch in Texas.

In Camellion's coat pocket were papers that identified him as Senor Ricardo Jose Mentira. In Rossana's large black pocketbook were documents which proved she was Senora LaDonna Maria Mentira. There was also a Plainfield .380 automatic in the pocketbook.

Rossana guided the Plymouth carefully past the Plaza de San Fernando, drove another block, then made a left turn onto Avenue Durango.

"I gather you're taking a short cut?" In his seedy brown suit, frayed dark topcoat, and cheap felt hat, he looked like what he was supposed to look like—an old *mestizo* going either to a funeral or a wedding.

"We can save about fifteen minutes by going this way," Rossana explained. "There isn't much point in staying with the heavy traffic. We'll take side streets and use Alvaro Obregon to get to the section of the Old City."

"A good idea. Unless I have a bad memory, that address on San Juan de Letran is in the Santo Domingo section, which is little more than a slum."

"Something like your American Spanish Harlem in New York City," Rossana said, the irritation plain in her voice. "Oh, no one will bother you in the daytime. It's your crazy scheme! As yet, we don't even know if the address is for a single dwelling or an apartment house. Suppose it is a single house? Walking right up and knocking on the door—it's *loco*!"

"Do you know of a better way?" grinned the Death Merchant. Through the mask, he felt as if his face were cracking.

"I know that if it's a trap, there might be as many as a dozen revolutionaries waiting for you. Your complacency isn't going to change anything."

"Whoever is there won't expect a senior citizen to come calling. I'm counting on those few seconds of surprise to swing the odds to my side."

"You mean if they open the door! If you want my opinion—"

"I don't, doll. All I want you to do is drive."

Angrily Rossana closed her mouth.

They were in one of the hilly sections of the city and ahead, far in the distance, they could see the hazy blue outlines of the mountains surrounding the city to the east, the south, and the west. To the southwest were the volcanic, snow-crested peaks of Popocatepetl and Iztaccihuatl.

Presently Rossana said, her voice more friendly, "I have always been amazed how some people, lost in a foolish idealism, can pick up a gun and become revolutionaries who think they can change the world. I would suppose the answer lies in psychiatry. Who knows? Perhaps Maria

Sojeda might consider herself a modern Joan of Arc?"

Richard placed another Triumutrolin tablet on his tongue.

"People become revolutionaries for different reasons—rancor, greed for power, dislike of themselves, or a hatred of stupidity which gradually develops into contempt for humanity itself, since stupidity is its most salient characteristic. Few of them are ever Galahads. Most are Robespierres of the most vicious kind." He smiled and thought for a moment. "If Sojeda is anything, she's a female Adolf Hitler."

Rossana stopped the Plymouth for a red light. "Your analysis is very interesting. But I believe there are exceptions."

" 'Ho!' as Huff would say. In this case it means 'Yes,' " Camellion said. He felt in the left bottom pocket of his vest to make sure the large Chlortopheosaron ampules were secure. "Dr. Ernesto Guevara could be called an exception —at least at the beginning of his career. Che had the desire to heal. He had a great capacity to feel genuine pity for human misery and suffering. One could say that it was out of dedication to fight corruption that he joined Fidel Castro. Then Che became a victim, a victim to power which corrupts. In the end, Che became a murdering knight in the charging forces of communism."

"Mexico City once had a Lord Mayor—Ernesto Uruchurtu—who was a humanitarian," Rossana said gravely. "Of course, he wasn't a revolutionary. He was responsible for getting rid of the slums of the Nonoalco-Tlaltelolco district. He had the entire area demolished. In its place he built dwellings to house thousands of people. He put up schools, self-service shops, playgrounds, markets, department stores, and parks. Uruchurtu was Lord Mayor from 1952 to 1967. He was so loved that the people called him Señor *Flores y Fuentes*—'Mr. Flowers and Fountains.' "

"Yes, Senor Uruchurtu was a good man." Not in the mood for conversation, Camellion thought of what Mexico City really was—a conglomeration of different and sometimes contrasting cities. Most of the middle-income groups lived in the newly developed suburbs, such as *Ciudad Satelite* —Satellite City—while low-income families were condemned to the 450 slum districts called *ciudades perdidas,* or lost cities. In these slums, tens of thousands vegetated in shelters put together with clay bricks, corrugated iron, poles, and cardboard . . . rat-traps that lacked the most primitive elements of hygiene and privacy. One had to see the misery—as Camellion had—to believe it. There were narrow alleys filled with mud, excrement, and potholes. Streets filled with garbage. Chickens picking in the dirt. Lines of ragged laundry that were little more than patched rags. And the children all about, with spindly legs, matted hair, and swollen bellies. There was the stench, the sour stink found only in the poorest slums of the poorest countries. The worst of these slums was Netzahualcoyotl—the "Bombay of Mexico!"

Yeah . . . Como Mexico no hay dos—Mexico is unique!

In contrast to Netzahualcoyotl and other slums, there were suburbs like San Angel, Tlatelolco, and Lomas de Chapultepec—where Eldridge Eubanks and his family lived—outlying areas where many homes overlooked ravines. But all were integrated into a landscape of rock, lava, and flowers. Some mansions even had streams coursing through their grounds.

Another ten minutes passed and Rossana turned onto Alvaro Obregon.

"We'll be in the Santo Domingo section shortly," she said. "We're in the Old City now."

"Yes, I see." Camellion looked at the buildings that were mostly of Baroque architecture characterized by elaborate ornamentation that employed *tezontle,* a light and porous rock, for facades. Gradually as the Plymouth Fury neared the Santo Domingo area, the *colonia,* or *barrio* residential district, became more shoddy and weatherworn. The cracks in the facings were unfilled. Brilliantly colored tiles became nonexistent.

Finally Rossana turned onto San Juan de Latran Avenue, and Camellion saw that they were in the twenty-eight-hundred block. She had done a good job of cutting across the city. Camellion reached down into a leather case on the floor between his legs, the kind of tote designed to carry two one-quart thermos bottles and a lunch box. He took two black metal boxes from the bag, one the size of a matchbox, the other slightly larger. He put the small box in a suitcoat pocket. He placed the larger box in the glove compartment.

"If you hear the signal, don't wait and wonder," he said. "Just drive off."

"I don't suppose you want me to drive up the forty-seven hundred block and look for the number?" Rossana asked, trying to make a joke of it. "We'll be there in a short while."

"Park in the forty-six-hundred block," Camellion said. "I'll walk the rest of the way. According to the city map, there's a tiny park across the street, at the end of the forty-six-hundred block. Park as close to it as you can. It will look more natural if you're watching the pigeons."

"The pigeons and the drunken derelicts," murmured Rossana, raising her eyebrows. "It's fifty degrees and the bums will be soaking up the sunshine." The lightness in her voice was strained, and Camellion noticed that her mouth was set in an odd little smile.

The Plymouth Fury ate up the blocks. Gradually, after they entered the Santo Domingo district, the street narrowed and Rossana had to slow and drive around peddlers and vendors selling produce, second-hand clothing, and cheap pottery from pushcarts.

They came to a marketplace, a stone square with a bronze statue of Benito Juarez in the center. The square was filled with people and carts, noise and scurrying, dust and bright sunshine. There were donkeys and goats, turkeys and chickens. Full-blooded Indians, descendants of either the Mayans, the Aztecs, or the Zapotecs, mingled with *mestizos,* the Indian women wearing wide hats and hand-woven woolen *jorongos* to protect them from the cold. Everyone in the market had something to sell—ceramic pots, brightly colored and beautifully decorated with animals, flowers, or butterflies; rugs, copper goods, sugar, coffee beans, chile peppers, corn, rice, and all kinds of fruit—aguacate, zapote, oranges, bananas. . . . Other vendors were hawking shredded tortillas, tacos, and coconut candies.

Rossana drove past the marketplace, and very soon the Plymouth was on the forty-six-hundred block. She slowed the car, both she and the Death Merchant looking to the left, watching for the small park at the end of the block.

"Park over there, doll," Camellion said. He took a round mirror from the glove compartment and gave himself a final once-over. He pressed down the long mustache and put on a pair of wire-frame glasses.

Not a bad job. I look old enough to crap rust!

Rossana pulled up to the curb and turned off the engine. She turned sideways and looked at "Senor Ricardo Jose Mentira."

"There is still time to change your mind," she said, her tone hopeful.

"And waste all this makeup?" Camellion grinned. "Not a chance."

He reached for the handle of the door. . . .

Chapter Seven

There were four young toughs loitering in front of a small hotel, but they ignored the elderly man shuffling down the middle of the dirty sidewalk with the aid of a cane. Not wanting to cross in the center of the block, or walk to the end and then go across the street, Camellion had chosen the side with the even numbers.

Different odors drifted to him: the smell of frijoles and frying onions, mixed with the stench of stale beer and rotting garbage. Odd, Camellion thought. The common stereotype of Mexico and its people rose in his mind. Each year thousands of American tourists spend a day in Tijuana, going by way of southern California; thousands more enter Mexico through Laredo, Brownsville, El Paso, and Nogales. After spending a day visiting bars and watching cockfights, drinking and eating, dancing and carousing, they return home thinking they've seen Mexico. The same myth prevailed about Mexican food. Chile is ever-present, but most of the food is bland, not over-spiced as many suppose it to be.

The Death Merchant glanced to his right—number 47740, a store selling colored *pepates* of various sizes, straw mats used as rugs or wall decorations. In the storefront window was a frightening display of life-size cardboard musicians in the shape of human skeletons. There was nothing unusual about such a macabre exhibit, since present-day Mexican society is still a victim of the beliefs and rituals which grew up around the subject of death. The average Mexican accepts the fact that his life might end suddenly, and even capriciously, at any time.

Next to the store was *El Mirlo*—number 47742. As a symbol of its name, the cafe had a large wooden blackbird hanging on a rod projecting outward over the door. From the Blackbird Cafe issued the strains of the famous birthday song *"Las Mananitas"* and the tongue-watering aroma of *Barbacoa de carnero*, pit-cooked barbecued lamb.

Carrying the leather case in one hand and the cane in the other, Camellion walked ahead, his eyes darting to the right. There was the number: 47744, painted in red over a door whose top was opaque glass reinforced with crossing wire. Camellion looked at the door.

73

The door has to open to a stairway. There's no other answer.

The next place of business—number 47746—was a cantina from which blared a song Camellion remembered from his childhood, *Pardon Me Boy, Is that the Chattanooga Choo-Choo?* The Death Merchant smiled slightly at the sound of the American tune that had been popular during World War II. Singing very softly, "Pardon me, boy, is that the cat that ate the new shoes," he moved to one side of the door, leaned his cane against the building, reached into his vest and took out two of the Chlortopheosaron ampules, which he put into the right-hand pocket of his topcoat. In the same pocket was a Hawes/Sauer 9mm automatic. He carried two SIGs in shoulder holsters.

He pushed his left hand through the straps of the leather case, so that the two straps rested on his wrist, and with the same hand picked up the cane. He opened the door with his right hand, stepped inside, looked around, and saw that he was in a tiny area at the bottom of a flight of wooden stairs. On both sides, at the bottom of the steps, were bare walls, the plaster so faded that the last coat of paint must have been applied when Pancho Villa was a baby.

At the top of the steps was another open space and a single door. To the left was bare wall. To the right was an open hallway that stretched from the space at the top of the stairs to the front wall of the building. Through the banister —which lacked most of its balusters—Camellion could see that there were two rooms to the right, both lacking doors, both apparently unused.

There was only one way to find out what the setup was— *Climb the stairs, knock on the door, and be prepared for anything!*

In case anyone was watching, he went up the stairs like an elderly fossil of flesh who had both feet in the grave and needed only a shove. With his hand in the right side pocket of his topcoat, his fingers a vise on two of the ampules, he paused at the top of the steps and looked at the door seven feet in front of him. There was no peephole. He did see the ends of two lock cylinders, the kind used with deadlocks, one several feet above the other.

I'll chance it! He hurried to the right, went to the first room on the side of the open hall and looked in. Except for several trash cans filled with beer cans and newspapers scattered on the floor, the room was empty. Panes were missing

74

from the two windows; the glass that was there was cracked and so filthy he could hardly see through it.

Camellion walked over to one of the windows and looked out, the pleasant aroma of *Barbacoa de carnero* slapping him full in the face. He saw the reason for the strong aroma, the chimney of the one-story *El Mirlo* was only twenty feet away. He turned around and looked up and down the two rooms and saw that while the doorway between the two rooms was minus a door, the door between the room in which he stood and the apartment beyond was also equipped with double locks.

He went back to the front door of the apartment, put his right hand into the pocket of his topcoat and knocked on the center of the door with the curved handle of his cane. He put his ear to the door, all the while keeping himself at full alert. Nothing. Not a sound. Again he knocked on the door, louder this time, thinking that the large teeth fronts, over his own upper teeth, were damned uncomfortable. Hearing movement, he pulled back and prepared to go into his act, his strong fingers ready to crush the two capsules the moment he pulled his hand from the pocket of the topcoat.

The door opened a foot and a man peered out, a fat-faced, hollow-eyed Mexican with a mustache that moved down the corners of his mouth into the top of a neatly-trimmed beard.

Sniffing loudly, the Mexican stared at the old man, who had a pushed-out mouth, leathery wrinkled cheeks, watery black eyes, and gray hair that showed underneath his hat.

"Francesca! She is here?" Camellion said in a high, cracked voice. He blinked rapidly and hunched his head forward, as if trying to see the man better. "I have come to see my daughter Francesca."

"There is no Francesca here, old man," the Mexican said in an odd voice. "Go away. You have made a mistake."

Camellion had a natural sensitivity that enabled him to detect the mood of others, even of people trying to conceal their fear or elation. There was deep fear in the Mexican. He had spoken automatically and in a tone that indicated his mind was somewhere else—*As if he's being ordered to speak! As if he's being watched!*

The Mexican tried to close the door, but Camellion jammed his right foot into the opening. Slowly he pulled his hand from his right topcoat pocket.

75

"But Francesca must be here," Camellion insisted, as if confused and in a daze. "This is number 47741. My daughter must live at this address. This apartment has to be hers."

The Mexican was getting ready to speak when another man inside the apartment pushed him to one side and opened the door wider, so that the Death Merchant could see him full length. In his middle thirties, the man was dressed in a brown suit, and he didn't appear to be Mexican.

"Senor—what is your name, Senor?" he inquired. He was polite, but did not smile. He spoke excellent Spanish; yet there was an accent to his words, one that was unmistakably —Russian!

Pig farmers! And where there's one, there are usually two and three and four!

"I am Senor Ricardo Jose Mentira, and I am looking for my daughter," Camellion said, sounding confused and uncertain.

Oh my! I'm about to have the triple miseries of Job!

The man stared at Camellion. "Senor Mentira, you have made a mistake," he said in a firm voice. "This is not number 47741. This is apartment—"

The man did not get to finish. With incredible speed, the Death Merchant brought up the cane and savagely rammed its metal-capped end into the Russian's solar plexus. A giant gasp jumped from Stefan Olenov's mouth. His eyes became as big as oranges and, making choking sounds, he started to double over, his hands moving jerkily to his stomach. Consumed with agony, Olenov never saw Senor Mentira crush the two capsules in his right hand and toss them into the room. Instantly a thin greenish vapor began drifting up from the broken ampules.

A blur of movement, the Death Merchant dashed to the first room to the right of the open hall. Realizing he was in the middle of a disaster area, he had only two immediate hopes: the first that he had taken enough Trimutrolin tablets; the second that he could do what he had to do quickly enough.

He twisted the handle of the cane and placed the cane on the floor of the doorway to the hall. Moments later, a thick stream of greenish mist began hissing from the center of the cane—Chlortopheosaron gas, commonly called CSN. CSN affects nerve endings. Whether CSN is inhaled or touches skin, the victim instantly feels as if he's been doused with boiling oil. There is a terrible burning sensation all over the body, accompanied by copious tears, paroxysms of coughing, and the feeling that one is being smothered. Nonetheless, CSN is harmless, the effects lasting only a half-hour. In this respect, CSN causes a wild mind trip by fooling the nerves into sending false messages of alarm to the brain.

The antidote is Trimutrolin, which renders nerve endings immune to CSN. The night before, Camellion had taken more than a dozen Trimutrolin tablets. He had swallowed another dozen since getting out of bed that morning.

He glanced apprehensively at the door with the double lock, drew a SIG automatic, reached into the leather bag, and pulled the length of cord fastened to the brown-paper-wrapped package at the bottom of the bag. He then got his first whiff of CSN—the gas smelled faintly of cinnamon—and knew he was safe. At least from the gas.

Standing to the left of the hallway door, the Death Merchant was about to put a couple of slugs into each lock, but hesitated when he heard a fit of savage coughing in the hall-way and saw the door ahead of him crack open, the one in the side wall of an apartment room.

The Death Merchant snapped up the SIG. Twice the Swiss autoloader roared, each 9-millimeter projectile tearing through the right side of the door. He heard a muffled cry. The door closed. For the sake of safety, Richard sent two more blobs of JHPT lead through the door, through the top center and the bottom center. It was not likely that anyone would open the door again, not for a while anyway.

Thinking of Cletus Huff—*That ding-dong daddy from the BATF had better be there!*—Camellion leaned around the side of the hall doorway and fired by instinct at the sound of coughing. He quickly saw that while his bullet had missed the man who was close to the banister and shaking with spasms of convulsive coughing, the projectile had hit another Camellion had not known about. The man had just come out the front door of the apartment, a handkerchief over his nose and mouth, and the slug hit him high in the left leg. He let out a horrified yelp and, with tears streaming down his face, fell to his side and made a pathetic effort to draw a weapon from underneath his coat and to warn the comrade by the banister.

"*Dimitri! Zhivu tam naoyu vse tirzyie!*" he called out weakly.

"*Dosvidanya, tovaritch*—when you land in hell, tell Nick I sent you!" the Death Merchant muttered grimly and twice pulled the trigger of the SIG. The first 9mm projectile bored

77

into the Russian lying in front of the apartment's door, which was half open, the lead smashing into him just below the throat. He jerked, threw up one arm, fell over on his face, and lay still.

Dimitri Gorkalov, staggering around at the end of the banister, was too submerged in a whirlpool of CSN-pain to know what was actually happening. The Death Merchant's bullet struck him in the left side, just above the belt. The Russian felt a tremendous stab of pain, an agony that spread throughout his whole body. The world had become one big dark shadow and, knowing he was dying, he felt like a man who had been play-acting all of his life and had now discovered that there had never been an audience. A dazzling flash of light burst before his eyes. Unconscious and dying, the Russian fell over the railing and pitched down the stairs.

The Death Merchant pulled back into the room, dropped to one knee, and put the leather case gently on the floor. He pulled a full clip from the left pocket of his topcoat, thrust it into the SIG he had emptied and slide-slid a shell into the firing chamber.

He picked up the leather case, raced across the room, and took a position by the wall. The door to the apartment was now to his right. Camellion moved six feet forward, gently placed the leather case on the floor, reached out and, ever so gently, tested the doorknob. The knob turned all the way; the door was unlocked.

Glancing now and then at the doorway to the hall, he turned the knob all the way, pushed open the door, jerked back his hand, and waited. He heard several men coughing from inside the apartment. From the sound they had to be several rooms away. Nothing happened. Not a single Russian came charging through the door. He didn't expect them to come after him. *They're waiting for me to come to them. And so I shall!*

Camellion picked up the leather case and tossed it through the doorway into the room. He pulled the second SIG and waited. When he had pulled the string on the package, it had separated the packing from two thin glass tubes filled with Chlortopheo and Saron-C. When the two tubes broke and the contents came into contact with each other, the result would be the formation of CSN gas.

The Death Merchant waited a few moments, then stormed through the doorway, a SIG in each hand. All set to dodge at a second's notice, he spotted a man lying face-down on the floor and assumed it was the Russian he had shot through the door.

Camellion received his first slight surprise when he saw the weapon lying close to one outstretched hand of the corpse. The gun resembled an American Benjamin CO_2 pellet pistol. Camellion knew it was actually an IVOS dart gun, the kind favored by KGB and GRU agents, the type of weapon they used to tranquilize a kidnap victim into unconsciousness.

The other surprises came instantaneously, all piling into each other. The leather case lay on the bare boards of the floor, but no clouds of CSN gas were issuing from it.

Chort vozmi! Camellion thought the Russian equivalent of "damn." *The glass tubes didn't break. I've walked right into the spider's web! Or rather, in this case, into the den of the Bear!*

Within those few seconds he saw that, near the front door, the Mexican who had first opened the door, and the Russian who had shoved the chili-bean to one side, were down on their knees crying and imprisoned within an involuntary net of uncontrollable coughing, both men looking as though they were undergoing the tortures of the damned. At least they had gotten doses of the gas from the crushed capsules.

But the two men behind them, one on each side of the door, had not. Neither had the pig farmer rearing up from behind an overstuffed chair in one corner of the room, an IVOS dart gun in one hand. Karol Tinkon raised the dart gun at the same instant that Valin Zaboriye, to Camellion's right, and Josef Bor-Kamokovsky, to his left, moved in fast. But the Death Merchant had a few seconds' edge. He snapped up the SIG in his left hand and jerked to one side at the same moment that Tinkon's dart gun made a noise like a child's pop-gun, and a tiny hair-thin dart zipped between Camellion and Valin Zaboriye and went bye-bye through the doorway.

The SIG in the Death Merchant's left hand roared, the 9mm bullet bashing Tinkon just below his ridiculous bright green bow tie. Gurgling blood that bubbled out of his mouth onto his yellow sports coat, the Russian KGB captain dropped the dart pistol and sank behind the chair.

A micro-moment later, Josef Bor-Kamokovsky grabbed Camellion's left wrist with both hands, Valin Zaboriye seized his right wrist and threw a brawny arm around his neck. As Zaboriye tried to put a knee into the small of the Death

79

Merchant's back, Georgi Dobrudja, a 6.35mm Tokarev pistol in his hand, ran out of the bedroom.

"*Zanskie oaya Amerikanski obkom po trevoge!*" he shouted at Zaboriye and Bor-Kamokovsky. "*Poc v dvizheniya iz gondochy!*"

Zaboriye didn't succeed in placing his knee in the small of the Death Merchant's back, although Bor-Kamokovsky did manage to twist the SIG automatic from Richard's left hand. But neither Bor-Kamokovsky nor Dobrudja nor Zaboriye expected Camellion's next move.

Thinking of what Dobrudja had said—*The old man must be the American in disguise. We must take him alive!*—Camellion raised his right foot and, with trip-hammer force, slammed his heel down on the left instep of Valin Zaboriye, who cried out in pain as the astragalus, cuboid, and scaphoid bones shattered. The sudden agony caused the Russian to relax his grip on Camellion's wrist and, involuntarily, to let his arm around the Death Merchant's neck go limp.

The Death Merchant jerked himself completely free of Zaboriye and, using his right elbow as a battering ram, smashed it savagely into Zaboriye's stomach. The KGB agent gasped loudly, staggered to one side, tripped over the corpse on the floor and fell heavily against the wall, screaming when his broken foot became wedged in one armpit of the dead man.

Josef Bor-Kamokovsky yelled "You son of a bitch!" in Russian at Camellion and, still holding onto Richard's left wrist, tried to stab him in the side of the neck with a knifehand *Nukite* blow. Expecting something of that sort, Camellion ducked. Bor-Kamokovsky's hand streaked over Camellion's head a split second before Richard swung the SIG in his right hand to the left and shot Bor-Kamokovsky in the face. The 9mm bullet went through the man's cheek, just below a large mole, and departed out the back of his head. The Russian made weird noises; blood flowed from his mouth and nose, and his hand fell away from the Death Merchant's left wrist, his last look at life the cleverly disguised face of Camellion, who turned his attention to the Russian with the Tokarev automatic.

Intelligent and very experienced, Captain Dobridja was a realist. He knew that the plan to kidnap the *Amerikanski*—whoever he was—had failed. He knew, too, that the only way he was going to save his own life and get back to the Russian Embassy was to kill the human machine of lightning destruction who had just taken the life of Bor-Kamokovsky. Feeling his nerve going, Dobridja raised the Tokarev and, at the same moment his finger pulled the trigger, saw that Camellion had grabbed the sagging Bor-Kamokovsky, was holding the corpse in front of him like a shield, and was snapping down with the SIG.

Dobridja's 6.35mm bullet hit the dead Bor-Kamokovsky in the chest. Being already dead, Bor-Kamokovsky didn't mind in the least. Being alive and very healthy, the Death Merchant snickered and yelled at Dobridja, "You're a dead man, Pig Farmer!"

With a sickening sensation, Dobridja knew that he was up against a man whose expertise in killing could not be surpassed. In that blink of an instant, another terrible thought exploded in the Russian's mind, one that turned his backbone to jelly. There was only one human being in the world who possessed such deadliness, the man they whispered about at the Center in Moscow, the man known as—the Death Merchant. Deep down, Dobridja knew he was not going to live long enough to tell anyone at the embassy.

Dobridja tried to drop flat as he got off the second shot. He didn't bother to aim; he just fired and dropped. At the same time, from the corner of his eye he detected Stefan Olenov—down on the floor with the Mexican—coughing and making a feeble effort to draw his own weapon.

Georgi Dobridja had miscalculated. His own 6.35mm slug tore through Camellion's topcoat on the right side, but it didn't even tear the suit coat underneath. The Death Merchant deliberately fired low, having assumed that the Russian would make a postage-stamp play and try to paste himself to the floor. Instead of hitting the Russian in the groin, the 9mm projectile tore off the lobe of the Russian's left ear. Dobridja yelled in pain and—in a spray of blood—twisted around, his face taking on that fixed, frightening, frozen look of one who knows that the last thread of life is about to be severed. He heard the SIG crack again, but felt not a twitch of pain. He had died too quickly, the bullet having entered his temple and lodged in his brain. He pitched to his side and lay still.

In spite of the torture from the CSN gas, Stefan Olenov had succeeded in pulling a Vognennom machine pistol from underneath his coat, a VMP to which a Borjinsky silencer was attached. And somehow he found the strength to get off a stream of slugs at the weaving, darting "old man" who was only a blur in his tear-filled eyes. All ten 7.65mm projectiles buzzed out the side door, every single one missing the Death Merchant, who had rocketed far to the left and was by the front wall when the last 7.65mm bullet went *ZITTTTT* through the Borjinsky silencer.

"I've seen better heads on cabbages!" Camellion laughed to himself, looked at the tortured Olenov, and pulled the trigger of the SIG. There was was an odd-sounding thud. Olenov's head snapped back and he fell backward, a ragged hole in the center of his forehead.

Camellion went over to the fat-faced Mexican with the beard. The man looked worse than than an old inmate of Hell. His dark face was wet with tears; his beard was soaked with tears. Never had Camellion seen a man who looked so miserable. The Mexican had actually coughed so much and so hard that his lips were wet with blood.

Camellion got down and shoved the muzzle of the SIG several inches from Bartolome Tablada's mouth. Coughing, one hand pressing against his chest, Tablada scooted back into a corner on his knees. Slowly the Death Merchant followed, and when the wretched revolutionary could retreat no farther, he again found himself staring into the dark muzzle of the SIG. It might as well have been an open grave. . . .

"*Buenos dias, mi amigo,*" Camellion said, his eyes glittering. "I want answers. The first time you tell me a lie, I'll blow your brain all over the walls. I just might anyhow!"

"W-who are you?" Tablada gasped, sheer curiosity, for the moment, taking precedence over terror.

"The First Horseman of the Apocalypse, amigo—Death!" Camellion said in a soft voice. "Tell me, who set me up? Why were the Russians here?"

Tablada was too frightened (and too superstitious) not to tell the truth. Between bouts of coughing, he answered the Death Merchant's questions. All he knew—Tablada confessed—was that a messenger had brought word to him and to three other members of the Twenty-third of September Communist League—When?—Last night!—that an *Americano* agent might come to the apartment. If the *Americano* came—"We were to kill him." Who had sent the messenger? The High Command of the League. And how had the High Command known about the *Americano* agent? Had the messenger explained? No. He had only said that an *Americano* might come and, if he did, to kill him.

And the Russians? Two of them had arrived at six o'clock that morning. But were they really Russians? Shut up and get on with it. The two men had knocked on the door. They had given the proper password and Simon Delacava— "He is one of the dead ones in the bedroom"—had opened the door and admitted them to the apartment.

"Before we knew what was happening, the one you shot last pulled out his silenced weapon and shot Simon and Benito and Paul. One of the men took a walkie-talkie from his pocket and called the others. Then they came up. The men—you say they are Russians—carried Paul and Benito and Simon into the bedroom. Then the men settled down and waited."

"Why did they keep you alive?"

To answer the door, Tablada explained. "They said that the *Americano* expected Mexicanos. They said you would either come through the window or knock on the door."

Tablada's eyes, watery and filled with fear, stared at the SIG in the Death Merchant's hand.

"Senor, what are you going—"

Camellion slammed the side of the automatic against Tablada's head. The Mexican slumped against the wall, his bearded chin hanging on his chest.

The Death Merchant went across the room, picked up the SIG that Bor-Kamokovsky had twisted from his hand, then reloaded both Swiss-made autoloaders, thinking that Tablada would have a lot of explaining to do to the Federales. In this tough section, the *Guardia Civil*, or regular police, came only at the last minute—*But they'll arrive sooner or later, and I had better be gone when they do.*

He went into the bedroom and looked around. Three men lay by the side of the bed, face down. Tablada had told the truth. Camellion returned to the other room, picked up the Vognennom machine pistol and pushed on the safety. He next searched the Russian for more extra-long magazines that the weapon used. He found two, unbuttoned his topcoat, and put the long clips in one pocket of his suit coat. His mind racing, he continued to search the Russian, found the dead pig farmer's billfold and saw that the man's identification card and driver's license were made out in the name of "Jose Ternestes." The KGB was always prepared for any eventuality. KGB *Mokryye Dela* assassins invariably carried phony identification when on a kill mission. And since the fingerprints of these men in the room were not on file in

83

Mexico, the Federales would never be able to prove that the dead men were Soviet nationals. The Death Merchant was not concerned about his own prints, even if they had been on file at *Centrico Federales*. He could not leave prints because of the extra-thin gloves he wore, each glove resembling the wrinkled hand of an elderly man.

But what is going to protect me and the others from the leak?

The conclusion was obvious. Someone in the Polar Cold cover net was a Communist agent. Another deduction bothered Camellion: the KGB (or maybe they were GRU) boys had not been trying to kill him, not at first. The dart gun proved as much. Then again, an IVOS dart gun could just as easily shoot a dart tipped with a killing poison. The problem remained. Had the Russians been trying to kill or kidnap him?

That sound! The Death Merchant cocked his head. Again he detected the creaking of boards at the bottom of the stairs. It was time to get the hell out—and fast. Richard went over to the leather case and smashed his heel down on it. This time the two glass tubes broke, and the Chlortopheo and the Saron-C. mingled and reacted. Almost instantly thick greenish gas began to pour through the open end of the leather case. Stooping to pick up the case, Richard happened to glance through the open door on the side of the room and noticed that there was a fire escape outside the double windows of the empty room ahead. This meant there was an alley separating half the block, since the roof of the cafe was right next to the empty rooms off the hallway.

He ran to one side of the half-open front door, pitched the gas spewing case through the opening and heard it hit what he assumed to be the center of the stairs. Quickly he slammed the door and, careful not to stand in front of the door, threw the latches of the two deadlocks and secured the safety chain.

There was a lot of coughing now on the stairs, loud cursing and some shouts. Several shots rang out and there were thuds and tearing sounds when several bullets ripped through the door toward the top, the angle indicating that the shooters were not quite to the top of the stairs.

Now it was all a question of time. Camellion moved across the room, picked up the Vognennom machine pistol, raced out the side door into the empty room and leaped to the side of the doorway by the hall.

If only I had a few grenades! He looked around the side of the opening and saw that, twenty feet ahead, four men in the brown uniforms of the regular city police were rocking back and forth in front of the apartment's front door, consumed with coughing. Three men in civilian clothes were in no better shape.

He ran across the room to the open window and looked down into the alley through the iron rods of the fire escape landing. He couldn't see anyone. *But what does it matter? I can't stay here.*

He crawled through the window onto the landing, which shook under his weight. *All I need is for the damn thing to fall!* There were no let-down steps, only a short ladder fastened to one end—open—of the landing. Without a backward look, Richard crawled down the rungs of the ladder, dropped the remaining eight feet to the ground, and started sprinting down the alley, running past smelly garbage cans and other rubbish. A hundred feet down the alley, he came to a narrow walkway between the buildings. The width of two men, the corridor led north, the opposite end opening to Saint Marco Street.

Camellion turned into the passage and began moving toward its other end. He noticed that every fifteen feet or so there was a small recessed niche partially filled with garbage cans piled in front of a door.

Why not? He ducked into one of the gloomy cubbyholes, careful not to brush against any of the trash cans crawling with flies and other insects. He removed the gray wig, pulled the curved plate from his upper front teeth and, last of all, tugged the mask from his face. Feeling like a snake shedding its skin—*Or a chameleon changing its color*—he dropped the mask and the wig and the plate between two garbage cans.

Calmly then, he stepped out into the passageway, listening to police sirens screaming on San Juan de Latran avenue. *The hell with the police. By the time they halfway figured out what had taken place, I'll be out of the area! Oh my! More trouble, I think!*

Up ahead, three young men had stepped into the mouth of the corridor and were moving slowly toward him. They stopped ten feet inside the passage and grinned malignantly at him. The Death Merchant, who had also paused, saw that the men were three of the same *correosos* who had been hanging out in front of the hotel. It was just by accident that they had turned into the passageway between the buildings. From the way they were staring at him, it was plain that the three toughs were not going to invite him to lunch.

The leader, a muscular dude with a thin mustache and enormous sunglasses, pulled a stiletto lock-knife from his jacket and pressed open the blade. The freak next to him— he had a face like a pushed-in melon—drew an Italian WW II Carcano folding bayonet and threw open the ten-inch blade.

The man with the dark glasses smirked and called out in Spanish, "Give us your money and your watch, and we'll let you live. Don't try to run. We can catch you, and when we do we'll poke out your eyes."

Slowly the two street toughs advanced, moving their blades from side to side, grinning and making cutting motions. The man behind followed, a blackjack in his hand. The three Mexican hoodlums stopped in confusion at the sound of Camellion's light laughter.

"I'm not going to run," he said. "I am going to kill you."

The three drew back in fear and disbelief when he pulled the Vognennom machine pistol from underneath his topcoat and thumbed the safety to "fire."

"Wait, hombre!" the man with the dark glasses cried in a choked voice. "We were only joking. We—"

"I'm not," Camellion said. He pulled the trigger, raking the three men with a stream of 7.65mm slugs. There was a long *zzziiittttttt* from the Borjinsky silencer, three brief cries of agony, and three fresh corpses in the passage.

Camellion shoved the VMP back into his belt and, with his hands buried in the pockets of his topcoat, walked over the bodies. He didn't feel the least bit uncomfortable about having killed the three toughs, feeling that he had saved the lives of many elderly Mexicans by executing the three parasites.

He walked to the end of the corridor and stepped out onto Saint Marco calle, expecting trouble. None came as he turned east. People passed him, but no one looked in his direction. He didn't give a second thought to the bodies in the passageway. In the Santo Domingo section, people were always "blind," their attitude being *no cuenta*—"it is of no account." Life was hard. Death was certain. Why become involved with the Policia?

Camellion came to the corner, walked across Retablosa

calle, then crossed Saint Marco and proceeded north on Retablosa. Presently he saw the green car parked at the end of the block and smiled to himself. Every time he looked at a Mexican-made Caboza, he thought of a 1969 Rambler. Of course, he couldn't be sure, not yet. Cabozas were as common in Mexico as Fords in the United States.

When he was even with the green Caboza, he bent down, as if to tie a shoelace, and glanced at the driver.

The man was Cletus Huff.

Camellion straightened, hurried over to the car, and got in.

Huff turned the key in the ignition. "Where to?"

"Back to Chapultepec," Richard said. As Huff pulled away from the curb, Richard took a small metal box from his suit coat, opened a tiny panel on one side, and extended an antenna to its full six inches. He then pushed a small red button next to the antenna, holding it down to the count of seven. He waited. A minute later the box made a brief humming sound. Good. Rossana had received the signal.

Camellion pushed back the antenna, closed the panel, and put the d-F Signalizer in his pocket.

"They were waiting?" Huff asked, slowing for a red light.

"They were—and guess what? They were ivans."

Surprise tightened Huff's mouth. "What's our next move?"

"Did you send the message on the short wave at Eubanks' house?" Camellion asked, opening a package of Life Savers.

"Ho, but Washington said it would take several days to check. Washington said they'd reply on a C-6y priority directed to 'Capella.' " The BATF agent grinned. "I didn't realize you were interested in astronomy!"

Camellion ignored Huff's attempt at levity. "Let's just hope that Eubanks and the others believed you remained behind because of an upset stomach. But they seemed to. Anyhow, they would have no reason to believe otherwise. You did instruct Washington to keep your inquiry from Polar Cold?"

"Ho. There's no danger. But what the hell do we do now?"

The Death Merchant thought for a moment.

"You and I and Korse—we're going to visit a sugar mill."

Chapter Eight

The Learjet, at 18,000 feet, streaked northwest toward Guadalajara, Leland Moore at the controls. Below were rolling storm clouds, the crest of blue-black thunderheads slowly twisting and turning. Above the jet was the round, wide bowl of deep blue sky, stretching out to infinity.

"The nice part about our going to Guadalajara is that I was scheduled to go there this week on business," Moore said. He looked at the directional gyro indicator, then half-turned his head to Richard Camellion, who was sitting next to him . . . the motion also directed at Cletus Huff and Harley Korse, who sat side by side in the rear seat of the cockpit-cabin. "The Rivera Packing Company in Guadalajara is going to install a complete refrigeration cycle. Polar Cold is handling the job. General Electric makes our equipment, but we do the planning and installing."

"I gather the company is making a profit," Richard Camellion said, vaguely interested. He leaned down and took a box of figs from the attaché case at his feet.

"Naturally the company makes a profit!" Moore sounded surprised. "P-C pays for itself ten times over, every year. It's true that we are a small company, but we're good, damned good. Last year we made a net of almost two hundred and ten thousand American. Eldridge is president. I'm the vice president and field layout man."

"Then you're saying that some of your people are experienced in refrigeration methods?" Harley Korse said, deep wrinkles creasing his high forehead.

"If we weren't, how do you think we could operate?" The irritation in Moore's voice was plain. "I myself have a master's degree in refrigeration engineering. How do you suppose I do field work? For example, this deal with Rivera Packing involves a complete R-cycle. That means cooling tower, condenser, compressor, and cold storage rooms, plus the know-how necessary for installation."

"I see," Korse said stiffly.

"I don't think you do," Moore said harshly. "Hell, we have four Mexican salesmen on the road. And all of you saw our offiices. No less than twenty-seven Mexicans working for us in the office, and another thirty out in the field."

Cletus Huff laughed in a lighthearted manner. "The way you are talking, one would think Polar Cold was your company, yours and Eubanks'. I should suppose that sometimes it must become psychologically confusing."

"Not really," Moore said. "We're well aware that Polar Cold is Big Uncle's. But El and I are proud of what we have done. Uncle owns the company, but it was El and I who actually built up the business. We know it. Washington knows it. And now you know it."

Camellion put a fig into his mouth. "I assume the three of us are going with you to Rivera Packing?"

Moore grinned and winked at the Death Merchant. "Why not? You three are from the home office in Chicago, and you're here in Mexico to see how we operate. The three of you are in sales, so you won't be expected to know anything about the engineering side of the business."

"Uh-huh, that makes sense," Camellion mused.

"We'll land in about an hour," Moore went on in a brusque manner. "Tomorrow we'll get things going with Rivera. I can't ignore Polar Cold business. Our technicians will have to begin installation at Rivera within several months."

"And the P-C-net agent we're going to meet?" asked Camellion.

"That's set up for seven tomorrow night," Moore said. "He'll phone the hotel first. Hopefully he'll have the information about the sugar mill."

The Death Merchant nodded. For any number of years he had known that he could do very little with only faith. The rub was that he couldn't do a thing without it. For now, he would have to be patient, await development, and hope—have faith—that he made the right moves. There was no other way to handle the situation.

Being in the front seats, Camellion and Moore did not see the shadow of doubt that had crept over Harley Korse's tired-looking face.

"I don't like it; I think we're moving too fast," the big-boned drug agent said in a funereal tone. "What none of you have said is that Guadalajara is a hotbed of revolutionary activity and that the Federales will be all over the place, including Zumerdia Airport. And what about the Mexican Security Service. Damn it! The MSS must have some inkling of what's going on!"

"Most of the MSS efforts are concentrated in watching

the commie embassies in Mexico City," Camellion said, "especially the *Sovyetskaya koloniya*, or Soviet colony. It's the Federal cops who handle the home-grown Marxist idiots."

"Harley's right, though, about Guadalajara," Cletus Huff said. "It was in 1972 that six thousand students rioted at the Plaza of Three Cultures. The Mexican government maintained that the riot was sparked by young men and women who had been trained at Lumumba University in Moscow. The newspapers said that other students had gone to North Korea and North Vietnam for training as specialists in riots and street fighting."

"So what?" Moore grunted. "All that doesn't have anything to do with us. Your perspective is off, Huff."

"Ho!" You misunderstood me," Huff said quickly. "I know that what happened in 1972 has no direct bearing on us now. I was only pointing out that Guadalajara was and still is a center of revolutionary activity." He turned and looked at Korse. "And I think that Harley was really referring to Camellion. How about it, Harley?"

"Yes, I was thinking of Camellion," Korse said, his eyes fixed on the back of Camellion's neck. "All of us must admit that we've been leaving a lot of bodies lying around. And you, Camellion, you've done more than your share of killing. The Federales must be damned angry about it! I'll give you odds that we're skating on thin ice."

Watching the clouds below, the Death Merchant smiled, his lips pulling back over his even teeth.

"While we're at it, let's not forget the *Departamento de Narcotico*," he said. "Its agents are still searching for 'Justin Lawrence.' It is not very likely that Mexican drug agents and the Federales and the Mexican Security Service will connect the Englishman Lawrence with either the operation at Diego Tuchilan's farm or the fracas at the pigsty on San Juan de Latran Avenue. The revolutionary I left alive will have told the Federales by now that the 'old man' was not really so old." He tapped the end of his chin. "They might believe him. Then again, they might not. It doesn't matter. They still have no idea what I look like. They don't have a single fingerprint."

"What about the Maria Isabel-Sheraton?" Korse asked. "Or would you have us believe that you went around wearing gloves all the time you were there?"

For a moment, Camellion didn't answer. He thought of the special "shellac" he had used to coat his palms before boarding the plane, a coating so thin that, while it permitted him to wash his hands, it distorted fingerprints and palm impressions.

Korse is the type of jerk whose hobby would be collecting used echoes! Camellion swung around and stabbed a hard stare at the U.S. narcotics agent. "I don't care what you might believe. I am not in the habit of saying what I don't mean, and I always mean what I say. Now I am saying that there isn't a single fingerprint at the Isabel-Sheraton. Period!"

Korse was not the kind of man to back down from anyone. He stared right back at the Death Merchant and spoke in his usual doomsday voice.

"Very well. I won't argue about fingerprints. But in no way do prints have anything to do with the fact that a trap was waiting for you at the apartment on San Juan Avenue."

"Ho, I'll buy that," interjected Cletus Huff, lighting another cigarette from the one he had been smoking.

"We'd have to be optimistic noodle-heads if we didn't assume that the Commie League isn't all prepared for us at the sugar mill near Zacoalco," Korse said mournfully. "It's clear to me what happened."

"Go on. I'm all ears," Camellion said and turned around to face the front of the plane.

"Let's hear your theory," he said, and settled back against the seat.

"Somehow, Hector Mudejar, Sojeda, and the rest of the League bosses learned that we knew about the farm," Korse intoned, the other three men detecting the note of enthusiasm that had crept into his voice.

"Well, don't put the blame on Emerald–4," warned Leland Moore.

"Why not? It's as good a theory as any!" persisted Korse. "There's no question in my mind that the terrorists knew we were going to attack the farm. That's why the top people pulled out and just by accident let the stooges overhear them talking about the apartment on San Juan and the sugar mill. The—"

"Ho, but the Russians showing up at San Juan don't add up," cut in Huff. "The KGB guns down the commies and tries a kidnap act of its own—unless you were wrong, Camellion. If you're right, then you have something the Russians want—and how did the KGB know about you to begin with? OK, so they didn't know they were after 'Richard Camellion!' But they did know that they were after an American agent! They must have!"

"I'm not wrong," Camellion said. "It was an attempted snatch. Why try to kill a man with a dart gun when a firearm with a silencer would work even better?"

"Someone had to talk, or else the Russians have a pipeline of their own!" Huff drawled. "Another worry we have is the Mexican Security Service. I'm inclined to think the MSS boys will know ivans when they see them. They probably have photographs of those guys going in and out of the Russian embassy!"

Looking sideways at Huff, Harley Korse twisted his face into an expression of disgust. Not only had Huff interrupted him, he had also dropped ashes all over the place. What a pig.

"The Mexican Security Service won't bother us," Camellion said confidently. "We can forget the MSS."

Korse's thick eyebrows raised suspiciously. "You sound pretty damned certain!"

"I am," Camellion said in a flat tone.

Moore became very serious. "I admit that something screwy is going on. But whatever it is, it's got nothing to do with any of our people in the Polar Cold cover." Methodically his eyes scanned the instrument panel. "There's a few other things I can tell you. If the guerrillas are waiting at the sugar mill, they don't know how we're coming or when. They can't know. We haven't even planned the operation!"

Korse made an indignant noise, looking as if he might be smelling rotten fish. "It's bad enough if they even know about us," he said with brutal frankness. An uncomplicated man who lived without pretexts or apologies, Korse said exactly what he was thinking. "You're too trusting, Moore. People change, and any network can be infiltrated."

Moore ignored the insult. "The second thing is that, with his new disguise, Camellion doesn't look anything like 'Justin Lawrence.' He doesn't need a visa because he's an American. It's that simple."

"Unless we're stopped for some reason and Mexican Feds decide to do some hard-nosed double-checking!" Korse was quick to point out. "The names of passengers are taken on Mexicana flights. Or did you arrive on Pan Am or one of the other airlines?"

"I didn't fly to Mexico," Camellion said. He sounded amused. "A Polar Cold salesman, vacationing in Texas, drove me in by way of Nogales. There isn't any name check-list on the Nogales route."

"He's got you there, Harley!" Leland Moore turned sideways and gave the dour-faced drug agent a big grin. Korse was quick to realize that the grin was more a reaction of nervousness than a sign of amusement or pleasure.

Korse settled back in his seat, his cheeks moving in and out with anger. These damned CIA thugs! No wonder the country was in such a mess.

"It all sounds good," he finally said. "But tell me, Camellion. What are you going to do if, for some reason, we're stopped and the Federales get to thinking that maybe your present face is a Hollywood makeup job?"

The Death Merchant didn't bother to answer. Not only was he watching the instrument panel, but he didn't want to give Korse the pleasure of having to admit to the truth—*If we're stopped and they think this is makeup—I'm in trouble!*

Moore did not comment either. He was occupied with banking the plane.

Seeing that neither man was going to answer, Korse turned to Huff, who was lighting another cigarette.

"It's ridiculous to even discuss this mess," he said. "All Moore is worried about is 'plausible deniability' if the Mexican Feds close in. Camellion sits there like God and says he 'knows' the MSS won't bother us! They're running the show. We're only along for the ride."

"Stow it," Huff advised in a low voice. A cigarette dangling from the corner of his mouth, he gave Korse a long look of disapproval. "The nitwits in Washington have ordered that we follow Camellion. That's what I intend to do."

Korse's mouth clamped shut. He turned away from Huff, looked out the window and remained silent, feeling the seat press up against him as Moore started to climb for altitude.

Camellion watched the altimeter and the airspeed indicator.

"You're going to climb over the thunderhead to the west," he said. It was a declaration and not a question.

"There are too many mixed-up thermals in that big black bastard," Moore said. "We'd be bounced around like a ping-pong ball. All we need is to go down and make a forced landing in some farmer's field and have the moronic Rurales find all the weapons in the back."

He leaned forward slightly and checked the oxygen flow into the cabin. "We should land at Zumerdia about two-thirty. That gives us the whole afternoon to get settled."

Harley Korse's yawn was extra loud. . . .

Chapter Nine

Listening to rain drops dripping from *campeche* trees and to the men moving around him through the undergrowth, the Death Merchant looked up at the black sky, empty of moon. Had he made any actual progress? Since the jet had landed at Zumerdia Airport, everything had gone well. In a rented car Moore had driven to a three-man pottery factory behind a neat little whitewashed house several miles from Ixrenntes, a small town ten miles to the southeast of Guadalajara. While the others had waited in the car, Moore had hauled two large Samsonite suitcases from the trunk of the car and, without a word, given them to one of the Mexicans, a young man with a bronze Aztec face. The party of four had then driven to Guadalajara, Moore reminding Camellion of a tourist guide as he explained that Guadalajara had been founded in 1530, was situated 5,000 feet above sea level in the Sierre Madre Occidental, and enjoyed a spring-like climate.

"Polar Cold does considerable business in Guadalajara," Moore had concluded. He had laughed. "I'm speaking of the refrigeration end of the business." He had added as an afterthought. "We'll be staying at the *Camino Real*. It has all the conveniences, even girls, but only if the management knows you."

The next day, the four men went to the Rivera Packing Company, and Leland Moore signed the contract with Aldo y Rivera-Sartorius. Installation of the complete refrigeration cycle would begin in six weeks.

That evening of the same day, while Camellion and the other three were in the bar of the *Camino Real*, Moore received a telephone call. Time: 7:10. At 7:45, the four of them were parked half a block from the Cholulaz Plaza, waiting for a man whom Moore had referred to only as "Rafael." Some minutes later, Rafael walked up to the car, got in, and Moore started the drive to the pottery factory, driving slowly over the twisted roads after he left the bright lights of Guadalajara. A light drizzle was falling and the concrete was slick and treacherous.

Four Mexicans, other than Rafael, were at the pottery factory—the young Aztec-featured man and three older men in their upper thirties. They listened solemnly as Rafael pulled a square of folded paper from his pocket and explained that he may have found a way to get inside the unused sugar-processing plant. Rafael was a chunk of a man in his forties. Clean shaven, he had a nose too large for his small mouth, heavy-lidded eyes that gave him a sleepy appearance, and fine black hair that seemed to have been carefully disarrayed on purpose. He didn't bother to remove his black plastic raincoat as he told the others that he had obtained the information by checking old land grants and surveys at the geodetic office of the Mexican Interior Department, which had a section in Guadalajara.

"This entire region is subject to earthquakes," Rafael said. "There were plenty of charts to use for reference. The latest chart shows that the tunnel was never sealed after the mill stopped operation twenty years ago."

Midnight. Two Cabozas and a long, black hearse pulled away from the pottery. Driving the lead car, Rafael headed in the direction of Zacoalco, which lay 50 kilometers south of Guadalajara. Very close to Lake Chapala, Mexico's largest body of fresh water, Zacoalco had tourism as its main industry.

"You're sure you have the exact location of the mill?" asked Moore, who was in the front seat next to Rafael. "We'll park a mile from the mill and go the rest of the way on foot. If we meet any Federales or Rurales on the road, they will think we are transporting a body for a funeral tomorrow or the next day."

"Suppose they become suspicious?" asked Harley Korse.

"Then we kill them!" came the prompt reply. Rafael added, with a delightful little laugh, "Do not worry, Senor. The police are brave, but they are not fools. It is only with army troops that the Federales come out into the countryside. As you would say in your country, Senor, the Federales 'play it safe.' "

Richard Camellion's eyes had adjusted to the darkness, and he had no difficulty in seeing Rafael, who still wore the black raincoat; only now he had a black beret pulled down over his hair.

"Amigo, how is the terrain around the sugar mill?" Richard asked.

"The entire area is hilly and rocky," Rafael said. "Do not forget, we are in the southern end of the Sierra Madre Occidental, at the lower level. The immediate vicinity around

96

the mill is level ground. Even without a moon, it would be very dangerous to try to sneak up on the building. We should thank God for the old Aztec tunnel. . . ."

There came the time when Rafael turned off the road and headed the car across a plain filled with cactus, short grass, and scattered rocks. For half an hour the two Cabozas and the hearse bounced over the rough ground, the springs of the three vehicles taking a terrific beating, the beams from the headlights raking the desolate countryside like sharp, yellow broadswords.

At last, Rafael drove underneath a tremendous slab of granite sticking out one side of a long sloping hill. The second car and the hearse followed.

"We're almost a mile and a half from the mill," Rafael said, turning off the engine of the Caboza. "I chose this place because our headlights cannot be seen from the mill."

The nine men went to work. They opened the casket in the hearse and removed equipment. The men slipped black coveralls over their clothes and exchanged their shoes for leather boots. Obregon pistols were strapped on. Canvas bags filled with grenades and machine-gun clips were thrown over shoulders. Sub-guns were loaded, walkie-talkies and heavy-duty flashlights checked.

Within fifteen minutes, the men had begun the sneak-in and were on their way to the mill. Being blind in one eye, Rufo Glaza remained behind to stand guard over the two cars and the hearse. He would keep in contact with the rest of the party by walkie-talkie.

The water dripping from the trees and vines became heavier as the men moved into dense growth to the west of the mill.

It's time I take over! The Death Merchant quickened his pace, moved past Urbaldo Ryan, the Irish-Mexican with red hair, and caught up with Rafael, who was at the point.

"I intend for us to reconnoiter the mill from a safe distance," Camellion said. "According to my calculations, we should be less than a quarter of a mile from the mill."

"Yes, that is so," Rafael said, glancing over at the Death Merchant. "Presently, this growth will thin and we'll move into a hilly region. From there we can get to within several hundred yards of the mill."

"The sewer runs north and south, doesn't it?" Camellion

switched to English. "What I'm getting at is, how far is the mouth of the tunnel from the mill, and when we stop to survey the lay of the land, what will be our distance from the mouth of the tunnel?"

Rafael thought for several long moments. He shortened his stride and put one hand on the flap-holster on his right hip.

"From our observation point, we'll be about six hundred feet west of the mill," Rafael replied in perfect English. "To get to the tunnel's entrance, and not risk our being seen, we will move several hundred feet to the south, to a dry creek bed."

"The creek could be flooded?"

"It won't be. It would take an hour's downpour to flood that big ditch. Once we reach the creekbed, we must move east another four hundred feet to reach the entrance to the tunnel. The tunnel is a good three hundred feet from the mill. If we know the tunnel is there, the revolutionaries also know. There will be guards, my American friend."

"The guards will have to be neutralized," Camellion said.

Rafael made a sound that could have been the beginning of a laugh.

"You find that amusing—killing the terrorist guards?"

"I was thinking of what Jose Ortega y Gasset once wrote. He said that civilization is nothing else but the attempt to reduce force to being the last resort. Yet with each passing year, man uses more and more force. Ironic, is it not?"

"Most of man's concepts about himself are Janus-headed," Camellion said, somewhat surprised that Rafael was speaking in a philosophic vein. "The politicians' promises of yesterday are the taxes of today; yet fools still hope they might effect change for the better."

"Yes," laughed Rafael. "It is similar to religion here in Mexico. When many people tell you that they are religious, they are only saying which church they're staying away from!"

Rafael stopped and touched the Death Merchant on the arm. "There! Ahead are the hills."

Camellion, Moore, and Rafael leaned against the side of a large rock shaped like an egg, their elbows on the top of the granite, and studied the mill through MK Star-Tron binocular viewers. Harley Korse and Cletus Huff used regular wide-angle, day-or-night binoculars with zoom controls.

"Hmmmm, I didn't realize the mill would be so big," Moore said despondently, the eyepiece of the S-T scope glued to his right eye. "Christ! The damned building is half a block long! And not a single light. But it stands to reason that the revolutionaries would cover up windows and not let any light filter out."

"I feel somewhat like a midget about to start a fight with a water buffalo!" Huff said to no one in particular.

The Death Merchant carefully studied the supposedly deserted sugar mill, which loomed darkly several hundred yards to the east. Raw cane sugar manufacture is a highly developed process which requires machinery of massive construction because of the tough nature of the material to be ground. All this requires a lot of space.

The mill was something out of a bad dream. Made of large, square-cut stones, which apparently had been removed from Aztec temple ruins close by, the sugar mill was a tremendous one-story building shaped in the form of an obtuse angle of more than 90 degrees. There was a second story on the east side, the west wall of this second story extending to the middle of the first floor's roof. Sections of the large roof were dotted with the remains of skylights and chimneys. The tall windows, on both the first and the second floor, lacked glass and appeared to be boarded up from the inside. To the east, fifty feet from the end of the building, were four twisted steel legs constructed of I-beams and girders. At one time they had supported a water tower. But the tank was nowhere to be seen.

Rubble and junk filled the yard around the mill, at each end and on the south and north sides. There were wooden barrels and metal drums with layers of rust. The tubes of an old boiler were piled on each other in a crazy pattern. A large molasses tank, to the south, was propped up with massive timbers overgrown with moss and creeper vines.

The entire mess represented the past . . . something that had been but would never be again. *A fallen giant that doesn't know it's dead!* thought Camellion, who lowered the Star-Tron scope and placed it in the case fastened to his wide cartridge belt, behind the holstered Obregon. The other men lowered their Star-Trons and binoculars, an expression of extreme concern on each man's face. The four Mexicans didn't appear as if they were getting ready to go to a fiesta.

"Let's proceed to the creek bed," Camellion said in a bored voice. "Rafael, lead the way. All of you keep a low profile. No smoking, speak only in whispers, and be prepared for anything"—*even death!*

The eight men moved toward the south, the Death Merchant right behind Rafael, the other men strung out behind Camellion. They picked their way through the rocks and brush, careful not to trip on vines and bare earth made slick by the light rain that had fallen earlier. Their eyes had adjusted to the darkness; yet their vision was still very limited. Nor could they use their flashlights; the beams would have been seen from the mill.

Fifteen minutes after they had begun to head south, the ground began to slope sharply. Rafael stopped and turned to the Death Merchant.

"Another twenty or thirty feet is the center of the creek bed," the Spaniard whispered. He put his arm through the sling strap of the Largo submachine gun, shouldered the weapon, and drew a .45 Obregon automatic, saying, "The entrance of the tunnel is about four hundred feet east. Getting there without being heard is the problem. The creek bed is full of pebbles and loose stones."

"It seems to me we can use our S-T scopes for the deal," offered Leland Moore.

"That's a good idea," Camellion said, then turned to Rafael. "How's the terrain on the other side of the creek? Is it possible to go east on the other side of the bed and get directly across from the tunnel entrance—without being spotted?"

Rafael nodded. "It could be done, yes. There's a lot of rocks for cover on the other side. Once we were opposite the tunnel, we could look in with a S-T scope and kill whoever is there with a silencer."

Moore said, "It sounds good. What about it, Camellion?"

"If guards are posted, there's the danger that one of them could slip back into the tunnel and that we wouldn't get him," Camellion said. "On that basis, I go forward alone. The rest of you can wait here—except you, Rafael."

The Spaniard shoved the .45 back into his holster. "I'll go across the dry bed and move east on the other side. Is that the idea?"

"With some modification," Camellion replied. "I'll wait here until you have a look-see with the S-T and radio back a report. It's possible that there are no guards, in which case we'll all go ahead together. Otherwise, I'll go it alone and put them to sleep forever."

Moore whispered huskily, "What happens if you scatter some stones and make a noise? There's no guarantee that you won't."

"*Ninjutsu!* You're no stranger to the Asian fighting arts, Moore."

"I am to *Ninjutsu*," Moore decided to tell the truth. "I don't even know what it means."

Rafael interjected. "I'm going to move on across the bed. I'll contact you by walkie-talkie as soon as I see what we have to deal with."

The Spaniard turned, moved forward, and very soon was lost in the darkness. No one heard a sound.

"What about this *Ninjutsu?*" Moore asked, his voice curious.

"It's Japanese. The word, translated, is the equivalent of 'to steal in.' That's what I'm going to do, steal in by using special methods of walking."

"It's your life," commented Moore. *Damn it! Camellion was always a hard act to follow.* "We might as well get on with it. The sooner the better."

"*Antes de harcerlo, vamos a sondear el ambiente!*" warned Mario Fuertes. Camellion, Huff, and Korse assumed that Fuertes, as well as the other Mexicans, were agents of the Polar Cold network in Guadalajara.

"That's what I meant, damn it! After Rafael gets the lay of the land!" Moore snapped in anger. "Quit splitting hairs!"

A half hour passed. At last Rafael contacted the group by walkie-talkie, reporting that there were four terrorists grouped just within the square mouth of the tunnel opening.

"They're sitting at either a table or a crate. I can't be sure." Rafael's voice floated tinnily through the walkie-talkie. "They have a shield on one side of the table. I believe it's a box open on their side, and that there's a light in the box. I think I'm looking at a faint glow. Is that what you wanted, Camellion?"

"Hold your position," the Death Merchant said. "I'll be coming along momentarily—over and out, buddy."

Richard put away the walkie-talkie, removed the sub-gun from his shoulder, and took off the two shoulder bags, handing all the equipment to a stony-faced Moore. Camellion pulled the Hawes/Sauer autoloader from a front pocket of his coveralls and took a foot-long silencer from the leather tube-holster on his belt. Expertly he screwed the silencer onto the muzzle of the specially grooved barrel of the H/S autoloader, put a cartridge into the firing chamber by pulling back the slide, and thumbed on the safety. While the others watched he shoved the odd-looking weapon between his gunbelt and coveralls. He then sat down on a rock and pulled off his leather boots and socks.

"Good God Gerty! You're going to do it barefooted?" exclaimed Cletus Huff. He tacked on, "I wish I could smoke!"

"Hell no!" Harley Korse smirked at Huff. "He's going to take a bath, dummy!"

"Bare feet shape themselves into the ground," Camellion said.

He stuffed his socks into the boots, stood up, and pulled the H/S from his belt. "Okay. Wish me luck."

"You'll need more than we can wish you," Moore grumbled. "But you have it, anyhow."

"I have an ace in the hole," laughed Camellion, who turned to go. "I've gone this route many times."

"You're going to have your butt in a hole if you're not careful!" Korse said mournfully.

"*Buena suerte, amigo,*" Urbaldo Ryan and Luis Guillermo whispered.

The Death Merchant pressed forward, and within minutes the men behind had been swallowed in the darkness. Employing the *yoko aruki,* or "sideways" walk of a trained Ninja, he crept across the rocky ground, gripping the stones with his bare feet. Very soon he came to rocks that were small, smooth, and pebbly—the creek bed.

Time for my ace in the hole! He took the Star-Tron scope from its case, switched the viewing to binocular vision and held the electro-optical device to his eyes. Instantly the darkness was replaced by what could be called the beginning of twilight. This was possible because, even in apparent total darkness, there is actually a considerable amount of low-intensity "back scatter" light. The 135mm f1.8 lens of a Star-Tron amplifies this background light 50,000 times. When the device is switched to monocular vision, the light is amplified 87,000 times.

Camellion saw he was in a creek bed that was nothing more than a wide ditch with sloping sides. There were, however, places where the sides were steep, even wall-like. On both sides of the creek bed were patches of trees and rocks.

Some of the rocks were as small as baseballs, others half the size of a small car.

Richard stared east, estimating that the creek bed continued on an almost straight course for several hundred feet, after which it curved sharply to the north. There was no sign of a tunnel.

Which means that the mouth of the tunnel is around the bend! Unless Rafael miscalculated.

Mentally imprinting the area ahead in his mind, Camellion returned the Star-Tron device to its case and once more began to move, this time proceeding east. This time he used *shinso toho no jutsu*—the Ninja "deep grass rabbit way" of walking, his bare feet making not a single sound on the stones. He calculated the distance as he moved—so many feet to a stride—and when he estimated he had moved 200 feet, he stopped, again took out the Star-Tron and looked around. He saw that he was only twenty feet from the curve. *I must be getting rusty!* He lowered the S-T scope and moved ahead the short distance, wondering if Rafael might be watching him. He stopped and again raised the Star-Tron to his eyes. There was a new view, the section of creek bed he had previously not been able to see. It twisted on its way until, 500 feet ahead, it again curved sharply to the north.

Camellion switched to monocular vision. The brightness increased to "daylight." Slowly he inspected the side of the slope to his left, to the north. There was no tunnel entrance. Perhaps the answer lay in the angle of search, in his angle of viewing?

Camellion moved all the way to the south side, a distance of twenty-five feet, and once more began the search.

There was the opening. *I couldn't see it on the north side because it was in that tiny bend!*

This time, keeping to the south side, he approached the tunnel entrance holding the Star-Tron in his left hand. He carried the silenced automatic in his right hand.

About here! He stopped, put the S-T scope to his right eye and stared ahead. Very clearly he could see the mouth of the tunnel. A hundred feet to the northeast, it was larger than he had expected: ten feet high and twenty feet wide, the front-facing stones large and dull gray. A thousand years ago the Aztecs had built the tunnel as an underground irrigation canal to service Uaximalital, which had been built a half-mile from where the Death Merchant stood. Came the decline and fall of the Aztec empire, through sickness, Spanish conquest, stagnation of culture, and the same kind of moral sickness which had begun to erode the modern world of the West, and Uaximalital had become a city of the dead, standing isolated and deserted. When the city was discovered in 1841, its significance and importance to the new science of archeology was overlooked. Uaximalital was only a curiosity, something from the distant past that had been claimed by time. And by creepers, vines, and moss. Over the long years, as civilization had advanced and the land had been partially cleared, campesinos had used the stones for building huts and fences. Year by year, Uaximalital was ruthlessly dismantled. By 1910, all that remained were paved streets and a dozen or so massive walls that had been part of a temple. Finally, even the memory that there had been a Uaximalital was lost, except among archeologists who had visited the city many times, but had never found anything of value.

The Death Merchant changed the Star-Tron to binocular vision and began to creep toward the mouth of the tunnel. Holding the S-T to his eyes, he was forced to move very slowly; yet he had the advantage of being able to see as clearly as if the sun were just setting.

He found the four guards. The four slobs were sitting at a card table, two on one side and one at either end. A box rested on the other side, the side of the box, facing the men, emitting a faint glow.

Not a man to underestimate the odds, Richard knew that this last 100 feet was the most dangerous. One sound on his part—if one stone moved—and the four terrorists heard it, they would snap on flashlights and investigate. Once they spotted him, they would give the alarm. Worse, since he was out in the open of the creek bed, he wouldn't have any chance. *They'd blow me all the way back to Texas!*

The distance between the Death Merchant and the four communist terrorists narrowed. Seventy-five feet. Sixty five. Fifty feet. He paused, took several deep breaths, tensed his muscles, then crept forward. He put down each bare foot with utmost care, very carefully testing the rocks before putting down his full weight.

Thirty-five feet!

I'll risk it!

As silent as a drifting shadow, he moved another ten feet. He was now so close he could hear the commies talking.

'Pon my soul! The meatballs are playing chess!

More than luck was with the Death Merchant. So was the night. The lantern inside the box on the table, invisible from the outside but casting a radiance over the chessboard and the men, made the darkness outside the tunnel seem twice as black to them.

Ever so slowly, Camellion lowered the Star-Tron and placed it on the ground. He didn't want to take the chance of returning the Star-Tron to its case. The leather might creak.

He stood there, as immobile as an iron statue, all the while calmly watching the four men twenty-five feet ahead. Damn it! His left ankle had begun to itch.

Two minutes. Three. Five. His eyes had adjusted to the darkness and he could see the four men. The job would have to be quick and sure. There had to be some sort of electric signaling device on the table. *If one man sounds the alarm, there will be no attack.*

He raised the Hawes/Sauer automatic. *You who are about to die, I salute you!*

Holding the H/S with both hands, the left hand on the bottom of the right hand, he sighted in on the first man. Closest to the boxed lantern on the far side of the table, the target was facing Camellion.

BBBzzzzziittttttttt! There was a splatttt. The man's head snapped back, a ragged hole in his forehead. Dead, he crumpled to the smooth stones that composed the floor of the canal.

The next terrorist to have his life switched off was one of the Latin cruds with his back toward the Death Merchant. He and the two other communists were still petrified with shock when a 9-millimeter projectile blew out the back of his head and knocked him over the chessboard.

Instinctively, the last two jumped up, the fatter one stumbling over the box on which he had been sitting. His fall to the left didn't matter. Camellion had assumed some of the creeps might jump like a grasshopper on a hot grill. *Didn't they always!*

"*Hasta la vista, estupido!*" The H/S jerked, the silencer went *Bzzzziittttttttt*, and the bandit cried out when a bullet busted him in the back and broke his spine. Fat-face, dressed only in sandals and walking shorts, was still trying to pull himself up on handfuls of air when the second bullet hit him in the side of the neck and solved all his problems.

The last man alive tried to jump back and pull a pistol from a holster around his waist. His pants were so tight they looked as if he put them on with an oversized shoe horn!

Camellion's first 9mm bullet hit the Marxist terrorist in the left side of the belt, bored in at an angle through his stomach and lodged against his backbone, the impact knocking him against the wall. His body had not even begun to sag before the second projectile stabbed into his right eye and burst his brain. With part of his eye dribbling down his cheek, the terrorist wilted to the floor.

The Death Merchant streaked through the mouth of the square-shaped tunnel and inspected the bodies. All four men were dead; all four were now less than leftover garbage from a week-old picnic.

Camellion went back to where he had laid the Star-Tron on the ground, picked up the device, and put it in the case on his belt. He took out the walkie-talkie and turned it on.

"The four guards are kaput," he said. "All of you get up here."

"We're on the way."—Leland Moore's voice.

"What does kaput mean?"—Rafael's voice.

"Finished. Over and done with," Camellion replied with a slight smile. *"Muerto! Perdida absolute!"*

"Excelente, amigo. I'm right across from the entrance. I will now come down."

In short order, Rafael was standing next to Camellion and commenting on the hit. "I had them in the sight of my sub-machine gun, in case they spotted you. If they had moved from the table, I would have fired."

"It's a good thing you didn't," Camellion said. "The racket would have warned their *companeros* in the mill."

Rafael give Camellion an odd, perplexed look. "Si, amigo. But you would have remained alive."

Finished with putting on his socks and boots, Camellion stood up and slipped into his shoulder bags. Last of all, he accepted the Largo submachine gun from Moore, glancing in the direction of Harley Korse as he put an arm through the sling strap. Korse was walking back from having a look at the bloody corpses of the four terrorists.

"It was cold-blooded killing," Korse muttered. He wasn't looking at, or speaking to, anyone in particular; nor had his tone implied condemnation. He had only declared a simple statement of fact.

Huff said with equal unpretentiousness, "What other kind is there?"

Ignoring Huff, Korse forcefully changed the course of the conversation. "If the tunnel was part of the Aztec city, why does it only lead to the sugar mill? That doesn't add up in my book."

"Ah, but it does, Senor," Rafael said. Each corner of his mouth moved upward, but it was less of a grin than usual. "The canal does go all the way to the City of the Old Ones. It just happened that the sugar refinery was built over the tunnel. When the passage was discovered, the mill owners realized that they had a ready-made warehouse. You see, one can store a lot of sugar sacks in, say, a 500-foot-length of stone tunnel. A short shaft was dug down to the tunnel and a freight elevator installed. That's all there was to it."

"We'll be coming up through the shaft?" Huff sounded worried.

"No, we will not," Rafael said. "The shaft is in the above-ground warehouse of the mill. That is all open area and the terrorists could be camping in there. We will enter at the west end of the building.

"Another shaft is there, or what?" Korse asked, rather sharply.

"I have information that there is a ladder from the basement to the canal," Rafael explained, speaking slowly. "A kind of secret emergency exit, only three meters from the ceiling to the floor of the basement."

"That's ten feet," Camellion said, eyeing the mouth of the tunnel. "We shouldn't have any trouble—I hope!"

Korse stared suspiciously at Rafael in the darkness. "You sound very positive!" This was his way of asking for an explanation of how the man with only one name knew such facts.

"I am positive!" was all Rafael said. Then he started after Camellion, who was walking toward the mouth of the tunnel. The omission angered Korse, but he didn't make any kind of comment. He knew it wouldn't have done any good. It was that damned Camellion who was calling the shots. Him and that spook, Moore, and now this "Rafael!" Jesus, the Mex looked like he was about ready to fall asleep on his feet! Oh boy! The characters the CIA employed!

The eight men moved north down the tunnel, three men keeping close to the wall on one side, three on the other side. Leading the way were Camellion and Rafael. They moved down the center of the tunnel, between the two groups, the beams of their flashlights probing the darkness.

They made good progress. Going through the tunnel was like walking in a long black tomb that reeked of age and led to nowhere, a crypt of endless darkness. The walls were long carpets of moss and lichen, the covering of vegetable matter so thick that one could not see the stones. For that matter, not even the stones of the floor! The dust was so thick that it registered deep footprints.

To a man they knew they were in great danger. There was the chance that other revolutionaries might be coming through the tunnel, either toward them, from behind them, or—the ultimate nightmare—from both directions!

Aware of the danger, they scurried as quickly as they could toward their destination. Closing in on the shaft of the freight elevator, they got into single file formation, keeping to the east wall. In the manner of grave robbers creeping into a cemetery, they crept past the open four-beam shaft of the elevator. The gray-painted I-beams were rusty, the cables and wooden floor of the freight elevator coated with dust. Next to the shaft were wooden steps that curved upward to the floor of the warehouse. More dust. The two railings broken, one section of the left railing hanging downward toward the floor.

Once the force had left the elevator behind, the men quickened their pace, but continued in single-file formation as they followed the tunnel, which began to curve toward the west. At one point the beam of Camellion's flashlight found a *palanca* slithering along. The six-foot snake, a cousin to the vicious fer-de-lance, quickly retreated when the light touched it, so Camellion didn't bother to kill it with the silenced H/S.

At length, they saw what appeared to be a tiny light, a single beacon in the blackness ahead—a gasoline lantern hanging on the wall.

Rafael snapped off his flashlight and turned to Camellion, who shut off his own flash. "By the light is the ladder," Rafael whispered. "It is really two ladders fastened together. The entrance at the top is underneath one of the cane-feeder tables. The opening is covered by old cane stalks fastened to thin boards."

"I am wondering about guards." Although Camellion could barely see the outline of Rafael's face in the almost total darkness, he stared oddly at the man—*There can be only one answer!*

"There shouldn't be," Rafael whispered. "But who knows. The guards you killed did not have time to give any warning. Yet, you and Senor Moore suspect a trap. You say the terrorists expect you to come here! And if other gangsters have discovered the dead guards by now. . . . Amigo, who can say what is waiting for us up there?"

Methodically Camellion scanned the light far ahead.

"There is only one way to find out," he said.

Again he and the others advanced, this time without the aid of their flashlights. They had the pinpoint of light to guide them, a tiny eye of yellow that grew brighter as they advanced. When they reached the lantern, they stood back from its light and stared at the wooden ladder that pushed its way upward through the dark hole in the roof of the tunnel.

"I suggest we all go home!" Cletus Huff whispered with a nervous little laugh.

The Death Merchant said in a quiet voice, "Rafael, you wait at the bottom of the ladder. If all is clear at the top, in the basement, I'll signal with my flash."

Rafael squinted warily. "Senor, you are taunting death!"

The Death Merchant laughed. "That's the only way to live a full life. Besides, there is no other way."

With the silenced automatic in his hand, he walked to the ladder, looked up for a moment, then began to climb. . . .

Chapter Ten

Why should there be cane-feeder tables in the basement? The Death Merchant wondered as he climbed the ladder, which was set perpendicularly. It was not that he didn't believe Rafael. He had no choice but to trust the man. But, since cane-feeder tables were always at the very beginning of a sugar processing "production line," they shouldn't be in any basement. They should be on the first floor of the refinery.

Camellion climbed quickly. As he neared the top, he estimated that, from the ceiling of the tunnel to the floor of the basement, the brick-lined shaft was no more than ten feet high. He paused at the top of the wooden ladder, which was fastened to the bricks by means of two iron rods several feet long. Hooking one arm over the top rung to brace himself, he reached up overhead and, with his other hand, gently tested the wooden covering over the top of the shaft. He pushed, ever so slowly. The cover moved slightly. He pushed again, this time exerting more strength, and found that the cover could be pushed aside with little effort.

By feeling with his fingers, he could tell that the cover was similar to a barrel top. He shoved the cover completely to one side, crawled up several rungs, pushed his head up through the opening, then pulled himself through the hole, coming out on the side opposite the cane-stalk-covered boards. He didn't move a single muscle. For a full minute he listened. All he could hear was the pounding of his own heart. All he could see was—blackness.

Resting on his knees, he pulled the flashlight from his belt. Why waste time? The time for extreme caution was past. If any of the communists were waiting in the basement, they had heard him push aside the covering and knew he was there. In theory, they wouldn't open fire until the other men in the tunnel had climbed the ladder and were in the basement. Anyhow, he had the edge. If communist guerillas were in the basement, he would catch a glimpse of them when he turned on the flashlight.

Let's see what happens! He turned on the flash, the bright glare hurting his eyes for a moment. He saw that Rafael had not lied. *By George, I am under a feeder-table!* He moved the flashlight around and raked it over one wall, twenty feet away. He crawled out from underneath the table, which was shaped like a long, wide slide, got to his feet and inspected the basement.

The beam of light revealed that he was in a large 40 × 60-foot area and that it was deserted. The cane-feeder table, crumbling with dry rot, was apparently old equipment that had been stored in the basement while the mill was still in operation. The rest of the floor was littered with junk . . . hand trucks, several sets of Liston scales, all coated with dust and rust and spider webs. Empty wooden barrels lay scattered in complete disorder. Some were right-side-up; other barrels were on their sides, many without staves.

Suddenly the light fastened on two glowing objects—the eyes of an iguana. The Cariban lizard hissed loudly, then scampered away, seeking refuge behind a barrel in one corner of the basement.

The Death Merchant found the stairs to the first floor. They were behind him and to his right, in what he knew was the southwest corner. He crawled back underneath the table and shone his light into the shaft, switching it on and off twice. Instantly Rafael signaled a reply. The rest of the men began coming up the ladder.

As soon as the other seven had climbed the ladder, the Death Merchant led them up the basement steps, again in single file. He paused toward the top of the stairs and this time, since the entire force was with him, he decided to use the Star-Tron to reconnoiter the forward area. He moved up a few more steps and eased himself up so that he could look over the first floor. Well now! He was pleasantly surprised to see moonlight tumbling in through some of the tall windows, those that had not been boarded up. Every ten feet or so, a long pillar of subdued light slanted down, exposing machinery in faint but eerie outline. If Camellion had been superstitious, he would have sworn that Little Old Mother Nature was on their side. Between now and the time they had entered the tunnel, the weather had cleared, the clouds had parted, and the moon was out.

His hand relaxed on the flap of the Star-Tron case, and he looked out over the floor of the refinery. In the moonlight, he could see the contours of the cane-feeder tables, the massive cutters, the huge shredding equipment, and the line of roller mills.

The rest of the men had crept closer to Camellion, who

turned to them and whispered, "I can see a hundred-foot stretch ahead. It's all clear. There's a wall between the cutting and shredding department and the chemical processing section. I can't see through walls! Not that it makes any difference because we have to take one section at a time."

Leland Moore whispered in a voice ragged with tension, "Listen, since the warehouse is built off the other end of the building, why do we have to wade through the whole damn floor? We've got it figured that the commies are holed up in the warehouse!"

"Clarify!" Camellion was terse.

Moore answered with a hard stare. "Why don't we ease out a side door—there has to be one—and go to the warehouse on the outside? Think of the time we'd save?"

"And the lives we might lose!" Richard told the CIA spook. "We don't actually know where the commies are. If they caught us out in the open—the outside—they'd chop us apart. There's almost no cover out there. It's better we dirty-trick on the inside."

"All right. We'll do it your way," Moore conceded. "How do we proceed?"

"We go up, spread out in a V-formation and move ahead," Camellion whispered. "Before all this is over with, we're going to have to ace out a lot of trash. But keep in mind that we want some of them alive. We can't question dead men. Or dead women!"

Camellion went first, then Moore and Rafael. The other five men followed. They spread out, formed into an attack V-formation and, with Camellion at the point, started the thrust toward the east. Their eyes probing the darkness ahead, they moved past the feeder tables and went on to the enormous cane cutters, Camellion and Luis Guillermo, to Richard's right, and Cletus Huff, to his left, pausing to look at the deadly blades, caked with rust but still sharp enough to decapitate a man.

It was Guillermo who first spotted the light, hissing, *"Electrico linterna! Delanta!"*

A flashlight up ahead could only mean trouble. Automatically, the Death Merchant and the men dropped down behind various pieces of machinery, all of them wondering if one flashlight indicated one Red gunman, two commie killers, or two dozen!

The Death Merchant looked around the side of the cane cutter platform he was using for concealment. Now there were four bright beams, but the bright glare made it impossible to tell whether there were only four men or forty behind them. Camellion was sure that, from the way the fingers of light were moving, the Red guerrillas were coming up fast. He was also certain that the enemy didn't know he and his men were there—*Or they wouldn't be coming at us with flashlights on. They'd be waiting in ambush.*

The terrorists had to come ahead another fifty feet before Richard and his men saw that there were two dozen of them. It was difficult to tell, what with the enemy moving behind various pieces of machinery. From his own center position, Richard now could see that more of the Reds—both men and women—were coming through the door of the chemical processing section.

"Why don't we fire?" demanded Cletus Huff. He stared accusingly at the Death Merchant. "Another minute and they'll be sitting in our laps!"

As Huff was speaking, Urbaldo Ryan moved to a better firing position. As he did so, he accidentally stepped on a trip-pedal that controlled a 300-pound iron shredder hammer. The pedal released the brake lug and the hammer dropped on its runners to the bed with a thundering sound, the crashing noise resounding throughout the entire area as Camellion's mouth was forming the word "Wait."

Now, why waste time saying anything? Quick as chain lightning, Camellion swung up his Largo Llama submachine gun and fired at the communist killers who, warned by the falling hammer, were diving pell mell for cover.

At the sound of the hammer hitting the crusher-bed, Rafael and Justo Mario Fuertes, both quick thinkers, also cut loose with their automatic weapons. The other five men of Camellion's force wasted precious kill-time by being as startled as the enemy.

All the same, the three streams of 9mm slugs cut down seven of the enemy unlucky to have slow reflexes. There were screams of fear and pain and a dozen loud whines of copper-coated lead ricocheting from metal machines, then nothing but dying echoes, followed by an agonizing silence.

"What do we do now?" Huff turned to Camellion, fear in his eyes.

"We use grenades, then charge, and do a lot of hoping on the way," Camellion said. He was about to tell Huff to pass the word but was stopped by a voice up ahead shouting to someone in Spanish—*"Go outside and get around them!"*

Doing some fast brainwork, the Death Merchant moved from his position and dodged between equipment to where Leland Moore was waiting behind a large cane cutter blade braced on the floor between four steel barrels. Camellion quickly looked around and saw three of the other men.

"Moore, take Korse, Ryan, and Fuertes and work back to that door we passed when we moved by the tables," Camellion ordered. "The four of you stop them on the outside, and the rest of us will use grenades and see what we can do in here."

Half a dozen blasts of automatic rifle and machine gun fire erupted from the enemy and there were shrill shrieks of high velocity slugs glancing off machinery, some of the ricochets close to the Death Merchant. Huff, Rafael, Guillermo, and Fuertes triggered off a reply.

"Get going!" Camellion said to Moore. The other man stared fearfully at him for a moment, then nodded, turned, and motioned to the other men close by.

With enemy slugs zipping all around him, Camellion dodged back toward the cane-cutter platform. This time he stopped next to Cletus Huff, who was firing short bursts as a delaying action.

"We'll use grenades," Camellion said. "Two each. We'll all throw together. Hold off until I get word to Rafael and the other bowl of chili sauce."

"What about Moore and Gloomy Butt and the other two?" Huff asked, his eyes filled curiosity. "Are they taking a coffee break?"

"Yeah, outside. They're going to stop a split-off force from giving it to us in the back. Remember! Two each. And we throw as a unit."

Richard crawled off and finally made it back to the cutter platform. He picked up several empty shell casings, ejected previously from his Largo Llama, and tossed them at Luis Guillermo, the Indian-faced young Mexican to his right, eight feet away. One of the casings pinged on Guillermo's sub-gun, and the Mexican turned and looked at Camellion. The Death Merchant took a grenade from a bag, pointed to the grenade and held up two fingers. He next pointed to himself and to Huff, then at Guillermo and Rafael, who were six feet to the right of Guillermo. Camellion held up four fingers, then moved his hand forward, indicating that the four of them would throw together. The Death Merchant next pointed to Rafael.

114

After nodding that he understood, Guillermo used the same shell and finger technique to communicate with Rafael, who looked as if he might be enjoying himself.

Working together, the Death Merchant and his three companions in misery pulled out two Mexican fragmentation grenades each and glanced at each other to make sure they were in synchronization. His mouth twisted in a wolfish snarl, the Death Merchant nodded. Each man pulled the pin from his grenade, let fly, and then got down behind whatever he was using for protection.

The world exploded. There were one-two-three-four bright flashes of red, and as many terrific explosions, a cacophony of crashing sound that was a reminder of the reality of existence: that everyone lives and dies for himself alone. An aria of screams followed, and a clanging symphony of blown apart equipment slamming upward against the ceiling or crashing against the floor; as a finale there was the final pinging of rocketing shrapnel and jagged pieces of metal, torn from the machines.

Once the monsoon of flying metal had subsided, the Death Merchant and his three men followed up with the second four grenades, this time throwing them as hard as they could, in an effort to blast forward areas as yet untouched.

The explosions of the four grenades jerked up the curtain on the second act of total destruction. Again there were more yells and the screams of men and women asserting their right to live, and the deafening crash of heavy objects being bent, broken, crushed, or crammed into each other.

The Death Merchant waited until flak city had passed. A piece of flying metal could kill you as efficiently as a bullet. Taking a deep breath, he looked around him to make sure that the other three men were ready, then moved out from behind the cane-cutter platform and charged forward, his finger close to the wide trigger of the Largo machine gun. Spread out on each side of him, Huff and Rafael and Guillermo moved ahead as fast as they could in the dim moonlight. Their eyes burned from powder fumes, but they ignored the tears and did their best to see through the layers of smoke in front of them.

The sound of machine guns firing from the outside didn't improve their dispositions—nor Camellion's; yet they didn't worry about what might be taking place outside the building. The instinct for survival was too strong.

Almost instantly, Camellion and the three men with him saw that their eight grenades had had the effect of a baby blockbuster. The heavy metal rollers of the roller mill had been torn loose and tossed aside as if they had been cylinders made of tissue paper. A dozen of the long tubes had been wrenched from their bearings. Even the roller mill housing and canopy were twisted and bent, the control panel nothing but jagged metal.

Everywhere were bodies, and that one-of-a kind saccharine odor. But it wasn't the smell of sugar or molasses; it was the special stink of death. The Death Merchant had inhaled its fragrance all over the world, and the scent was always the same. . .

The bodies of the Twenty-third of September Communist League terrorists lay in tumbled confusion. Those who had not been killed by machine gun fire had been torn apart by the grenades. Bloody and butchered, the bodies were in grotesque positions which indicated that arms and legs had been broken in numerous places. A few had jagged ends of rib bones protruding. Others lacked an arm or a leg. The Death Merchant noticed that one man lacked a head and a foot. Not far away, a woman was on her back, her torn slacks and halter caked with blood mingled with dust, the end of an enormous roller resting where her face and head should have been. But she wasn't the only League terrorist to have been killed by falling equipment. Other cockroaches lay mangled, some almost completely covered with parts of machines. One has-been killer lay on top of several rollers, both arms spread out, his head hanging down, mouth and eyes open in statue-frozen horror. Nonetheless, part of a machine had killed him. A rusty brace protruded from his chest, as though he were a bug pinned to the roller by a giant pin. The bodies and the sides of the bulky equipment were coated with blood, great splashes of red that, mixed with gray dust, had a peculiar dark color. The blood alone was enough to make one want to vomit, particularly Cletus Huff, who was finding it more and more difficult to keep down the dinner eaten hours earlier. Already he was tasting bile.

The ATF Fed forgot all about regurgitating as the Red killers who remained alive recovered their senses and began to fire. One commie guerrilla jerked from around a continuous juice clarifier, saw Huff, and tried to rake him with a stream of CETME automatic rifle slugs. Huff jerked frantically to one side a hair of a moment before the Red fired, surprising himself with his speed and coolness under fire. The hail of 7.62mm projectiles cut the air to his left and zinged off one of the metal rollers. The blobs of lead were still completing their paths of ricochets as Huff automatically aimed, fired, and saw his burst play tic-tac-toe on the cotten shirt of the terrorist and smash him to the floor. Again Huff was astonished. Killing a man was so easy! And so was dying!

The Death Merchant was past being shocked at anything, especially death, which he considered as natural as living. What people really feared was the *when* and the *how*. Unlike the man eight feet ahead of Camellion who very suddenly knew when and how! Camellion blew apart his head with a four-round burst of 9mm slugs and watched the yo-yo's hate-twisted features and skull part company, explode, and vanish into the rest of the bloody surroundings.

Camellion laughed—*We are such stuff as dreams are made of; and our little life is rounded with a sleep! Bull excrement! I wonder what Shakespeare would have said about a mess like this?*

He stepped over the headless corpse, almost slipped on thick blood and, storming forward, came to the end of the quadruple vacuum evaporator, where he came very close to the end of his short life on planet Earth. He almost bumped into three of the enemy who had been creeping toward their left on the other side of the Q.V.E. The three commies were far more surprised then Camellion, who recovered and instantly put two slugs into the stomach of Velasco Jorge Murillo, a tall man with a crooked nose and cow-like eyes.

Murillo fell back with a hoarse cry while Andrew de Oca —all muscles and not over twenty—grabbed the barrel of Richard's Largo with one hand and, at the same time, tried to bring up his own Spanish Parinco sub-gun.

The third man, Ruz Legue—his *companeros* called him "Little Coco"—tripped over the right leg of de Oca and fell against the side of the Q.V.E. tank.

De Oca cried out and jerked his hand away from the hot barrel of the Largo Llama. The Death Merchant shot out his left hand, grabbed de Oca's wrist, pushed away the Parinco and brought up the Largo, holding his right hand tightly around the top rod of the metal frame stock. Using the empty submachine gun like a spear, he stepped slightly to one side, jumped a foot off the ground, came down on his right foot, kicked out with his left leg and slammed inward with the Largo Llama.

The tremendous kick was a *Goiu-Rvu* karate *Sokuto Geri* —a "sword-foot kick" that brought the sole of his booted foot crashing into the left side of Ruz Legue's rib cage. Ribs cracked, Legue howled in pain and went down on his knees, his hellish surroundings swimming before him. As if from far far away, he heard de Oca cry out in supreme agony when the end of the Largo barrel smashed into the bridge of his nose. His mouth and throat filling with salty blood, de Oca felt the Parinco jerked from his hand. A few moments later, his inner world of pain clicked into total nothingness as the Death Merchant twisted the machine gun around and tore apart de Oca's chest with four slugs.

Little Coco attempted to crawl away, despite the hellfire pain in his ribs. He got all of six feet along the side of the tank. Coming toward him, Rafael killed him with two 9mm projectiles that entered the top of Little Coco's skull and spilled out his brain like half-cooked oatmeal.

Wanting to reload his own Largo scatter-box, the Death Merchant zig-zagged wildly, barely dodging a burst of slugs tossed his way by Hilda Sanchez, a shapely young woman with flowing dark hair. Several of her 5.56mm projectiles came within a fraction of Camellion's back, one only .16 centimeters from the back of his neck.

He reached the side of a scalding hopper, glanced around and saw that for the moment he was safe. Getting his second wind, he pulled a full magazine from his ammo bag, thrust it into the Largo, pulled back the cocking knob, and started moving toward the other end of the hopper. . . . *I'll catch that bitch from the other side and send her home to hell to join her companions!*

Camellion had calculated correctly. Hilda Sanchez was coming at him on a straight-in course, but Richard hadn't counted on Rafael's spotting the Mexican woman; he had assumed that Rafael would head straight for the door leading to the chemical processing department.

Sanchez had been joined by Elberto Granados and Hugo Nunez, two stone-killers who had a natural talent for assassination. Hilda Sanchez was hardly aware of them. Nor was she aware that her breasts had burst from the restraining halter and were flopping around like two melons tipped by red-brown strawberries. In her enthusiasm, she had also failed to spot Rafael, who suddenly rose up fifteen feet to her right. Then she saw him, fear and sudden recognition causing her to pull up short. Her eyes opened wide. So did her mouth! But the scream never came. A half-dozen 9mm projectiles did! Two tore off her left breast; the rest made her a bloody thing of shredded flesh and chipped bone, all of them knocking her back against Hugo Nunez, who was going through the motion of aiming down on Luis Guillermo. Before he could complete his aim and pull the trigger, Rafael cut his fat legs out from under him with another line of copper-coated lead that slammed the communist revolutionary sideways against the rusty condenser of a juice crystallizer.

Seeing Nunez die amid a shower of flesh and ripped patches of shirt, Elberto Granados tried to duck. He dropped, spun around, and succeeded in avoiding Rafael's blast which passed over him. Granados' elation was short-lived. He looked toward the south and let out a screech of fear at the sight of Camellion, who had succeeded in crawling around the end of the hopper. The Death Merchant and the flaming muzzle of the Largo were the last things Granados saw. Camellion fired. Four slugs hit Granados in his skinny chest. With a hurt, disbelieving expression on his face, he dropped and became part of the dirty floor.

Camellion looked to his right and spotted Rafael, who also saw him, grinned, and pointed ahead toward the wide doorway that led to the chemical processing department of the old sugar refinery. Richard nodded and started to move in the same direction.

In the meanwhile, Luis Guillermo was extracting himself from his difficulties. Earlier, he had come upon five terrorists, four men and a woman, all of whom had been trying to sneak around to the south side of the building, in an attempt to come up from the rear and trap Camellion and his tiny group in a cross fire.

Snarling *"Communista marranos!"* Guillermo had raked the group with a burst. But the magazine of the Largo machine gun had been almost empty and the short burst had killed only the blond woman and one man. The advantage of lag time had been on the side of Guillermo. During the few seconds that the men were recovering from their surprise, Guillermo had swung his empty machine gun like a baseball bat and had jerked the Obregon automatic from the spring-clip holster strapped to his chest. The barrel of the Largo had slammed against the head of one man, cracking his skull. Made desperate by fear, Guillermo had then kicked upward at the hands and arms of Byron Verdencia while he had placed a .45 bullet in the chest of Pablo Algaranaz. The toe of Guillermo's boot had smashed into one of Verdencia's wrists, forcing the man to drop the gun. Guillermo had then tried to swing the Mexican automatic to Verdencia, but Verdencia, equally terrified, had grabbed his wrist and, with the other hand, had thrown a fist at Guillermo's head.

Guillermo ducked and decided on a desperate gamble, his feeling being that very soon the much heavier man would succeed in tearing the Obregon .45 from his grasp. He faked a left jab at Verdencia's bumper-like chin, and when the terrorist ducked and blocked with his free hand, Guillermo's left hand darted to the slim wooden handle of the burin sticking up underneath the back of his collar. An engraver's tool with a six-inch blade, the burin was in a special holster fastened to the top of Guillermo's back.

Too late did Verdencia realize the trap. The burin was coming straight at him. Hideous pain exploded in the hollow of Verdencia's throat. He tried to scream, but the welling blood and the blade of the burin buried in his windpipe wouldn't let him. The world began to swim. His knees began to buckle. He was unconscious when Guillermo pulled the burin from his throat and jumped back to avoid the rush of scarlet.

Detecting someone to his right, Guillermo swung around with the Obregon automatic and saw Cletus Huff, who hurried over to him and stared down at the dead guerrilla. On its knees, the corpse had fallen forward, so that the top of its head was resting on the ground.

"Well, good God Gerty!" mumbled Huff. "He reminds me of a Moslem saying his prayers." Wiping sweat from his smoke-dirty face, he looked at Guillermo in disgust. The grim-faced man was wiping the thin-bladed Burin on the shoulder of the corpse. Trying to keep a stone face, Huff swallowed hard. His mouth was dry and he had a headache. He thought of the estimated eight million Mexican aliens in the U.S., and thousands more pouring in every week, while the fumble-butts in Washington did nothing!

He watched Guillermo return the odd-looking knife to its

120

holster, then reach down and pick up the Largo submachine gun. Only then did the Mexican, after he straightened up, look directly at Huff, his mouth twisted into what could have been either a smile or a sneer. Huff could not decide which.

"Amigo, have you seen Senors Camellion and Rafael?" asked Guillermo, shoving a full magazine into the Largo.

"I caught a glimpse of Camellion headed straight for the door," Huff said, thankful that he had kept the cracks out of his voice. "I haven't seen Rafael for the last fifteen minutes."

Both men cocked their heads to the northeast. It was impossible to tell how many submachine guns were firing outside the building.

"Those guns! It has to be Moore and the rest of our men," Huff said hopefully. "The enemy wouldn't be firing from that far back. It can only mean that Moore and his bunch are advancing."

"Come, amigo," urged Guillermo. "We will go find our *compadres*."

Machine gun in hand, he turned to go, not bothering to see if Huff were following.

A .45 automatic in one hand, the Death Merchant stood against the wall on one side of the wide doorway. Rafael was on the other side, an Obregon autoloader in his hand. Twenty feet in front of the dark opening were Cletus Huff and Luis Guillermo, each man crouched at the side-end of a fork-lift truck that was minus its batteries.

The Death Merchant had outlined the plan during a brief conference with the other three men, his strategy having formed after he had heard the roar of gunfire at what he estimated to be the northeast corner of the long building. Some facts were in evidence, the first being that since the chemical processing section was twice as dark as the area just cleared, most of the windows in the east side of the mill had to be boarded up.

All was quiet from within the darkness beyond the door. If any commie rebels were there, they were waiting with the intention of letting the Death Merchant and his minuscule force come to them; and this time the commies wouldn't make the mistake of being close to the doorway. They would go beyond the range of grenades. Another certainty was that every commie weapon had to be trained on the doorway.

The Death Merchant switched on the walkie-talkie. It was a good thirty seconds before Moore answered.

"What's the situation out there?" Camellion asked.

"We don't have a scratch," Moore said, his voice weighed down with fatigue. "We didn't see any of them after we left the building. Harley came up with the idea that we wait for them. We hid behind a stack of steel drums and gunned down fourteen of them when they went past. Come to think of it, the man with the red hair thinks he has a sprained ankle. He tripped on—"

"Where are you?" cut in the Death Merchant.

"On the east side, not far from the northeast corner. We ran into another bunch, but we saw them before they spotted us. How's the situation on your end?"

"Other than being unable to move, we're all right, all four of us." Camellion was mildly condescending. "We can't move without a diversion from you and yours."

"You're all set to attack the next section?"

"We can't until you start lobbing in grenades from your end."

There was a pause. Finally Moore responded. "Give us five minutes. Anything else?"

"Five minutes—out."

Camellion switched off the walkie-talkie, looked over at Rafael and nodded. He wasn't the least bit satisfied with the way the operation was going. In the first place it was not likely that they would capture any of the terrorists. In the second place, if the terrorists had prepared a trap, they couldn't have done a worse job—*It was we who surprised them! None of it fits, because I was expected at the apartment on San Juan Avenue!*

Anger at himself? Yes! And anger at the CIA DD/P section. Counterespionage men like Moore did not belong on this kind of mission. Men with families were always too cautious. As for Huff and Korse, it wasn't that they were nonprofessionals. In the States they would have been experts. Here in chili-pepper land, Huff and Korse were like city boys who had been teleported to the wilds of Canada with only a compass that they didn't know how to use. They didn't have the experience for this kind of intelligence-gathering-and-kill mission.

Camellion pursed his lips. *Yet I must admit that, so far, all three have done their share. Hmmmm. Either heaven is on our side, or else hell has stopped helping the terrorists. The eight of us are still alive. Not one man is wounded. When you get down to the nitty-gritty of it, what's the difference whether we die now or do it a day at a time. Karma? The Hindus and the Buddhists would call it that. We in the West might say Destiny. Yeah, Destiny shapes our ends. So do rich foods. But we're still free to go on reducing diets!*

A violent series of grenade explosions from the east end of the building terminated the Death Merchant's philosophical wool-gathering, the half-dozen concussions shaking the old building. Richard caught Rafael looking expectantly at him. Camellion shook his head, which was another way of saying, not yet.

He heard submachine guns chattering from the far end of the building. Other music boxes roared in reply. *The second blast was about a hundred feet up, about the center of the south side. Moore couldn't have come that far, not yet.*

More explosions of grenades. One-two-three-four-five shattering blasts rattled broken equipment lying on the floor and made roof braces, made of girders, tremble along their lengths.

Mrs. Camellion's son Richard took the last three fragmentation grenades from one of his shoulder bags and looked over at Rafael. He wanted to be absolutely certain that the talented Spaniard was prepared on his end of the strange symbiosis that existed between him and the Merchant of Death. Especially now did their lives depend upon each other. There is a time and place for everything. Now was the time and this was the place for teamwork between experts.

And for the use of thermite grenades. But not yet.

Holding a fragmentation grenade in one hand, Camellion nodded at Rafael and held up four fingers. Four grenades each. Another nod. Let's do it. And then the two men did. Each man threw four grenades as fast and as far as he could, yet doing his best to place each grenade in a different position.

The blast from the last grenade, thrown by Rafael, was still slamming broken parts of machines with the force of cannon balls when the Death Merchant pulled the first thermite grenade from the smaller Musette bag on his hip. Filled

123

with concentrated thermite, the fire bomb was larger and heavier than a conventional grenade. Listening to more of the rataplan of machine guns to the east, he moved his hand up and down, weighing the thermite grenade. He then pulled the red ring, stepped out several feet from the wall, and flung the T-grenade sideways through the doorway, on a course that took it on an angle toward the south side of the building.

The thermite bomb did not explode in the conventional sense. There was only a muffled plop, then a huge blossom of pure white fire, which resembled the bursting of an aerial bomb—the kind used by various American communities in a fireworks display on the 4th of July.

There the similarity ended. Thermite is not a harmless 4th of July Big Bang. Thermite is a mixture of powdered aluminum and powdered iron oxide which, when ignited by black powder, burns at a hellish temperature of about 4,000 degrees F. When thermite burns, white-hot molten iron is released, acting as a heat reserve to prolong and spread the incendiary effect.

Molten fire was everywhere. Molten iron hissed in puddles on the floor and on pieces of machinery, some of it dripping down, moving in crooked streams, like tiny rivers of volcanic magma. Yet there had not been one scream. Not one blob of thermite had splashed on an enemy.

Lightning speed was essential. With only the Obregon .45 in his hand, the Death Merchant tore through the north end of the doorway. Dodging and weaving, keeping as low as he could. Camellion moved like a wild man, all the while expecting a hail of slugs to whack him into the next world. He wasn't disappointed.

There was fire from numerous small arms, as well as several streams of submachine gun slugs. A bullet stabbed through his close-cropped hair. More slugs came close to his head. A tug at his pants, down by his inner left calf! Another jerk and pull at his right hip, the bullet tearing through the top of a canvas shoulder bag! A jerk at the holster on his right hip. A slug had torn through the leather! A loud *pinnnggg* when another projectile cut through one of the ammo bags and flattened itself against one of the Largo machine gun magazines.

The Death Merchant dove to the side of a boiler that had once supplied the heat for the boiling pans which had been used to make molasses. Bullets whistled and buzzed all around him, metal bees trying to sting him to death.

The fragmentation grenades had transformed this part of the chemical processing department into a smoking junkyard. Gears and panels had been ripped from machines; juice heaters had been blown apart. A huge metal section had been torn from a catalyst hopper and thrown to the top of a cyclone separator. There it rested, balanced precariously on top of a rounded flange coupling that connected two pipes, the end of one pipe attached to a regenerator, the end of the other to a cooling precipitator. Three times the size of a manhole cover, the heavy piece of metal rocked gently back and forth, as if trying to make up its mind whether it should crash to the floor. Its edges, jagged and razor sharp, were mostly shredded and in strips. Some of the strips were curled back. Others were a foot long.

Within the stark white light of the burning thermite, Camellion saw that the communist terrorists were behind masses of equipment at about the center of the south side, bottled up there by Leland Moore and his men, who had entered the building by way of the only entrance on the east end, a door not far from the northeast corner. There was a large truck door in the center east wall, but the chains were gone from the mechanism, and the door could not be raised. Some of the rebels, having torn loose boards, had tried to escape through windows. They had been quickly cut down by Moore and his group.

The Death Merchant pulled the Largo from his back, stuck it around one end of the boiler and fired a short burst of six rounds. In reply, several sub-guns and four or five automatic rifles sent streams of high velocity projectiles at the boiler. There were the screams of ricochets, metal glancing off metal, all of it familiar to the Death Merchant, who now knew, from the enemy fire, that the enemy was concentrated seventy-five feet to the southeast.

His features highlighted by the ferocity of determination, the Death Merchant moved back from the boiler. He was careful to insure that he remained within the safe distance that kept each end of the boiler between him and the enemy. *If I tossed shellac at them, they'd go to hell with a fine finish!* He took the second thermite bomb from his bag, mentally calculated the range, pulled the ring, then threw the deadly little fire grenade over the boiler.

The Death Merchant did not hear the faint *plop* nor see the huge white blossom of bursting flame. He did hear the intense shrieks of pain and, glancing behind him, toward his right, see Rafael and Huff and Guillermo charging through the doorway from the other section. Although the three were moving as fast as they could, to Camellion they were as slow as an old maid opening and closing her hope chest.

Before the three men could reach him, he pointed ahead, then dashed from around one end of the boiler, his Largo ready for instant firing. He leaped over rubble and parts of machines torn loose by exploding grenades. Within seconds he came to the hell created by the thermite grenade.

The molten iron had splashed on half a dozen of the communist band, two of whom were women. Horrible screams of unbearable agony poured from the throats of bodies rolling and twisting on the floor—human torches whose clothes were masses of flame and whose flesh was, in places, melting away from the bones. Thermite consumes flesh the way an ordinary fire dissolves tissue paper. Thermite "eats" quickly, too. One man's face had become a living skull and a deathhead's grin. The left arm of one of the women was utterly denuded of flesh, the radius and the humerus bones showing, the dull, sticky whiteness made more hidious by the sickening stench of burning cloth and leather, flesh and thermite. It was a wiener roast of hell.

Only two of the enemy tried to fire at Camellion. However, they were retreating and their streams of fire went wild. They ducked very quickly when Camellion lunged to one side and triggered off a ten-round volley of his own. One man, too slow to live, received four slugs in the left side of his chest. He fell back and crashed to the floor while Camellion, not wanting to press his luck, leaped over a tiny pool of burning thermite and dropped down behind a large rusty tank marked *Miel de Cana*—molasses.

He caught sight of Moore and the red-headed Irish Mexican sixty feet to his left, both men crouched behind stacked boiling pans. Seeing Camellion, Moore held up one hand, making a circle with the thumb and trigger finger. Very slowly the Death Merchant nodded.

The sharp but very short scream behind him was totally unexpected.

Camellion turned. His mouth became a tight line, and he

126

focused his eyes with dark and bitter intensity. At once it became apparent how Rafael had been killed. Bent over, Rafael had paused by the side of the cyclone separator, on top of which, on a flange, had been balanced the metal strip torn from the catalyst hopper. The vibration of gunfire had finally caused the heavy piece of junk to topple off the flange. It had crashed downward and had fallen on Rafael, one jagged tooth stabbing him between the shoulder blades. The Spaniard lay face down, a pool of blood forming under him. The ragged slab of metal was still on his back, held in place by the foot-long "tooth," most of it buried in Rafael's back.

Death is final. Rafael's time to go bye-bye had come—and gone.

Like the old song—"It was just one of those things . . ."

Camellion saw Huff and Luis Guillermo reach Rafael's body. While Guillermo only glanced at the corpse, Huff put on the brakes, stood like a pillar of salt and gaped in disbelief at the dead man, as if he were seeing Christ at the Second Coming.

The Death Merchant watched Huff, his face showing no emotion. Poor Huff. He didn't know that when men and women let the sight of death overwhelm them, they become aware of their own vulnerability. It is the price man must pay for being human. The horror of death is but the bitter fruit of man's having risen to the level of consciousness.

The Death Merchant turned around and looked toward Leland Moore, who was holding a walkie-talkie in his hand. The W–T on Camellion's belt buzzed. He pulled the instrument from his belt and turned it on.

"That scream! Who got it?" Moore asked.

"Emerald–4," Camellion replied, the words coming out in a positive tone. "It was an accident. Rafael was under a machine, standing by the side of it, and a piece of metal fell on him, speared him like a fish. He's dead."

"How did you know that Rafael was E–4?" Moore's voice was miles distant.

"He knew too much about the setup here," the Death Merchant said laconically. "Who else but a member of the League, a man who had actually hidden out here, would know about the ladder from the canal to the basement? The tinkle of a little bell turned into the ring of Big Ben. The answer had to be that Rafael was E–4."

Camellion wished he could have seen the surprise on Moore's face, but in the dim light all he could detect was the outline of the CIA agent's face. Continued Camellion, "Since 'Rafael' was Efran Rebaderos, or E-4, and since E-4 was a lieutenant of Alvar Gomara, I have concluded that Rebaderos was hiding out here with the others. Somehow he managed to slip away and meet us at the farm. What interests me now is the possibility that Gomara himself might be around."

Moore's voice came out crackly from the walkie-talkie. "The last of them, as far as I know, are bottled up ahead of us. Unless we've already killed Gomara, he has to be up there. Any ideas?"

"I'm going to try to talk them into surrendering," Camellion said. "We won't earn any brownie points by killing all of them."

"Surrender? I think you're nuts. But go ahead and play God in your own private Genesis if you want to."

The Death Merchant was unruffled. "I am inclined to think that they might fear thermite more than they love communism. It's worth a try."

He turned off the walkie talkie, replaced the device in its holster and called out in a loud voice, speaking Spanish:

"None of you can escape. You're hemmed in. Either surrender right now or we'll burn you alive with thermite. We're giving you sixty seconds to come out. Hold your flashlights with the beams pointed upward and keep your hands above your head. If anyone tries to get clever, we'll cremate every single one of you. I'm starting the countdown right now. When I reach sixty, we'll use thermite. You will not get a second chance."

Ten seconds passed. Fifteen. The first yellow beam shot toward the ceiling. Then a second and a third and a fourth. Finally, nine shafts of light were pointed upward and moving outward toward the Death Merchant.

Leaning out, he saw the first three guerrillas, their arms above their heads. In each man's hand was a flashlight.

The battle of the sugar mill was over.

Gradually, all nine terrorists—six men and three women—stood with their arms upraised, their dirty faces sullen and fearful, their eyes slits of hatred. Murder is the father of power; treachery is its mother. These terrorists, like political terrorists everywhere, were the pawns of that power. All shared the same delusion: that within Marxism lay the social and economic salvation of the human race.

Alvar Gomara was not among the nine.

Paul Torres Escutia was!

Chapter Eleven

From the way Richard Camellion glared up at the sky, the full moon might have been his personal enemy. He dropped his cold stare to the nine captives who had been taken from the building and lined up against the south wall on the outside. They looked pathetic, standing there in the moonlight, staring at the muzzles of the Largo Llamas held by Urbaldo Ryan, Justo Fuertes, and Luis Gillermo.

Leland Moore touched Camellion on the arm, leaned over, and whispered urgently, "We can't take them with us. We don't have the room. I suggest we get back to the pottery. If you want my advice, I—"

"I'll ask for it," Camellion cut in equably. "When I was ten, my father told me, 'Richard, my boy, never eat at a place called 'Mom's,' and never play cards with a man called 'Doc.' That's all the advice I have ever needed." He smiled, then said somberly, "Don't get any termites in your testicles. We'll be leaving very shortly."

Moore sighed and remained silent. Why argue with a man who could follow you through a revolving door and come out ahead on the other side? Well, this was a weird business, and orders were orders. The prime directive was still in effect: follow the orders of Richard Camellion. Damn the Center!

Camellion's eyes looked up and down the fat form of Paul Escutia. The man's average height made him seem rotund. A shorter man, weighing 300 pounds, would not have appeared quite so spherical. The revolutionary leader was dressed in blue cotton pants, a dirty, short-sleeved white shirt and chukka boots. Around his waist was a webbed cartridge belt and an empty holster. Escutia stared back at Camellion, who approached him slowly, stopping within three feet. The bandit leader's face was coarse and cruel and, with his triple chins, somewhat comical. But, paradoxically enough, there was a remarkable expression of dignity on his face, and an almost poetic fervor in his solemn eyes.

"Who are you?" Escutia gazed at the Death Merchant, his words precise and demanding. "As prisoners of war, we have a right to know who our captors are. I say this: I will tell you nothing. None of us will. Go ahead and shoot us."

The Death Merchant only stared at Escutia, smiling.

Justo Mario Fuertes' lips twisted in disdain. "Your bravery is touching, you communist pig, but rather belated," he said, sneering. "A little while ago you were not so anxious to meet your Maker."

Urbaldo Ryan brushed a lock of rust-red hair from his forehead.

"A bullet is quick," he said, his voice heavy with sarcasm. "Thermite can be slow and very painful, depending on what part of the body it hits."

All the time, Ryan kept his eyes on the woman standing in front of him. She was about thirty, a thin, flat-chested bitch, with a slightly flattened nose, framed by high cheekbones. Her chestnut hair was cut short like a boy's. Her eyes were bright with fierce hatred.

Luis Guillermo mocked, " 'Prisoners of war,' he says. "Why you're nothing but damned terrorists trying to tear down society and the established government. 'Prisoners of war!' "

"We are partisans fighting the cancerous forces of imperialism!" one of the captives spit out in defiance.

"You're a bunch of murderers, brainwashed by Marxist bull-shit!" Leland Moore cracked. "Now shut your damn mouth, or I'll close it for you."

The Death Merchant studied Paul Escutia, his search careful and professional. Escutia was not a coward. But he still was not superman. Camellion smelled fear, a fright that was as distinguishable as expensive perfume on a beautiful woman.

Richard sucked in a slow breath and a twinkle crept into his eyes. He smiled pleasantly at Escutia.

"I agree. You do have a right to know who we are. We're missionaries from the Eskimo Church of Greater Icebergia. We are here to convert you." Camellion's smile vanished and his voice became a direct threat. "In short, fat-boy, you can't tell us what we want to know if you're in hell being fried like a piece of bacon."

"Go to hell!" Escutia looked directly at the Death Merchant, his black eyes glowing with Satanic hatred. "I will never tell you anything. Go on! Shoot me!"

Camellion's eyes locked with Escutia's. "Just as people are more afraid of love than they are of hate, so it is that life can be a thousand times worse than any death," he said acidly. "For example, my fat friend, picture yourself living

131

with both your arms and your legs so crippled you can neither walk nor feed yourself. Try to conceive of yourself, in addition to being crippled, going through life without a nose, without your lips, without your eyelids."

Paul Escutia drew back, his expression revealing his conflicting emotions—disbelief and horror vs. reality.

"I give you my word, such a half-live, half-dead condition will be yours within a week if you don't tell us what we want to know." Camellion then tossed in the carrot. "If you co-operate, you will be flown to the United States and there given a new identity and a new start in life."

"The United States!" Escutia had the look of a man who knows he's trapped, but is fighting resignation and acceptance.

Ignoring the terrorist leader, the Death Merchant turned to Harley Korse and Cletus Huff, who stared at him the way victims of the Spanish Inquisition must have gaped at Juan de Torquemada!

"Handcuff him," Camellion ordered. He nodded toward Escutia, then looked up and down the line of guerrillas, who stood with their hands on top of their heads. Camellion indicated the woman standing in front of Urbaldo Ryan and the man to her right. "These, too. Move all three of them off to one side."

Leland Moore looked oddly at the Death Merchant. "What are we—what are you going to do?"

"Haven't you ever heard the expression that riots are poor people's press conferences?" Camellion said with a laugh. "Sometimes people have to improvise. I'm only going to do what the Mexican government would do if they caught these gentle people."

Huff and Korse snapped handcuffs on Escutia and the two other communist revolutionaries and shoved them away from the side of the building. The Death Merchant removed the Largo submachine gun from his shoulder and addressed the six prisoners still standing against the mill wall.

"Do all of you believe in Marxism?" His voice was jovial.

"And we're proud of it!" the remaining woman sneered, thrusting out her chin.

"That's nice. You'll be talking to him very shortly," Camellion said. He raised the Largo to hip level, switched the safety to "fire," and pulled the trigger, the raking sweep of projectiles cutting into the line of six revolutionaries. Riddled, they were knocked back against the mill wall where, dead and bleeding, they sagged to the ground—all except one man. He took several faltering steps, blood dripping from his mouth, his eyes as wide as saucers; then he fell forward on his face.

"Messy, very messy!" Huff stared at the bodies and nervously reached for his cigarettes. The two terrorists with Paul Torres Escutia stood ashen-faced, staring with intensified hate at the Death Merchant, who was reloading the Largo submachine gun.

"Well, that's one way of solving the problem of transportation," Moore sighed. "Effective, too."

"Murder usually is!" Korse said accusingly. He stuck out his jaw and his eyes jumped to Camellion.

"And you have the nerve to call us killers!" Escutia said quietly. "We kill, and you kill. What's the difference?"

"The difference is, we're the good guys in the white hats. You're the baddies in the black sombreros," mocked Camellion, putting the leather sling strap of the machine gun over his shoulder. He jerked a thumb toward the six bodies on the ground. "They were lucky compared to what will happen to the three of you if you don't answer our questions, starting about two hours from now."

Camellion realized that he had not been mistaken. His earlier assessment of Paul Escutia had been correct—*He's afraid of pain and he's afraid of death.* . . .

He turned and looked straight at Harley Korse, the amusement gone from his eyes. "Murder, you say! Suppose we have a good solid round of 'ain't it awful?' Will that make you happy?"

The Death Merchant's words and manner niggled at Korse, who was caught off guard. However, he quickly recovered his composure and stood his ground.

"I call it murder when unarmed men are shot down!" he said firmly.

"It was an execution made necessary by circumstances," Richard said, his voice calm but militant. "I was judge, jury, and exterminator who rid Mexico of six cockroaches. As for you, Korse. You're in the wrong business. Everytime you sit down hard, you shake up your brain. I suggest you go into politics!"

Harley Korse's big face reddened and his mouth became sullen. It was Leland Moore who saved him from further embarrassment.

"It's time we started for the cars," Moore said, his voice

133

impatient. "We have a long way to go and a lot to do before daylight. With any kind of luck, we can fly back to Mexico City in the afternoon." He glanced at Paul Torres Escutia and the two terrorists with him. "On the assumption that we can force them to talk."

"They'll talk!" Justo Mario Fuertes said with a wide grin. "Or beg for death."

The Death Merchant bowed graciously before Moore, an arid smile tugging at his mouth. "Lead the way, amigo."

Chapter Twelve

Eldridge Eubanks' house on the outskirts of Chapultepec, one of Mexico City's swank suburbs, reminded Richard Camellion of British colonial bungalows he had seen in India. The residence was a one-story affair, spread out and roomy, with sweeping lines and a wide veranda. The only difference was that there were a lot of palm and jenacara trees around Eubanks' house and that the blue tile roof was in a pantile pattern—longitudinally curved roofing tile, laid alternately with convex covering tiles.

Another difference was the short-wave MHz VHF antenna that stretched from the peak of the roof to a sixty-foot-high steel pole a hundred and fifty feet away. Neither the police nor Eubanks' neighbors were suspicious of the antenna, nor of the Americano who lived at Camino Pedregal 217. Eubanks was a ham radio operator. His call letters were E.B.D.W., and he was licensed by the Mexican Communications Department.

Eubanks kept the transceiver in his study, a large room toward the rear of the house. There were no windows in the room; only Eubanks had the key to the door which, while appearing to be wood, was sheet steel. The inside of the room was protected by infrared and ultrasonic alarms, although it was not likely that any burglar would find the two code books in the safe behind an old painting of a sunrise. The safe itself had triple tumblers. Should anyone force it open, a small charge of TNT would have blown the code books into nothingness—and the unlucky burglar right along with them.

Esther Eubanks, knowing that her husband's real business was counterespionage, never entered the study. She didn't want to, nor did she ever want to ask questions about various people who sometimes stayed in one of the guest rooms. She realized that such strangers were connected with her husband's work in U.S. intelligence. For example, this latest guest, the quiet and polite man whom Leland had introduced as Richard Camellion ("That's only his cover name," Esther had told herself at the time). He was in his middle fifties, had silver-gray hair, a thick mustache, a purple birthmark on his right cheek, and walked with a limp. His right shoe had a sole three inches thick, and Mrs. Eubanks assumed he had a clubfoot.

"It's still one giant gamble," Eldridge Eubanks intoned solemnly. He shifted his weight in the chair and recrossed his legs. "The entire plan is based on the assumption that Escutia told the truth."

"Ho, but the man and the woman agreed with him, and we questioned them separately," pointed out Cletus Huff, who was seated across the study from Eubanks, a cigarette dangling, as usual, from his mouth, his feet propped up on one end of the folding table. "What surprised me was how he withstood interrogation. I don't think Ryan and Fuertes missed a single spot of his fat hide with their electric cattle prods. And by God Gerty, the son of a bitch still kept his mouth zippered."

Leland Moore, who was sitting next to Eubanks, gave a tiny laugh.

"Escutia was quite a man," he said. "Getting him to talk was like trying to pull a crocodile's teeth, until Fuertes started giving him two hot feet with a blow torch. After that, he couldn't talk fast enough."

"That explains why he told the truth," Huff said encouragingly. "He knows that there will be a repeat performance if we find out he lied." He looked questioningly at Richard Camellion who was relaxed in one of the Dina Lounge chairs. "You're not actually going to have Escutia taken to the States are you? There's no way of knowing how many murders he's committed. The right thing to do would be to put a bullet in his head."

The Death Merchant smiled tiredly. "Did I ever tell you about a Chinaman named Wong who went to court and asked the judge for a divorce?"

Huff and Moore looked surprised. Korse and Eubanks smiled. So did Rossana del Moreno. She was lying on the chaise longue, her legs off the floor, the upper part of her body resting against the top section that was propped up.

"The judge asked Mr. Wong why he wanted a divorce," Camellion continued. " 'Because my wife gave birth to a baby that was white,' Mr. Wong said. The judge granted the divorce, saying, 'Two Wongs couldn't possibly make one white.' "

Everyone laughed but Cletus Huff. Looking perplexed, he

looked at the Death Merchant. "What does that have to do with the disposition of Escutia?"

"It means that you ask too many questions," Camellion replied reprovingly. He then reassured Huff with a broad smile. "But there's no harm in telling you though. Escutia and the two other revolutionaries will be kept alive until this operation is completed; then all three will be neutralized. . . ."

"That's what I thought," Huff said, brushing ashes from his lap. "So they'll be executed the day after tomorrow."

"Or we'll be dead tomorrow night!" Eubanks said, looking at the Death Merchant, a deep frown furrowing his forehead. "Let's assume that Paul Escutia didn't lie. I still maintain—"

"We established that he didn't four days ago, six hours after we captured him," Camellion said coolly, his eyes remaining fixed on Eubanks.

Disliking the interruption, Eubanks made an angry face. "I still say that what you propose is foolhardy. Flying out to Copper Canyon in the Sierra Madre Occidental—and landing at night, yet—is madness. I don't mean to insult you. I am saying that I think you're over-reaching yourself. To me, your scheme is far-fetched."

Having said what he had been determined to say, Eubanks adjusted his eyeglasses and shifted nervously. He continued to look directly at the Death Merchant. An astute judge of people, Eubanks sensed that Camellion was one of those rare individuals fortunate enough to enjoy detailed planning for its own sake, a man who very carefully thought out each tiny move in advance; furthermore, Camellion had been gifted with the even rarer ability to act decisively without the least trace of remorse over adverse results. All good qualities, yes! But damn it, this time Camellion was wrong. This time what he was planning was nothing more than a suicide mission!

Harley Korse's gloomy face came alive. His pocked cheeks hollowing slightly, he turned to his left, to Camellion sitting six feet from him.

"I agree with El, but for a different reason," he said, speaking slowly. "As Escutia tells it, 'The Parrot,' Alvar Gomara, and Maria Sojeda are to meet in Huatabampo— they must be there, or on their way there, right now. Thursday night the three of them will pretend to go fishing in the Gulf of California, where they'll make contact with the

Sea Hawk, the yacht that's carrying the arms. Then they'll use a helicopter, carried on the yacht, to transport the cases of weapons and ammo to the Sucker Flats in Copper Canyon. On the return trip from the canyon, the mobsters will carry the six hundred and forty kilos of Mexican Brown back to the yacht."

"Damn it to hell, we know all that!" snapped Leland Moore peevishly. "What's the bee buzzing in your bonnet? What's your point?"

"The yacht! The *Sea Hawk!*" The words jumped from Korse's mouth. He glanced at Moore, then swung around to the Death Merchant and addressed Camellion directly. "Why exclude the yacht from your plans. Why let those garlic-snappers sail away into the sunset? You want to set the chopper down in the dark and play war in the blackness when we could just as easily blow the *Sea Hawk* out of the water, after the thirteen hundred pounds of 'H' is on board. We have the explosives and you have the know-how!"

"Hold on there, Harley!" Huff was brusque to the point of rudeness. "Blowing the *Sea Hawk* to kingdom come would work out just fine for you. Your concern is the 'H.' And it would be on the bottom of the Gulf of California. But what about the guns? The heroin won't be on board the yacht until after the crates of weapons are in Copper Canyon. Well, it just so happens that I have a job to do, too. That job is stopping illegal weapons from coming into Mexico!"

"There isn't any way we can sink the yacht and get both the guns and the drugs," Korse grudgingly admitted. "It has to be one or the other."

"You're right, Harley. I've chosen to grab the heroin in the canyon," the Death Merchant said, his voice as laconic and unruffled as ever as it broke up the clash between the DEA agent and the BATF Fed. "If you two could think your way out of a paper bag, you would realize that if the revolutionaries don't have the heroin, they won't be able to get the weapons. The guns will fly into Mexico, and they'll fly right back out again. The only things the mobsters are going to find in Copper Canyon are a lot of dead bodies."

Korse snapped his mouth shut and shook his head from side to side, his disappointment unconcealed. Moore and Eubanks glanced uneasily at each other, while Cletus Huff removed his feet from the end of the table and lit another cigarette.

All this time, Camellion had been watching Rossana del Moreno without looking directly at her, his furtive glances taking in the curve of her hips beneath the figure-hugging chocolate slacks and the swell of her breasts pushing against the tight vanilla blouse.

Now, Camellion let his gaze wander straight in at her. She smiled—a smile of promise?—and he remembered the smooth contours of her naked body and how fierce and raging she was when she made love.

He enjoyed the curve of her lips as she talked. Nor did he mind what she said.

"Richard, yesterday, when you explained your plan, you said that our helicopter would land within half a mile of Sucker Flats." Her eyes bored into his, her voice vibrant and sure. "What puzzles me is how we can land, or even make an approach for that matter, without the enemy's hearing us. A helicoper can be heard for miles."

"Ho! That's a good point," Huff said. He turned and looked at Rossana, who swung her legs off the chaise longue.

"Another thing that bothers me is that none of you seem to be the least bit concerned about internal security," she said incredulously. She stood up and walked over to the portable bar pushed against the wall, between the chaise longue and Leland Moore. When she reached the bar, she turned to face the Death Merchant. "Richard, have you forgotten the trap on Avenida San Juan? We should face the fact that the KGB has intruded itself into our operations. Polar Cold has been penetrated!"

"There's no hard evidence that the network has been infiltrated," Moore said stubbornly. "To jump to conclusions and make hasty moves at this point could be dangerous."

"I remember only too well what took place on San Juan Avenue," Camellion said, his voice bitter. "But apparently, you have forgotten that the revolutionaries hadn't set up any trap at the sugar mill. They weren't expecting us. Escutia told us that he hadn't been warned that we were coming, and he couldn't shed any light on how the KGB had learned I was going to the address on San Juan Avenue. I don't think he was lying.

Rossana spoke as she turned to the bar and reached for a glass and bottle of Fleuri Blanc. "What Escutia said and what the truth might be are two different things. By believing Escutia, you're risking the lives of everyone in this room. I would think about that, Richard."

"Not the lives of everyone," Moore said cheerfully. "You're not going with us, Rossana. You'll handle the office."

Leaning toward her, he gave her an affectionate pat on her backside.

"Don't do that!" she said angrily, turning to Moore, who drew back in surprise and embarrassment. As suddenly as it had come, her anger subsided. Her face softened. She turned and her level gaze sought out the Death Merchant. "The Barranca del Cobre could be a trap, just as it is possible that Escutia lied about everything, regardless of how much he was tortured."

"Nothing is certain in life, except death and taxes and the protestations of R. Nixon," Camellion said stoically, his face dead-pan. "We take our chances. This isn't football. We're not getting paid for yardage, but"—he looked straight at Eldridge Eubanks—"we're not going to commit suicide getting the job done."

"We will if we use a helicopter!" Moore said warily, watching Camellion, who began taking off his tan dress boots. Moore supposed the right boot, with its built-up sole, must have made walking very difficult.

For days, Moore had wondered about Camellion. Who was he, really, this tall machine of death and destruction whose changes of mood were infectious? Moore had also sensed that Camellion never actually lost his temper, which, like his charm, was always under firm control. Whether it was temper, politeness, or persuasion, he used each in carefully measured amounts, just the right amount required for the specific situation. Richard Camellion had charisma, and was very much aware of the effect he had on people around him.

Eldridge Eubanks said defensively, "There's another problem that's only been touched on: getting out of Copper Canyon if our helicopter is damaged. Being stranded in that giant canyon would be the same as being dumped on a tiny uncharted island in the middle of the Pacific Ocean. We wouldn't last a week!"

He searched the Death Merchant's face for added justification of use of the Polar Cold freight helicopter. All he got was an amused look.

"The Parrot, Gomara, and Miss Sojeda are supposed to meet the *Sea Hawk* around ten at night, the day after tomorrow," Camellion said. "Escutia said the heroin would be

140

taken into Copper Canyon by pack train. It's logical to assume that the same revolutionaries who will take the mule train into the canyon remain and guard the stuff. There won't be too many of them. The pack train had to start from a village. Too many men with a pack train would arouse suspicions; and once in the canyon, not many men would be needed to guard the train. Copper Canyon is deserted. There aren't any Indians or bandits—nothing! Ten men at most could do the job."

Eubanks carefully adjusted his glasses. "Let's assume you're correct. What does that have to do with our using a chopper?" he probed in a mild voice.

"We're going to land while it's still daylight in the canyon," Camellion said, quick to notice the frowns deepen on the faces around him. "We shouldn't have too much difficulty neutralizing the guards. After that it will be a piece of cake. All we'll have to do is wait for the whirlybird from the *Sea Hawk* and ambush the occupants after the bird sits down."

"I can think of a lot of ifs, ands, and maybes," Harley Korse said, his face remote and withdrawn. He looked even more drained when Camellion ignored him, like a poor relation at the funeral of a rich relative.

"Let's go to the table and I'll show you what I have in mind," Camellion said. He pushed himself up from the lounge chair and in his bare feet padded to the long folding table, on which was spread a topographic map of Mexico.

The four other men and Rossana del Moreno gathered around Camellion and looked down at the 1:24,000 scale map, the kind best suited for orienteering. The thin brown lines were contour lines, with every fifth line, heavier than the others, containing a number that indicated that every point along that line was so many feet above sea level. Red straight lines, marked off in squares, indicated laps traveled by compass. Longitude and latitude were marked off, as well as compass declinations. There were meridian lines that that ran true north to true south—lines which homed in on the North Pole in one direction, the South Pole in the other. The numbers attached to the lines were degrees of longitude, figures westward from the zero degree line that runs through Greenwich, England.

The Death Merchant focused on the map, then tapped a spot with his finger. "Here is Sucker Flats," he said, glancing up and around him. "As you can see, it's a flat area, open, about a mile long and a thousand feet wide. The area is surrounded by cliffs that go into mountains cut up into gorges, gullies, and valleys. It's here that we'll find the rebels."

Moore was leaning over, his hands flat on the table. "Where we'll land has to be here," he said without looking up. "It's the only open area within a half mile of the Flats." His finger moved slightly on the map. "There's this spot, but it's—let's see—almost two miles to the south. *El Cuchara Diablo,* it's called."

"The Devil's Spoon," Camellion said. "As you can see, the area is shaped like a spoon, with the handle pointed to the north. But that area is too far from the flats to be of use to us."

An inch-long piece of cigarette ash fell on the map. Huff mumbled, "Sorry!" and brushed the ash to one side. No one paid any attention to him, except Korse, who looked as if he were about to have the nervous breakdown of the month as he looked up at Camellion.

"I'm going on record as saying that I think your scheme is something right out of a grade-C movie," he said, his tone grating. He moved back from the table, raised up to his full height, and turned to face the Death Merchant. "Why even with night-vision gear our chances are only fifty-fifty. There's literally hundreds of places where the commie terrorists could ambush us; and with Escutia out of the picture, how do we know that the others won't call off the operation?"

His glare demanded an answer from Camellion.

"That's a good point," Eubanks chimed in. He glanced from Korse to Camellion. "Escutia told us he was supposed to meet The Parrot and the other two in Huatabampo. They're not exactly going to feel like dancing the samba when Fat Boy doesn't show up!"

Leland Moore regarded Camellion narrowly and slowly moved one hand across the top of his wavy brown hair. Finally, he said, "Rossana went directly to the heart of the matter when she brought up security. I'm not referring so much to the Russians as I am now to the efficiency of the 23–9 League. We can't ignore what happened three days ago. Bunuel and Moncada were both found shot to death in Magdalena. Executed! Slugs in back of the head!"

The Death Merchant rolled his wide shoulders in a shrug. "We expected it. By killing them both, by sacrificing their own man, the League made sure we'd never find out who the traitor was. It was a wise move on the League's part."

Camellion left the table, went back to the lounge chair and sat down, wondering with a quick side-thought why anyone would furnish a room with furniture made of PVC pipe painted brown.

Moore went on patiently as he walked back to his chair. "Camellion, let's not play games. You know very well what I'm saying: that the commie terrorists have woven threads of intelligence into the overall fabric. Harley was right. The big three of the League could call off the transfer, could postpone it until a more opportune time. For all we know, maybe they already have."

"There's so much we don't know," Korse said irritably, looking past Camellion. "To go into that canyon would be playing Russian roulette." He glanced then at the Death Merchant, to see what effect his words might have had.

Camellion's face was oddly expressive. *'There's so much we don't know!' That fool! Of course there is! I wonder what he and the others would think if they knew that Wink-Eye-1 has crashed somewhere in the rain forest of Surinam and that I've been elected to find the satellite?*

Camellion leaned back in the chair and stretched out his legs.

"I didn't say Harley was wrong," he announced, addressing Moore. He smiled pleasantly at the puzzled Moore. "Come to think of it, I think you're right, too. Unfortunately, we can't sit by and take the chance that the guns-for-drugs trade might be made. The Center says to go ahead. Gentlemen, we shall proceed as planned."

There was an uneasy silence. Moore's eyebrows peaked more than usual. The muscles in Korse's face tightened in frustration. Huff, a master at concealing his true feelings, lit another cigarette.

Eldridge Eubanks pulled a silk handkerchief from his coat pocket and began the ritual cleaning of his glasses. "You used the short-wave this afternoon," he said thoughtfully. "I assumed that is what you were going to do when you asked me this morning to give you the key to this room." He paused and looked up, his eyes steady. "Your own special cipher?"

The Death Merchant nodded. "And memorized!" He added the lie, "One could call it a kind of pig-Latin Choctaw with a mixture of Ojibway." Camellion consulted his wristwatch; then his eyes swept the room. He noticed that Rossana, lying back on the red cushions of the chaise longue, was studying him with cool appraisal, her lips curved in a slight smile. The others seemed to be sitting on the edge of a razor blade, waiting for an earthquake.

The Death Merchant gave them the first shock. "We'll leave tomorrow morning," Camellion said firmly, "before noon. We'll fly to Guadalajara, refuel, and then go on to Durango, where we'll spend the night. We'll refuel the next morning and then make a straight shot for Copper Canyon. We'll time the last lap so that we land while we still have the sun."

He leaned down and reached for his boots, then paused and looked up at Eldridge Eubanks, whose face wore an unfamiliar pinched expression.

"The Bell is in tiptop shape, isn't it?" he asked, his tone sharp.

"Polar Cold's equipment is always in excellent condition," Eubanks said indignantly, as if Camellion had insulted him. "We operate the company at peak efficiency. I was thinking of the excuse we're going to have to give our regular copter pilot, who flies the bird when we ferry equipment and supplies to distance jobs."

"There's the flight plan," added Leland Moore. "What do we put down as our destination after Durango? The Mexican Flight Authority is rather strict."

"I'll pilot the Bell," Camellion said indifferently, putting on his boots. "Tell the regular pilot that a Polar Cold efficiency expert from the States is testing the bird. On the F.P. we'll list Ciudad Obregon as our final set-down. I know that Polar Cold has done business in Ciudad Obregon. Such a stop will seem reasonable to the M.F.A."

Eubanks settled down in his chair and thought for a moment. "Yes, that's all very reasonable. It's not likely anyone will check to see if we touch down at Ciudad Obregon. I guess we'll dismantle our firepower and put the weapons in suitcases?"

"Do you know of a better way?" Richard said drily. Once again he looked at his wristwatch. "It's almost midnight and I need my rest. I'll go into the city tonight to save driving time tomorrow morning." He deliberately tossed his words at Rossana, his voice a challenge. "If somebody invited me to spend the night, I wouldn't have to go to a hotel."

Swishing the wine around in her glass, Rossana looked at

him for several long moments, a slight smile on her face, laughter in her lovely eyes. If she noticed the prudent glance that passed between Korse and Eubanks, she pretended not to.

"Richard, you can ride back to Mexico City with me," she said softly. "We can spend the night star-gazing."

The Caboza had just passed the city limits when Rossana, who was driving, gave Camellion a puzzled, sideways glance. Richard was leaning back, his head on top of the seat, a big grin on his face.

"A very private joke, or the simplicity of true genius?" she murmured with a slight, throaty laugh.

Camellion didn't change position or look at her. "I'm not a mind reader. What are you talking about?"

"The look on your face," she said mildly and slowed the car. She glanced at him again. "The look of a fox watching the hounds go off in the wrong direction!"

The Death Merchant licked his lips and sighed. "I was thinking of the surprise that Moore and Eubanks and the other two Feds are going to get when we land in Copper Canyon."

"Surprise?" Rosanna shifted gears, fed gas to the engine, and the car speeded up.

The Death Merchant's laugh was low and sinister. "They don't know it, but I'm not going to set the Bell down half a mile from Sucker Flats. Half a mile is too close. Instead we're going to land right smack in the middle of The Devil's Spoon. What a hike they're going to have!"

Her voice was low. "Are you sure your plan will work?"

"The only thing I'm sure of is that I'm a direct descendant of my parents . . ."

Chapter Thirteen

The Bell 212 had lifted from the field at Durango and been airborne only fifteen minutes when Cletus Huff, checking a pocket compass, noticed that Richard Camellion was flying southwest instead of northwest. Huff looked again at the compass to make sure he was correct.

"Camellion, I thought you said you were familiar with navigation!" the Bureau of Alcohol, Tobacco, and Firearms agent called out in a loud voice from where he was sitting, on one of the metal seats fastened to the side of the fuselage. "In case you don't know it, we're on a southwest course! If we keep going in this direction, we'll end up in the Pacific Ocean!"

Harley Korse and Eldridge Eubanks paused in their work of assembling 9mm Spanish Parinco submachine guns and turned and stared at Huff. Leland Moore placed his Parinco on the floor, turned, and looked at a portside window; all he could see were patches of brown and green below and cloud-littered sky above. For all he knew, he could be headed for the moon! He got up and headed for the copilot's seat.

"I know we're headed southwest!" the Death Merchant called back to Huff. "We're not going to Barranca del Cobre in the Sierra Madre Mountains; and put away the machine guns. You won't be using them."

Camellion adjusted the cyclic control and glanced at Leland Moore, who was settling into the cushioned seat beside him. In the windshield of the cabin, he could see the partial reflections of the three other men, who were coming forward.

"See here, Camellion. I want to know what is going on!" Moore demanded angrily, leaning toward Camellion. "We put together all the details to land and attack in the Copper Canyon, and now you tell us the whole god-damned thing is off!"

"Yeah, that's what I'm saying." The Death Merchant smiled.

Eldridge Eubanks had come up behind Camellion and sat down behind him. "With the amount of fuel we have, we can't stay airborne more than four hours," he said. "If

146

we're going out over the Pacific, we're going to rendezvous with either a sub or a surface vessel. No doubt a surface ship—we couldn't land on the deck of a sub. Well, which is it, Camellion?"

Every bit as mentally quick as Eubanks, Leland Moore instantly sorted the bits and pieces of the puzzle and came up with the only answer possible: Richard Camellion had pulled a fast one.

"I don't give a damn if we're meeting Jesus Christ," he said, almost shaking with rage. "Whatever plans you've made, you did it behind our backs, several days ago when you used the short-wave to contact The Center. I don't like that kind of bull-shit!"

"He doesn't trust us." Harley Korse's voice was bitter. "Or haven't you figured that out yet?"

Moore glanced at Korse, then jerked back to Camellion. Moore became more disgusted when he saw that Camellion was not the least bit concerned. Who did the son of a bitch think he was?

The Death Merchant finally said, "We're going to a point three hundred and eighty miles southwest of Durango. There's a PG class U.S. gunboat waiting where twenty-two degrees latitude intersects a hundred and ten degrees longitude. From Durango the flying time will be three hours and, roughly, forty minutes."

Harley Korse pulled a map from his pocket, unfolded and began to study it.

Moore sat straight up in amazement. "All right. The gunboat has a pad and we're going to set down on it. But are you saying that a United States gunboat is going to move up the Gulf of California and attack the enemy yacht? It can't be done! Unless Paul Escutia is twice the liar that Baron Munchausen was, the *Sea Hawk* is going to be ten miles due west of Huatabampo." His face screwed up in thought. "The gunboat would have to travel more than two hundred miles up the gulf to get to that position. By the time—"

"The U.S.S. *Chanticleer* is the name of the gunboat," Camellion said. He put a pill in his mouth and swallowed it.

"I don't give a damn if it's called the B.S. *Hitler!*" Moore shouted. "By the time we meet the gunboat this afternoon, land, and whatever else has to be done gets done, there won't be enough time for the *Chanticleer* to sail up the Gulf. What else are you holding back?"

Harley Korse thrust his head down between Moore and Camellion.

"The intersect point is a hundred and fifty-four miles due south of the southern-most point of the peninsula of Baja California," he said. "Of course, that's still on the high seas. The *Chanticleer* has a right to be there."

"The *Chanticleer* isn't going to do the job," the Death Merchant said, his voice as calm as his hand was steady on the Bell's control stick. "None of you should be surprised, either, at the sudden switch. You should have realized that I had no intention of letting the *Sea Hawk* off the hook. Before this day is done, I intend to send that yacht to the bottom of the Gulf of California."

Leland Moore turned to the right and looked fearfully at Eldridge Eubanks, who carefully pushed his glasses up on his nose and locked eyes with the sour-faced Harley Korse. Intuition told each man what the others were thinking: that Richard Camellion was one very clever individual; he was also a man who suspected one of them of being a traitor, a double agent. Now that the shock had passed, none of them really blamed Camellion for his duplicity and supercautiousness. Vital information had filtered out of the network. How? Was it possible that one of them was an agent for the Twenty-third September Communist League? Or even for the KGB? Unthinkable!

Poised behind the Death Merchant, Korse finally shattered the lull in the conversation. "You said we wouldn't be using machine guns. How are we going to do it? Are we going to board the yacht or just blow it out of the water?"

"*We* aren't going to do anything," Camellion said warily. "I and maybe a dozen Black Berets are going to board the boat. The four of you are too valuable to risk in this kind of an operation. Polar Cold is one of the main intelligence networks in Mexico, and there's a shortage of BATF and Drug Enforcement agents. Another factor, the deciding one, is that none of you have the experience for a fire-fight on water. You'd only get in my way."

Not wanting to show his ignorance, Harley Korse remained silent. He wondered, too, about the 1,300 pounds of heroin in Copper Canyon.

"What are the Black Berets?" Moore's voice was as puzzled as the look on his face. "Some kind of elite Navy outfit?"

Cletus Huff wanted to stand up and shout. Attacking a yacht had not been his idea of enjoyment.

"The Black Berets—so-called because each man wears a black beret—are attached to the First Ranger Battalion," the Death Merchant explained. "The old Green Berets operated behind the lines in small, eleven-man teams. The Black Berets are capable of conducting deep-penetration, commando-style raids—in and out in a hurry, to attack enemy targets or to protect a variety of U.S. interests, such as the raid that will take place today."

Moore's curiosity jumped ahead of his natural caution. Before he thought about it, he asked, "How do you fit into this, Camellion? I know you're not a regular 'company' man. You're too independent."

The Death Merchant glanced at the VSI dial, then calmly turned and smiled at Leland Moore. "That's none of your business. But I'll tell you anyhow. I do what I do for money, lots and lots of money, and all of it tax-free."

At a loss for words, Moore didn't know what to say. Somehow he felt that he had made a complete fool of himself, that Camellion was secretly laughing at him. He pulled away from the Death Merchant and leaned back in the copilot's seat, listening to the steady drone of the rotor blades.

"What about all the heroin in the canyon?" Harley Korse poked his head forward again. "What are we going to do about it?"

"I've made arrangements to take care of the 'Brown,'" Camellion replied. "You'll get all the details about midnight."

Korse was persistent. "You're not going to tell us the plan now?"

"No."

Eldridge Eubanks' tone was as glacial as his eyes. "We're just along for the ride, but for the record I'd like to know how you're going to take that yacht! The gunboat isn't going to do the job, and I don't think you're going to use this helicopter."

"Stick around and you'll see," Camellion said monotonously.

Hours later, Eubanks saw—and so did Moore and Korse and Huff.

Camellion began to lower the Bell 212, and, peering through binoculars, the four saw the U.S.S. *Chanticleer* sitting there in the calm blue water of the Pacific Ocean, the midafternoon sun reflecting from her pilot house.

To the gunboat's port was a much smaller craft, a PCH— a sleek U.S. Navy submarine chaser, with bow and stern turrets and a 20 millimeter cannon mounted on the center bow deck.

"Now you know," the Death Merchant said.

Chapter Fourteen

Almost twice the size of a World War II PT boat, "Little Willie" (as the Navy boys had nicknamed the PCH sub-chaser) was a lean, gray ghost cutting swiftly through the moonlit waters of the Gulf of California, her sharp prow tossing back a constant spray.

Richard Camellion stood in the control compartment of the pilot house with Lieutenant Commander Dean Hackmon, a young sailor at the helm, and Major Robert Whitespear, the leader of the Black Berets, who was half Sioux.

Camellion was well pleased with the sub-chaser. The control compartment, elevated in the port side of the middeck housing and completely surrounded by double-strength bulletproof glass, offered a 360-degree view of the ocean. The craft was very fast, traveling now at an incredible 54 knots (or 54 nautical miles per hour).

The Death Merchant looked at the green-lighted chronometer on the panel to the left of the wheel—2100 hours—and turned to Lieutenant Commander Hackmon, who was studying the water ahead through a pair of Bausch & Lomb "night glasses."

"Commander, how are we doing on plot time?" Richard asked. "Twenty-two hundred hours is the maximum. We don't have to board at ten, but we must be there before the enemy copter lifts off."

Hackmon lowered the binoculars and reached out for a handhold as "Little Willie" cut slightly to starboard.

"We're fifteen minutes ahead of plot-schedule," he said. "We can either cut speed or continue at full speed and arrive ahead of P.S.M. It's your decision."

Of medium height and about 35 years old, Hackmon had an easy manner and wore his hair even shorter than Camellion. A professional career man, Hackmon knew better than to ask questions; nevertheless, he had done a lot of thinking about the tall man in the jet-black jumpsuit. There wasn't any doubt in his mind that Camellion was someone important. Probably CIA. Before the *Chanticleer* had left San Diego, several civilians had come aboard, one with a metal case, and conferred with Captain Lawrence, the skipper of the *Chanticleer*. Now Hackmon wondered if the case had contained the big stainless-steel pistols that Camellion was wearing in holsters on a wide belt around his slim waist. In the dim greenish light cast from the instrument panel, this man called Camellion appeared sinister, like some coiled spring, or a virus waiting for a victim. Hackmon had the impression Camellion was also an individual who took orders from only a few superiors, and that those higher-ups reported only to God, and perhaps to the President of the United States—when they felt like it!

"We'll keep our present speed," the Death Merchant said. "Better to get there too early than too late."

He turned and looked out over the ocean. The weather was perfect, the water a plain of gentle, breathing swells that were three furlongs from trough to barrel. The only trouble was the shortage of firepower. He had expected a dozen Black Berets. He had gotten six! Those six had better be good!

Robert Whitespear's low laugh came as a rumble from deep within his throat. Finally he said in his deep voice, "If we were marching on land, at this rate of speed we'd be passing up ostriches."

Hackmon smiled pleasantly at the barrel-chested Black Beret, who was dressed in khaki combat fatigues.

"This craft was designed for speed," Hackmon said. "When we catch up with the target, we'll be able to run circles around her. We have plenty of firepower, too. Other than the twenty-mil job, the turret aft has twin M-sixties. The heavy machine guns in the forward turret are M-thirty-sevens. I feel sorry for those poor bastards on the schooner!"

Hackmon vaguely wondered how Whitespear could be a Major. Whitespear had to be under thirty.

In the half-darkness, the Death Merchant's eyes sought out Hackmon.

"We're moving down the center of the slot, are we not?"

"As straight as an arrow," nodded Hackmon. He took a few steps forward and looked at the compass. "We couldn't be more on course if we got a prize for it." He reached out and patted the sailor at the wheel on the shoulder. "Mason here looks like he might be a junior in high school, but he could spin this ship on a nailhead if he had to—after he found the nailhead with one eye shut and the other one half-closed."

"I assumed he knew his job or he wouldn't be here," Richard said casually. "I asked the brass for the best crew and

152

the best commander, men who wouldn't have to think twice." His gaze pounced on the stoic-faced Whitespear. "That includes you and your men, Major."

"We try," Whitespear said. If he was concerned about the coming battle, no trace of it showed on his face.

Commander Hackmon felt a new warmth toward Camellion. He was on the verge of saying that he hoped Camellion would turn in a good report when it occurred to him that this mission was not taking place. It was a lightning strike no one would ever hear about. Only the enemy—whoever the "enemy" might be.

The Death Merchant pushed the swordfish cap back on his head so that the extra long blue visor was almost at a perpendicular angle.

"How far will we be from each shore when we reach the target? I've made a rough calculation that the Gulf is about eighty miles wide off Huatabampo."

Commander Hackmon leaned over and consulted the plot board, which was lighted with a soft, greenish glow.

"Eighty-two point four," he said. "Give or take a few miles, we'll be between forty-three and forty-five miles from the Mexican mainland and the same distance from the east coast of Lower Cal. We'll be in Mexican territorial waters." Hackmon said, his implication clear. He pushed his tongue to one side of his mouth, pushing out his cheek, and thought about how the American flag had been removed from the radar and radio mast. "In case we should meet a Mexican Coast Guard ship, what are your orders?"

Camellion didn't hesitate. "Sink her. If she's too big, then we run. But don't worry about it. We won't run into any Mexican vessels." He placed a Trimutrolin pill on his tongue.

Hackmon debated whether or not he should ask Camellion to put that last order in writing. No. Camellion would think he was stupid. Besides, Camellion had taken a Star-Tron wide-angle scope from the Trevis rack and was scanning the water all around "Little Willie."

Its diesels a powerhouse of sound, the sub-chaser cut north through the warm waters of the Gulf of California. Traveling at maximum knots, the PCH soon began to close in on the target.

There was a loud buzzing from the central intercom, and a red light began to flash on and off at the top of a plate marked "radar." The radar "hole" was directly below the center cabin.

Commander Hackmon flipped the switch that activated the voicecaster. "Yes, Houmis?"

"Sir, there are two objects ahead on the screen." The voice of the radar operator was disembodied, yet filled with tension. "The smaller object is moving west toward the larger object, which is stationary. I estimate the distance to both objects to be around seven thousand, five hundred yards. We're closing in fast sir."

"Thank you, Houmis," Hackmon replied in an even voice. "I'll leave the intercom on so that you'll know what's going on up here."

"A bit over five miles," Major Whitespear muttered thoughtfully and looked at his wristwatch. He glanced over at the Death Merchant, who had a crooked smile of satisfaction on his face. "That's damn good time."

"Full stop," ordered Commander Hackmon. At the helm, Mason DePugh cut the power; the diesels grew silent, and the sub-chaser glided to a stop in the water, bobbing slightly in the wash of the waves.

"We're going to use M3 grease guns and Colt autos," Whitespear said to Camellion. "We have several Colt CAR-15s as well. Which do you want?"

Patting the holstered weapons on his hips, Camellion shook his head. "I'll use only these Auto Mags. Machine guns are too clumsy in close quarters. One more thing, Major—tell your boys to kill anything that whispers or moves on that vessel. This is what the Israelis call an *Ain B'rerah* situation, a No-Choice situation."

"I assumed as much."

"And Major—no grenades. I'll handle the demolition when we're finished with the kill operation."

Whitespear hunched his broad shoulders. "You're in command."

He grinned like a smiling cobra, gave a mock salute, turned, and went through the bulkhead at the top of the short length of steps that ran down to the compartments below deck.

In the meanwhile, Commander Hackmon had ordered his crew to battle status. Within minutes, the individual members of the crew began to report in over the intercom. The gunner was secure in the stern turret. The crewman in the bow turret was ready. The gunner and ammo handler were ready behind the 20mm cannon, the two men and the weapon protected by a shield of armor plate.

Major Whitespear's calm, deep voice came in over the speaker.

"We're ready down here. We'll move on deck through the stern walk-in hatch when you give the word. Give us a few minutes' notice, Camellion."

"Roger," Camellion replied. Seeing Hackmon nod to De-Pugh, Richard added, "We're going in for the run now."

De Pugh started the engines, and the sub-chaser leaped forward. He increased power, and soon the ship was cutting through the water at full speed, every member of her crew ready for action.

Camellion moved closer to Hackmon, told him what he wanted, and watched as the Commander gave an order to DePugh, then piped what was going to happen throughout the ship.

"ATTENTION! We are first going to establish identity to make sure we have the target. Fire only when I give the order."

"Sir, the smaller ship has reached the larger vessel," Roger Houmis reported from the radar hole.

"Very well, Houmis. Begin full-circle scan. Use full KWs and keep a constant reading on the pulse repetition rate. If any ship of cutter size approaches, I want to know about it at once."

"Yes sir."

"Little Willie" closed in rapidly on the target. Using the Star-Tron, Camellion could now see the schooner clearly. Only several nautical miles ahead, the ship was large and two-masted, her sails tightly furled. The sails were only there for ornamental purposes, since the ship would be equipped with a gasoline or diesel motor to turn her screw.

Camellion also saw the smaller "object," which was to his right, on the port side of the schooner, whose bow was facing the sub-chaser. The small cruiser, moored at midship on the port side of the schooner, had a deep-V hull, an 8' beam and a length of 25', the kind of outboard cruiser that had a folding bulkhead which opened to a small center cabin.

We have them! The thought was a pleasant one. The cruiser had to be the boat that had brought Mudejar, Gomara, and Sojeda to the *Sea Hawk. They're as good as dead!*

He smiled when he spotted figures running back and forth on the decks, and saw several men lean out of front windows on the small bridge and point toward the sub-chaser. No doubt, they were shouting orders—*For all the good it's going to do them.*

"DePugh, keep a distance of a hundred yards on the first swing," Camellion ordered. "We must make sure it's the right target."

"It will be a strange coincidence if she's not!" murmured Hackmon.

The PCH closed the distance very quickly, DePugh swinging the craft to starboard. During the angle-out, the motion of the ship was erratic, non-rhythmic, much like a drunk with the blind staggers. Then it was done: the PCH was on a straight course, running with the wind 10 to 30 degrees off her quarter.

At a distance of 300 feet, the sub-chaser roared by the port side of the much larger vessel. The Death Merchant and Commander Hackmon, both with Star-Tron scopes pressed to their eyes, saw the name on the metal plate attached to the side of the bow—*SEA HAWK!*

A beautiful vessel she was. Snow-white and big, the kind of pleasure craft that only a millionaire could afford, a millionaire many times over. From the schooner's appearance, it was evident that she had tremendous buoyancy both fore and aft. There was a long cabin—two decks—amidships, hatches fore and aft, and a raised cargo hatch at center stern. The stern itself was a raised transom with considerable overhang.

A lover of beautiful ships and the sea, the Death Merchant could easily envision *Sea Hawk* riding the high seas. Aft from the cutwater her wooden hull broadened, and Camellion knew that her bow, when surfing down in the troughs, would never cut through, would never bury itself in the wall of the next wave, but would always rise up and over. *A classic design. They don't build them like that any more!*

Camellion and Hackmon secured their Star-Trons on the rack and the Death Merchant took over command of "Little Willie."

"You men at the cannon. When we make the next pass, sink the cruiser. Blow out its bow, but keep your fire from the stern, from the fuel tanks. I don't want an explosion. Gunners in fore and aft turrets: fire when we come up on the schooner's starboard."

Richard moved over to DePugh, who was turning the PCH in a large half-circle. "Get in within a hundred feet," Camellion ordered. "Then swing back to port and come up

156

once more to starboard. We'll board portside by the bow. Do you have all that, DePugh?"

"Yes, sir," the young sailor replied. "That will be easier than going around a roller rink."

He turned the wheel to port. The PCH practically spun on her twin screws and, her bow splitting the waves in fury, she dove through the foam toward the *Sea Hawk*. When it seemed that "Little Willie" was about to cut across the stern of the larger vessel, DePugh spun the wheel and the bow turned. Only 30 yards to starboard of *Sea Hawk*, "Little Willie" shot due south.

"By God! They're going to fire on us!" Hackmon said incredulously, catching a flash of men at the long polished brass railing of the schooner.

"You could hardly expect them to throw flowers at us!" laughed Camellion, just as the enemy opened fire. Scores of projectiles ricocheted from the steel hull and the armored turrets of the sub-chaser, dozens more bouncing from the shield protecting the 20mm cannon and making spider-web patterns in the bulletproof plennen-glass on the port side of the control compartment.

Rifles, pistols, and submachine guns were still exploding when the heavy machine guns of the sub-chaser roared in reply. Two streams of .30-caliber slugs roared from the twin M37 machine guns in the forward turret, singing a deadly duet with the heavies in the aft turret, twin M60s which were spitting out 7.62mm projectiles at the rate of 550 rounds per minute.

Within ten seconds, a dozen sailors and three mobsters were cut to pieces by the hail of lead, some of the corpses looking as if they had been hacked with axes as solid, spitzer-shaped projectiles knocked them back from the railing and pitched them across the deck, soon awash with blood and gore. Several sailors, killed instantly on their feet, fell sideways into the hatch on the forward deck.

As the PCH charged along the port side of the *Sea Hawk*, Camellion noticed a long, canvas-covered object secured on the stern deck with guy lines. Camellion knew immediately that this was the fuselage of a helicopter, minus the main rotor blades.

Now, above the roaring of heavy machine guns, he yelled at the gunners of the cannon, *"You men at the cannon: riddle whatever is under the canvas on the stern."*

The two machine-gun turrets swung as the sub-chaser

157

turned across the bow of the *Sea Hawk*, then charged north again. This time the PCH was within 75 feet of the schooner.

More .30-caliber and 7.62mm projectiles raked the port side of the schooner, killing those crewmen who had not been quick enough to leap through the bulkheads of the midship housing. Other American-made machine-gun bullets sent up clouds of splinters from the wooden walls of the housing and the two masts. Safety glass shattered and fell from port holes.

No one on board the *Sea Hawk* had expected the attack, least of all Captain August Giffin, who had been assured by Angelo Catura, the representative of the three New York City mobs, that there would not be any trouble. Frantic with fear, Captain Giffin did not have time for any regrets. On the small bridge deck, Giffin, the First Mate and the Radioman went down in a splash of blood, patches of their clothes and chunks of their flesh flying off into space as 7.62mm slugs tore away their lives, and sent what they had been into immeasurable distances and unreachable heights.

The pilot house was instantly demolished, most of the instruments turned into junk. A dry chemical fire extinguisher exploded from slugs. A chronometer was wrecked. Bullets hit a barometer. The polyaxial compass was torn apart. The "Carib" 55-channel VHF marine radio and the RDF electronic navigational receiver burst and jumped as if hit by tiny hand grenades.

The chart room was next. A Weems parallel plotter and a three-arm protractor jumped from the chart table. A .30 slug ricocheted from a steel brace of a "Sport Spot" light and hit parallel rules, knocking them to the floor. More slugs smashed into a Davis artificial horizon device and knocked it through a window. The Mark XII sextant jumped. The Davis pelorus and corrector was blown apart.

As the sub-chaser moved north, there was a louder and deeper sound from the foredeck, the *bom-bom-bom* of the 20-millimeter cannon. A dozen of the shells found the cruiser moored along the port side of *Sea Hawk*. The shells tore into the deep-V hull at the bow, right at the waterline, and ripped out the fiberglass, leaving a jagged hole the size of a washtub. The cruiser shuddered from bow to stern. Water rushed into the hole and the bow began to settle.

Bom-bom-bom-bom! More 20mm shells hit the canvas that covered the helicopter on the stern deck. There were ripping and tearing and grinding sounds. Moments later, all that remained were torn strips of smoking canvas hanging from the shattered fuselage of the helicopter. Three of the guy lines had been torn loose by the blast and, as the PCH cut across the stern of *Sea Hawk*, the fuselage sagged a few feet, but stopped when checked by the other lines.

With Mason DePugh expertly handling the wheel, the sub-chaser executed a turn with such speed that the stern skidded to the west as the bow snapped around to the east. DePugh quickly righted the long, gray craft, and once more the sharp prow stabbed straight south, the port side only a scant fifty feet from the starboard side of the shot-to-pieces schooner.

"Major Whitespear, prepare to board the target," Camellion called out, turning his head toward the intercom, which was still on the voicecaster.

The turret machine guns and the cannon were silent, the gunners finding the deck of *Sea Hawk* filled only with corpses. To all appearances, the schooner was devoid of life. Those still alive had to be waiting below decks.

Camellion took a four-section photograph folder from one chest pocket of his jumpsuit, opened it, and studied the three photographs—two men and one woman. Hector "El Perico" Mudejar! Alvar Gomara! Juanita Maria Sojeda!

"Your family?" Lieutenant Commander ventured to say.

"The condemned!" Camellion said. "They will never see the dawn."

Hackmon flicked him an amused glance. "And all men are brothers," he said ironically. "I wonder what nut first said that?"

"Alle Menschen sind Bruder!—Schiller, for one," Camellion said.

The Death Merchant turned and went through the bulkhead. He paused on the first step, then turned to the commander of the PCH. "Once we're on board the *Sea Hawk*, move off a hundred feet and wait. One of us will call when we're ready to abandon ship."

Commander Hackmon nodded and Camellion started down the steps, on his way to join Major Whitespear and the four Black Berets, catching himself on the railing as the vessel began to cut across the bow of *Sea Hawk*.

DePugh had both hands on the wheel, his feet firmly planted in the metal footholds on the deck. He started to turn the wheel before the stern of the PCH was past the bowsprit of the much larger vessel. Again the sub-chaser skidded on the water, the stern swinging south, the bow cutting to the north. Quickly and expertly DePugh righted the vessel and the bow swung toward the port side of the schooner.

Below deck, in back of the control compartment, Dean Sweets (who received a lot of good natured kidding because of his name), one of the Black Berets, cursed as he was almost thrown across the small cabin.

"This is one of the damnedest rides I've ever had," he growled.

He caught a handhold in time to keep from falling, straightened up, and started for the opposite end of the area.

"Why complain?" laughed Jerry Lofink. "Suppose you were a civilian. Think of all the troubles you'd have then! Man, you've got a home in this man's army."

Lofink, too, weaved back and forth from the motion of the little fighting craft, yet he managed to reach the bottom of the steps and get behind Arch Hubbler. The Death Merchant was at the top of the stairs, his hand on the pull-open lever of the hatch bulkhead. Major Whitespear waited behind Camellion, a .45 M3 grease gun in his right hand. The men waited. No one spoke.

DePugh eased up on the power, until the engines were barely throbbing, and eased the PCH alongside *Sea Hawk*. There was no sign of the Sports Cruiser which had been blasted in the bow by 20mm shells.

Gently the hull of the sub-chaser touched the higher port side of the schooner, the two ships rocking slightly in the water.

Although neither the Death Merchant nor the Black Berets heard Commander Hackmon's "GO!" they knew it was time to attack, not only from the sound of the diesels, but from the way the two hulls were rubbing together.

The Death Merchant pulled his two Auto Mags, threw open the bulkhead and moved out onto the stern deck of the sub-chaser. Major Whitespear and the other four Black Berets pounded the deck right behind him, each man holding his M3 with the stubby barrel pointed upward.

The deck of the *Sea Hawk* resembled a ghost ship, the corpses looking particularly hideous in the moonlight, the only sounds being the two tall masts of the schooner creaking and the water breaking against the sides of both vessels.

The Death Merchant saw that DePugh had pulled into a position that placed the stern of the sub-chaser close to the Cosom boarding ladder on the center port side of the schooner. Camellion was about to swing over the short railing of the PCH, but ducked down with the five Black Berets when the M60 heavy machine guns from the rear turret started roaring, streams of 7.62mm slugs hitting the wooden walls and going through the port holes of the stern housing. It was this long, low cabin on which the blasted fuselage of the helicopter hung. In front of the cabin was a 6 × 7-foot cargo hatch.

The gunner stuck his head out from the top of the turret and yelled, "I saw several faces in the rear deck housing!"

"Give us cover fire and make sure you keep it high," the Death Merchant yelled back at the gunner, who then dropped back down and instantly began stabbing the stern housing with high-velocity projectiles. Camellion glanced up —the slugs were high enough for safety.

He shoved one of the AMPs into a holster, crawled up over the railing of the PCH, grabbed the middle rung of the Cosom boarding ladder, and pulled himself through the opening onto the deck of *Sea Hawk*. He got to his feet, pulled out the second AMP again, raced to the front port corner of the middeck cabin and glanced up at the bridge, its windows shot out. If anyone was inside on the bridge, it was not very likely that they would rear up while the M60s were thundering.

Major Whitespear and the four Berets scrambled up the Cosom ladder and took positions in front of the center cabin, posting themselves so that they could see the fore and aft sections of the schooner and watch the bridge.

The Death Merchant gestured with one of the "Alaskan" Auto Mags toward the sloping housing of the walk-down hatch twenty feet ahead.

"I'll go below through that forward hatch," he said to Major Whitespear. "You and your boys check out the bridge and the rest of the main deck and the rear housing. *No prisoners!*"

"I think you should take one of us with you," Whitespear said, rigid in his conviction. He stared at Camellion; never had he seen a man so calm under fire. "There's no way of knowing what you might run into down there."

"I work best alone," Camellion said quietly. Without another word, he turned and ran to one side of the hatch housing, the non-slip rubber soles of his moccasins noiseless on the deck. He stepped over the corpse of a man that had most of his face and chest shot away, eased to the front of the

161

walk-down hatch, and carefully looked around the side into the opening. The door was open, and he could see a dimly lighted passageway at the bottom of the stairs.

The two .44 Magnum autoloaders in his hands, the Death Merchant started down the steps. . .

Chapter Fifteen

The suddenness of the attack, of what had happened and would have to follow, had left Juanita Maria Sojeda stunned, the hideous reality being almost too much for her to bear. This had to be a preview of hell! Worst of all was the knowledge that there was no escape. Gripping a U.S. Armalite combat rifle, she had never hated with such intensity, with such completeness, her entire consciousness brimming with rage against the people responsible for the total collapse of the transfer. The cases of weapons in the hold would never reach the *Barranca del Cobre*. The heroin in the Canyon of Copper would never be flown to *Sea Hawk*.

She was physically miserable. Enemy machine-gun slugs had wrecked the air conditioner units above decks, and the salon was becoming unbearably hot. Her scalp was wet with sweat, her hair stuck to her neck, her thin blouse to her back and breasts.

On her knees besides an ice-cube maker, Juanita glanced angrily at Hector Mudejar. *El Perico* had pulled the fancy mahogany bar from the wall and was now behind it, at the end farthest from Juanita. The giant of a man waited, watching the tiny area that was filled with the steps from the stern hatch, his finger close to the trigger of the Nato M14 automatic rifle.

Across from Juanita Sojeda, Alvar Gomara stood, his slender body against the back of a food storage locker that faced the galley. He didn't appear frightened, only hot, patient, and determined.

"Are the three *Americanos* still in the front or did they go on deck?" Juanita's whisper was wrapped in tension and tied with fear.

Gomara didn't even bother to look at her. The attention in his eyes shifted to his ears. He cocked his head slightly, listening, and renewed his grip on the Thompson submachine gun.

The type of woman who felt more secure when she was talking, Juanita turned and verbally sought the attention of The Parrot.

"None of this would have happened if you and Alvar had taken my advice," she accused the hulking Communist leader. Her low voice shook with anger and despair. "I told you both that we should have canceled the operation. I warned you and Alvar that only serious trouble could have prevented Escutia from reaching Huatabampo. We know now what happened to him. He was captured and made to talk."

"*Ud. tiene razon en este caso!*" The Parrot said bitterly. "It was a calculated risk. We lost. But we're not dead yet. Be quiet. We can't hear anyone approaching with your senseless jabbering."

Juanita replied only with her eyes, a stab of hate that splashed over Mudejar's broad back. She thought of the *Americano* who had used the name of "Justin Lawrence." Somehow she knew that he was responsible for the disaster.

The Death Merchant reached the bottom of the stairs, looked around in the dim light and saw he was in a section that would have been known as the fore peak on a cargo vessel. Behind him were two compartments—the anchor rode and the chain locker. Ahead was a narrow passageway. On each side of the passageway was a gleaming brass railing and three doors of three staterooms. Beyond the staterooms, aft, was the mess, the galley, and the salon. Then came the stern hatch space, the food and water stores, the electric generator and the stern cargo hold.

Richard moved to the right and tiptoed to the side of one of the staterooms. He thought he heard a bilge pump, but couldn't be sure. He was positive about the three submachine guns roaring from topside. Major Whitespear and his boys had found some of the enemy. Camellion's concern was below decks. A vessel of this size had to have a sizable half-deck below the second deck on which he stood. The crates of rifles and submachines and ammunition—maybe even grenades—would be stored either on that half-deck or in the cargo hatch in the stern. Nonetheless, Camellion was puzzled. The helicopter on the stern deck had been a small four-man job. It couldn't be the bird that was to have flown to Copper Canyon. A piece of the puzzle was missing. Well, time enough for that later.

Camellion leaned around the corner and looked at the stateroom doors. Next to the third door on the port side was another door, this one more narrow. *Probably the head and maybe a shower. Let's see if we have guests in the staterooms*.

Camellion unzipped the left pocket of his jumpsuit and

took out two metal balls, each one gray-colored and about half the size of a golf ball. On each metal ball was a small pull-tab. Richard stuck one Auto Mag in his belt, pulled the tab on one ball and rolled it gently down the passageway. He pulled the second tab and tossed the second ball. Not being completely round, the first ball stopped in front of the third door on the starboard side. The second ball came to a halt in the middle of the corridor. There were two slight popping sounds, and light-green-colored CSN gas began to pour from each ball.

Camellion pulled the Auto Mag from his belt and waited. It would take a minute or so for the gas to filter underneath the doors into the staterooms. *If anyone is inside, I'll soon know it. I don't think they've taken any Trimutrolin pills to immunize themselves.*

Vincent Aiuppa and Sammy Piletroto, the two Mafia gangsters hiding in the middle stateroom to Camellion's left, had never heard of CSN gas, much less the antidote of Trimutrolin. Neither had Angelo Catura, who was standing in the head, a Smith and Wesson .41 Magnum in his right hand.

All three hoodlums suddenly were convinced that they had stepped into the middle of a nightmare. Green gas began to drift upward from underneath the two doors. They tried to hold their breath, but it was impossible not to breathe. They had to inhale the gas. The instant they did, it was as if their bodies had been dipped into liquid fire. Their skin burned with agony. They couldn't breathe. Their eyes filled with tears and the coughing began, the kind of uncontrollable hacking that comes with acute bronchitis.

Self-preservation is one of the strongest instincts in the human species. This is especially true when a person thinks he is being smothered to death; then, only one thought dominates the consciousness—air. The three mobsters forgot all about the attack on the schooner. All that mattered now was instant survival. At the moment, all they wanted was fresh air.

Shaking, in the grip of a fit of coughing, Angelo Catura was the first to open a door and stagger into the corridor. Through a fog of tears, he glimpsed the tall figure of the Death Merchant and bravely tried to raise his .41 Magnum. There was an enormous blast of sound from one of Camellion's Auto Mags, and a .44 jacketed soft-point Magnum projectile hit Catura in the lower chest, knocking him back as though he had been struck by a locomotive. Unconscious from the terrific impact of the bullet, the ugly-faced mobster dropped the .41, fell against one of the stateroom doors and sagged to the floor. With a hole in him the size of a grapefruit, Catura was only a few seconds from infinity.

Vincent Aiuppa and Sammy Piletroto, who also thought they were choking, were in the process of leaving their stateroom when the Death Merchant fired. Aiuppa's hand had turned the knob and he was pushing the door open.

Hearing the big boom of the AMP, Aiuppa made an attempt to pull the door shut, his mind a maelstrom of fear and indecision. But Sammy Piletroto, desperate for air and determined to get it at all costs, shoved violently against Vinnie before the latter could completely close the door. Coughing and gagging, Aiuppa was pushed forward, the momentum of his body throwing open the door and carrying him into the gangway.

An old-time hood who was street-wise, Aiuppa did have the presence of mind to throw himself flat and to begin triggering off shots with his .38 Colt Diamondback revolver.

Sammy Piletroto, coughing so hard it was a miracle he hadn't snapped his neck, stumbled from the stateroom, a .45 Colt Commander autoloader and a Smith and Wesson Model 59, 14-shot 9mm autoloader in his hands. As much of a pro as Aiuppa, Piletroto began firing both automatics the instant he cleared the door and was in the corridor.

After banging out Catura, the Death Merchant had moved to the left and taken a position next to the wall of the first stateroom. He made it a practice never to stay in one spot any longer than was necessary.

Aiuppa's first four .38 slugs went straight down the passage and buried themselves in the decorative paneling of the chain locker and the anchor rode. As Aiuppa pulled the trigger the fifth time, Piletroto opened fire with the Colt .45 and the 9mm Smith and Wesson automatic, the series of shots echoing up and down the long gangway. Two .45 flat-point slugs and two 9mm full-metal-jacket projectiles burned through the air as Vinnie Aiuppa's fifth .38 bullet came within several inches of Camellion's right shoulder as he leaned out from the side of the wall.

Neither Aiuppa nor Piletroto had time to fire again. The Death Merchant cut loose with both Auto Mags, firing four times at hip level. The big explosions sounded like field pieces going off; yet there was very little kick and recoil to the stainless steel autoloaders, because the muzzles of the 12½-inch barrels were Mag-na-ported.

But there was plenty of violent movement to Vinnie Aiuppa and Sammy Piletroto. One .44 JSP cut into Aiuppa's belly, blew apart his bladder, broke his spine, then tore out his back. The impact was pitching Vinnie against Piletroto, who had caught a .44 bullet in his right bronchus, when another .44 smacked him in the deltoid muscle and ripped off most of his left shoulder. The fourth .44 projectile, sounding like an egg breaking, chopped into Piletroto's right side. The lead sent tiny pieces of shirt flying, tore all the way through Piletroto's longs, shot out his left side, and struck the throat of Aiuppa, who was falling.

In the salon, The Parrot, Gomara, and Juanita Sojeda continued to wait, all three expecting the worst. Juanita remained by the ice-cube maker, her eyes mere slits. She wasn't afraid of being dead; her only worry was that she might not be able to take many of the enemy with her. Mudejar, not wanting to leave the stern entry unprotected, did not move from the end of the bar. He, too, had heard the loud gunfire, but from his position was unable to look up the passageway, any more than Juanita Sojeda could. The ice-cube making machine was too far from the length of corridor.

However, one side of the food storage locker in the galley was even with the corridor. All that Alvar Gomara had to do was stick out his head from behind the locker in order to see up through the galley, the mess, and the gangway beyond.

That is what the revolutionary leader did—just as the Death Merchant put the second .44 AMP slug into Sammy Piletroto.

Santo Madre Dios! To his sorrow and anger, Gomara saw Aiuppa and Piletroto jerking like two puppets—and the cause of their dance of death: a man in a dark jumpsuit, two big shiny pistols in his hands. And two objects on the teak floor, hissing a light green gas!

"There's only one man—and there's some kind of gas!" Gomara yelled at Sojeda and Perico. Then, with a speed that was astonishing, Gomara jerked the Thompson sub around the corner of the food locker and sent a storm of .45 slugs at the Death Merchant, the loud roaring of the

Chicago chopper shaking the glasses and bottles on the bar in the salon.

The Death Merchant, knowing that he did not have time to raise the Auto Mags and fire, jerked back to the side of the stateroom the instant he saw Gomara step out into the passage with the deadly Thompson chatterbox. Slugs cut into the corner of the stateroom, throwing out splinters and chips. Other .45 projectiles buried themselves in the wall paneling behind Camellion, who got down on his knees, leaned over and, holding an Auto Mag so low that the end of the butt was touching the floor, shoved the big weapon around the corner, pointed the barrel upward and fired four times very rapidly. He moved the weapon slightly with each shot. He then pulled the weapon back in, extracted the empty clip and dropped it into his pocket. He next took a full magazine from a leather case on his belt, shoved it into the butt, cocked the AMP, and sent a .44 cartridge into the firing chamber. He didn't enjoy his lack of progress. He hated a Mexican standoff. *We'll have to do something about it!* He reached into his right pocket and took out three CSN balls.

Alvar Gomara was in a quandary, although not one of the Death Merchant's .44s had come close to him. One had hit the end of the sink in the galley and bounced off. Two more had cut through the metal table in the mess and buried themselves in the thick wooden ceiling. The fourth had smashed into the front of the food locker behind which Gomara was standing, the powerful slug creating a lot of racket as it smashed through cans of food and finally came to rest inside a can of tuna fish.

Juanita Sojeda looked over at Gomara, who stood with his back to the food locker, his eyes set to the left, his head tilted, as if he were expecting Camellion to come charging down the narrow passageway.

"Do you know what kind of gas it is?" Juanita Sojeda's whisper was urgent, her eyes boring holes in Gomara. "See if he's coming this way. Together we can kill the dog."

"It's a greenish gas," said Gomara, "and it's drifting this way. Whoever the man is, he is good. The three *Americano bandoleros* are dead."

In front of the ice-cube machine, there was only a drop table hinged to the thin partition that separated the galley from the salon. Pushing her AR18 in front of her, Juanita Sojeda began to crawl to the side of the partition.

She twisted around in terror at the roaring of *Perico's* M14 A–R. Only The Parrot had seen what had happened. The figure of a man had suddenly appeared at the bottom of the steps in the areaway just outside the Salon. It appeared as if he had jumped. Mudejar had fired instantly, the stream of 7.62mm slugs ripping open the man from neck to navel.

At once The Parrot saw his mistake. The "man" he had just cut open with slugs was a corpse! He had been a corpse even before Mudejar had fired! The clever enemy had thrown the dead sailor down the steps to see if anyone was waiting, to draw fire, and *Perico* had fallen for the ploy.

Mudejar cursed with the rapidity of an electric typewriter. In desperation, he looked around him. Then he remembered that Gomara had said there was only one man attacking from the bow.

The Death Merchant, still on his knees, looked around the corner of the stateroom. He heard the chatter of M3 grease guns on the main deck, toward the stern, and knew that more of the enemy had been alive than he had anticipated.

Could Mudejar, Gomara, and Sojeda be among them?

Camellion stood up, pulled the tab from the first CSN gas bomb and threw the ball down the gangway with all his might. He was pulling the tab on the second grenade when he saw the first ball land in the center of the galley and begin hissing out gas. He tossed the second grenade, trying to place it farther than the first one. His right arm was coming down from the throw when he saw the two barrels moving into the gangway from the sides of the salon. He jumped to the right only half a second ahead of a storm of Thompson and AR18 projectiles that burned up the length of the passage and buried themselves in the wall behind him. *What a waste of ammo!* Camellion pulled both Auto Mags and listened. In a matter of seconds the CSN gas would reach the salon and whoever was holed up there.

The second CSN grenade had landed closer to the salon than the first bomb. Gomara and Sojeda had finished the cycle of firing, furious that they had missed Camellion, when they both got the first whiff of the greenish gas. Juanita Sojeda tried to scream, her entire body feeling as if it had been doused with boiling oil. But the scream was overpowered by a fit of coughing. She leaned against the partition between the galley and the salon, too miserable to think of anything but the agony flowing throughout her body.

Alvar Gomara was in the same fix, his own body tortured by a raging hacking he could not control. Incoherent thoughts flowed through his dazed mind, and he had the impression that an invisible entity was slowly pulling his soul through his lungs. But he held onto the Thompson; the sub-gun was the only emotional security he had.

Hearing the coughing, the Death Merchant started to race down the gangway, Auto Mags in his hands. During those same moments, Hector Mudejar left the end of the bar, in a last-ditch effort to stop whoever was attacking from the bow. Very fast for a man who weighed 270 pounds, *Perico* moved to the center of the salon and raised the M14 A–R, in that twinkle of an instant seeing a figure in some kind of dark outfit moving down the passage.

Only the Death Merchant's hair-trigger reflexes saved him from being cut in two by a dozen or more 7.62mm projectiles. While The Parrot was bringing the M14 into firing position, Camellion threw himself forward, pulling the triggers of both AMPs as his body was falling to the deck of the mess.

The Parrot pulled the trigger of the M14 at the same moment that the Death Merchant began to dive to the deck. The A–R roared and the stream of high-velocity projectiles screamed just above Camellion, three within inches of his head.

Mudejar felt the heavy M14 shuddering in his hands, heard the 7.62mm cartridges exploding, and was vaguely aware of the extractor throwing out hot shell casings. His only other impression was the big *whooommmssss* of the two Auto Mags, then a final micro-second in which he felt infinite horror, in which he realized that he had made the very last mistake of his life.

The first .44 JSP bullet hit The Parrot in the stomach, the second stabbing him high in the chest. Both projectiles, sending bits of cloth and flesh flying, hit with such force that Mudejar's body, instead of doubling up, was knocked all the way back to the spaceway that contained the steps to the stern hatch. Streaming blood, the corpse smashed against the steel steps, hung suspended for a moment, then slid slowly to the deck.

As if in a dream, Juanita Sojeda and Alvar Gomara were

aware of what had happened. Stark-naked terror gave them the strength to act, yet the agony caused by the gas had dulled their reflexes and dampened their consciousness.

Gomara did his best to shove his Thompson chatterbox around the corner of the food locker while Sojeda, who had dropped to her knees, attempted to thrust her automatic rifle around the end of the partition. Suddenly, she lost her balance, fell slightly backward, and sat down hard on her rear end.

Flat on his belly in the gangway, the Death Merchant fired both Auto Mags—once, twice, three times!

Juanita Sojeda screamed, and the lower part of her right leg seemed to slap against her left leg.

Alvar Gomara cried *"Ohhhh-uhhhhh,"* dropped his Thompson, staggered back and gaped at the stump of his left wrist from which blood was gushing. Through the tears in his eyes, he could barely see all that remained of the hand itself—a mangled mess of bloody flesh and bone lying on the deck. Odd! There wasn't any pain! Only a gigantic numbness reaching all the way to his shoulder. Half-unconscious and half-insane from his own shattered reality, Gomara stumbled outward from the rear of the food locker, doing himself a favor as he did so. By exposing himself, he ended his misery.

The Death Merchant, springing to his feet and advancing, fired again. This time the .44 Magnum bullet hit Gomara in the left temple and exploded his head. Parts of skull bone, blobs of brain and hair splattered the low ceiling, a giant jet of blood spurting from the neck of the toppling corpse.

A minute earlier, when Camellion had first fired at Gomara and Sojeda, he had fired at Juanita by instinct, judging where her body would be from the position of her hands holding the AR18. As he fired, she had stumbled backward and the .44 slug, first going through the thin metal partition, had only torn off the top of her right knee cap after she had sat down and her right leg was flying out in front of her.

In agony and only half-conscious, Juanita was lying on her left side and fumbling for the rifle when a moccasined foot pressed down firmly on the weapon.

Juanita Sojeda looked up and saw the calm face of Richard Camellion, his peculiar blue eyes boring into hers, blue eyes that might as well have been two death heads. By some sense she could not explain, she knew this man in the

171

black jumpsuit was the same agent who had called himself "Justin Lawrence," and by the same intuition she knew the name was only an alias.

"Who are you?" She stared up at him, her whisper barely audible. "At least tell me your name."

"El Mercader de Muerte!"

Juanita Sojeda's agonized expression changed to puzzlement. The Merchant of Death! What kind of name was that? It didn't make sense! Camellion ended her staring by sending a .44 bullet into her half-open mouth, a slug that blew out the back of her head. Juanita Sojeda fell back to the floor, her eyes still open and staring only now they were not seeing anything.

Richard started to move to the area beyond the Salon. From the top deck came the roaring of grease guns and, from much higher up, the racket of a helicopter moving from west to east. By the time Camellion reached the stern-hatch steps and hurried around the bloody corpse of Hector Mudejar, the machine guns had stopped firing and the sound of the chopper was fading in the distance.

"Can you hear me up there?" Camellion called up the steps.

"Yeah, we hear you!" one of the Black Berets replied.

"I'm coming up. Don't get trigger-happy."

The Death Merchant hurried up the steps. Soon he was standing in front of the stern housing, telling the Black Berets not to go below, because of the CSN gas. Then he used the walkie-talkie to contact Lieutenant Commander Hackmon and instruct him to bring the sub-chaser alongside *Sea Hawk*.

Watching the Death Merchant, most of the Black Berets lit cigarettes. Major Whitespear continued to chew on a small cigar.

"You heard the helicopter fly over?" asked Whitespear. "It was a big bastard, looked like a Sikorsky HH-3E, the kind they called the 'Jolly Green Giant' in Viet Nam. It had pontoons." Whitespear looked questioningly at Camellion. "Apparently it was going to land close by, that is until the pilot saw us. That's when the other guys on board opened fire."

"It wasn't a Mexican craft either," Dean Sweets put in.

The Death Merchant nodded. Watching "Little Willie" turning in a circle toward the port side of *Sea Hawk*, he put together half a conclusion: *The mobsters must have changed*

172

their plans. No doubt it was the big job that was going to ferry the arms to the canyon. Or could it be that the Mafia was planning to double-cross the revolutionaries? We'll never know.

"Down below—you did what you had to do and found what you were looking for?" Whitespear's voice was only slightly curious; his face remained impassive.

Camellion said, "Major, as soon as the sub-chaser is in place, I want you to go aboard and get the G.I. rucksack I put in the cabin in back of the control compartment. Will you do that for me, please?"

"Since you said 'please,' how can I refuse?" Whitespear smiled and started toward the port side of the ship. "Little Willie" was gliding in alongside, the diesels barely throbbing.

"What's our next move?" asked Wilbert Degenhardt. He looked up at the moon as he shouldered his grease gun.

"You fellows will return to the sub-chaser," Camellion said. "I have a job to do below. After that, we go home."

A half-hour later, Camellion had found the weapons neatly stored in the half-deck below the second level. Twenty-seven cases in all—grenades, M14 rifles, Colt CAR-15 submachine guns, AR-10 light machine guns and 5.56mm Stoner assault rifles. One case contained a Stoner medium machine gun and 10,000 rounds of ammo.

There were a lot of loose ends to the mission, but the Death Merchant was positive of one fact: *These weapons will never be used by Mexican revolutionaries!*

He opened the rucksack and took out two ten-pound blocks of M5A1, a penlight-battery-powered timer, a pair of wirecutters, and a coil of Pliofilm-wrapped electric cord. Working very quickly, Camellion made the necessary connections; when he had completed the job, the timer was connected to the twenty pounds of TNT. With the utmost care, he turned the knob of the timer until the red pointer was on 45MIN. Forty-five minutes. Two thousand, seven hundred seconds. When the timer reached zero, an electric spark would travel from the timer to the blasting caps in the blocks of TNT. Then—*bloooie!*

To the tune of the ticking timer, the Death Merchant left the half-deck and hurried to the bow of the second deck. Once more he stood in front of the bullet-riddled paneling of the chain locker and the anchor rode. Here he connected an electric timer to a ten-pound block of M5A1, put the block on the deck, and set the timer for twenty minutes.

"*Hasta luego, Sea Hawk,*" he muttered. "May you rest in a million pieces."

The job completed, Camellion raced up the steps of the forward hatch, rushed to the port side of the ship and lowered himself to the stern deck of the sub-chaser, which, as soon as he was on board, roared away.

In the control compartment, the Death Merchant looked directly at Mason DePugh. "Take us a mile away, then come to a full stop. We'll watch the fireworks." He turned to Commander Hackmon, who was admiring Camellion's self-assurance.

"What does the radar show?" Camellion asked.

"All clear," Hackmon said. "The way the Gulf is, you'd think the Mexican Coast Guard is on vacation."

The Death Merchant smiled, but did not reply.

The first explosion, in the bow of the *Sea Hawk*, came on schedule. Camellion and the other men could see the ship riding at anchor, silent, deserted, her outline dim in the moonlight. Suddenly there was a tremendous roar. The bow vanished, and wreckage began to rain down, peppering the water. Just as quickly, *Sea Hawk* started to sink where the bow had been. Within a minute the forward mast was under. The middeck housing followed. A few minutes more and the aft mast slid under the waves. For several long moments the round stern, the screw and the rudder, all three vertical, seemed to hang suspended, as though the water were made of concrete. Then they, too, were gone, and there was nothing but some floating debris, disturbed water, and an occasional big bubble that burst on the surface.

"That is that!" Major Whitespear said. Pleased, he laughed, almost brightly. "I don't know what all this was about, but I suppose it was a success."

"It will be," Camellion said, "just as soon as the second charge goes off." He pretended not to notice the surprised look on the faces of Whitespear and Commander Hackmon.

They waited, "Little Willie" bobbing gently in the water. Finally, there was a sound like distant thunder, only closer and heavier. A mile behind, where *Sea Hawk* had sunk, the shimmering water rose in a mound, a hill that expanded, rose, and spread in circumference. Slowly the mass subsided. The water became level, although the waves were heavier and higher as they rolled outward from the invisible circle.

"Gentlemen, let's go home," the Death Merchant said.

Chapter Sixteen

The six men waited in the boatdeck wardroom of the U.S.S. *Chanticleer*, cat-napping and drinking coffee. They spoke little; when they did speak, their conversation drifted among trivialities, "safe subjects." Not only did Moore and Eubanks have little in common with Huff and Korse, but collectively the four of them did not even know the names of the other two men, who had not offered to introduce themselves. One of the men was an ordinary-looking individual, the type of non-person one sees on the street but can't describe five minutes later. He called the big man "Vallie." The huge man, who looked as if his muscles had been welded together, addressed the smaller individual as "Walt."

Half a dozen times during the night the two strangers had gone to the radio room, never explaining why.

The six sat and waited. They smoked, drank more coffee, and occasionally went to the head. At 0300 hours a sailor brought a tray of sandwiches. They ate and went back to waiting.

"It will be dawn soon," Leland Moore said.

"Yeah," the man named Vallie said.

Eldridge Eubanks got up and started for the windows on the port side. "They should be coming back soon."

"If they're coming back!" Harley Korse said.

Eubanks didn't notice the first sign of dawn. Men of the land never realize that the first light, coming perhaps an hour before the sun reaches the horizon, is imperceptible. A slight grayness slowly becomes evident in the east. If the weather has been clear, as it was this night, some of the smaller stars disappear and the gray develops a faint pink hue. Time begins to quicken, and as the advancing sun pushes its light up over the edge of the sea, waves become defined.

This morning, as the white moon hung very low, the color intensified, playing off the thin, high clouds which roofed the early morning sky. The sea began to reflect the pink glow as it radiated its own awakening blue.

Watching, Eubanks reflected that there was so much in life he had missed, simple things no one ever thinks about until too late.

The lower clouds took on a bright reddish color, and then, at last, the top of the sun broke out of the depths in the east. At last, too, Eubanks saw in the distance that for which they had been waiting all night—the sub-chaser.

He cleared his throat, wanting to sound detached and professional.

"I think I see the boat," he said. "I'm not sure."

The five other men moved quickly to the port windows, Moore and the big man named Vallie carrying binoculars which they quickly focused.

After a short while, Vallie said, "Yeah, it's 'Little Willie' all right. Camellion's pulled it off. He always does."

Watching the sub-chaser grow larger—they still could not hear its engines—Harley Korse muttered, "I sometimes wonder whether Camellion's a hero or a maniac!"

Vallie lowered the binoculars. "More often than not, there's very little difference between the two." He turned from the window and walked to the coffeepot on the wardroom table.

After "Little Willie" had docked next to *Chanticleer* and the Death Merchant boarded the gunboat, he went straight to the wardroom on the boatdeck, acknowledged greetings, poured a cup of coffee, and sat down at the table.

"Damn it, tell us what happened!" Leland Moore said impatiently.

"What about the arms on *Sea Hawk?* Did you find them?" Nor could Cletus Huff contain himself.

"And the heroin?" Harley Korse was gruff. "Did you make contact with the revolutionaries?"

"*Sea Hawk* is scattered all over the bottom of the Gulf of California," Camellion said, taking a pillbox from his breast pocket. "And so are the illegal weapons and Mudejar, Gomara, and Sojeda. My end of the operation was a complete success."

He opened the small box, took out a 10-milligram, heart-shaped Benzedrine tablet, put it on the end of his tongue, and took a sip of coffee.

An angry expression fell over Leland Moore's face, and his sharp eyes stabbed at the Death Merchant. He noticed that Eubanks and Huff and Korse were also confused.

"What do you mean by your end of the operation?" Moore demanded.

"All in due time, after we get back to Mexico City," Camellion said evenly, but all the while he was looking at

177

Vallie West. "Val, how did the strike on the mainland work out?"

"Verbal or Eyes Only?" West pushed the end of a Carlton into a Tar Gard filter-holder and looked up at Camellion.

"Eyes Only," Camellion said and took another swallow of coffee.

"You were right," Walter Snibben said. He smiled at the Death Merchant, then looked at Vallie West, who was taking a folded square of pink paper from his shirt pocket.

Leland Moore's temper joined forces with his pride, and the counterespionage agent blew his stack. "I've had enough of this, Camellion!" he raged, half-rising from the table. "El and I are an integral part of this operation, and so are Huff and Korse. Yet we're being treated like pariahs. I demand to know why!"

"First you plan the strike behind our backs, and now you won't report the total results!" Harley Korse backed up Moore. "None of us are the 'leak,' if that's what you're thinking!"

Reading what was printed on the sheet of paper, the Death Merchant didn't look up. "You'll get all the facts as soon as we get back to Mexico City. We'll fly straight from here to there."

Korse and Eubanks drew back in surprise. Moore tried to read the Death Merchant's expression, but as usual Camellion's face did not reveal what he might be thinking.

"I suppose we're going to refuel in midair?" Huff tried to make the question sound like a joke. He crushed out his cigarette in a tray already so full that it resembled a crooked model of the Tower of Babel.

"In a sense, yes," Camellion said, giving Huff a smile. He folded the sheet of paper and tucked it into one of his hip pockets. "During the night, Navy technicians installed an extra fuel tank in the Bell. We'll take off as soon as we have some breakfast."

"None of this makes sense," said Moore in disgust. He glared furiously at Camellion. "When we make our report I—"

"I don't give a damn what you put in your report!" Camellion interrupted, but in a soft voice. "And who says it has to make sense? A lot of things in this world are a paradox and lack sense."

Moore exhaled with a slight shudder of tension and temper. Leaning back in the chair, he told himself that before this day was over, he would have all the facts of the mission. *I'm not going to wait forever!*

Nineteen hours later, after he and the others had flown back to Mexico City, Moore was still waiting! So were Eldridge Eubanks, Harley Korse, and Cletus Huff. All remained in the dark, even though the two Spanish-style swag lamps in Eubanks' study were burning.

Moore wondered how it was possible for Richard Camellion to keep going without sleep. His energy had to come from more than those damned Benzedrine pills. Here it was 11:30 P.M., and Camellion had energy to burn. Moore then remembered that Camellion had slept several hours after the Bell had landed and all of them had driven to Eubanks' home on the outskirts of Chapultepec. Eubanks had called Polar Cold's office, instructing Rossana to come to the house that night. Everyone had hit the sack and slept until 9:30 P.M., except Camellion, who had told the others he slept for only a few hours. "I had a lot of thinking that had to get done," he had given as an explanation.

Rossana had arrived at eleven-fifteen, and the six of them had gone directly to the study.

Moore leaned back in the Dina Lounge chair and saw that Eubanks, wiping his glasses with a tissue, was getting ready to speak. But Eubanks closed his mouth and waited when he saw Camellion take a square of folded yellow paper from his shirt pocket.

"OK, we'll get down to hard cases," said Camellion, who was dressed in a brick-colored nylon-knit shirt, slacks to match, and wore brown suede moc boots. Getting up from the chair, he handed the square of paper to Eubanks, who was sitting next to him, and walked across the room to a series of decorative storage cubes, on top of which Rossana had placed her handbag, a black grain leather job with an adjustable shoulder strap. Looking very clean and well-groomed in a peach cap-sleeve jumpsuit, Rossana sat next to the cubes.

"I'll be damned!" muttered Eubanks, who was staring at the yellow sheet of paper.

Rossana looked up in bewilderment at Camellion as he picked up her bag and opened it. "Richard, what do you think you're doing?" Her voice was sharp, and her expression of dismay had been replaced by one of anger.

Harley Korse and Cletus Huff sat as still as two schoolboys caught cheating. Both stared at Camellion and Rossana del Moreno. A look of shock on his face, Eubanks got up, took half a dozen steps, and handed the yellow sheet of paper to Leland Moore.

The Death Merchant pulled a .25 caliber Astra automatic from the middle compartment of Rossana's bag, grinned down at the infuriated young woman, dropped the gun into his pocket and closed the bag.

"I always carry a pistol," she said, her tone neutral, her eyes careful and watchful. "What are you trying to prove?"

"Baby, your career is over," Camellion declared. "The KGB here in Mexico City will have to scratch you from its list of active agents."

He swung around, his cold blue eyes raking the four astonished men.

"She's the 'hole in the dike,' the mysterious informer who's been making life unpleasant for us. At this point, I can't say whether she's regular KGB or a 'developed' agent. The Center can get that out of her once she's back in the States."

Camellion turned and smiled at Rossana, whose carmine lips twisted in confusion and whose eyes grew more fixed with worry. But her voice was remarkably calm.

"Richard, you're either crazy or you've made a very serious mistake." She uncrossed, then recrossed her legs; she next attempted a slight laugh, which only betrayed her fear and concern. "I think you must be joking! You have to be!"

"I wish I were," sighed Camellion. "But you're *it*, honey child."

Handing the paper to Harley Korse, Moore was dumbfounded. He stared from Rossana to Camellion, who had moved away from Rossana and was standing in the center of the study.

"This is ridiculous!" Moore stood up, his eyes bleak, his tone icy. "That report isn't any indictment of Rossana. It's only a report that Mexican Army paratroopers parachuted last night into Copper Canyon, shot the bejesus out of Twenty-third of September League terrorists, and found the 'H' that the commies were going to trade for guns. How does that make Rossana a Russian agent?"

"You could have told us that this morning on the gun boat!" Korse said harshly, and handed the paper to Huff. "Why the cat-and-mouse play?" He jerked a thumb at Rossana, who was sitting very still, her face expressionless. "She wasn't out there with us on the *Chanticleer*. She wouldn't have known."

"I wasn't sure what might be waiting for us on this end," explained the Death Merchant. "Rossana might have popped up here unexpectedly, or something might have come up that would have forced us to go to Polar Cold. I was afraid that one of you might inadvertently have made her suspicious and suspect that we knew she was a Russian agent."

"I don't know that she is! I want some proof!" Moore demanded cuttingly. "You've talked a lot, but you haven't offered one particle of evidence. Do you realize what you're really saying? You're telling us that the Polar Cold net has been penetrated!"

Cletus Huff said pointedly, "The report says that two groups of Mexican paratroopers dropped into Copper Canyon. One contingent dropped within half a mile of Sucker Flats. The other group came down close to *El Cuchara Diable*—The Devil's Spoon. According to the report, most of the terrorists were concentrated in the Spoon! Why there? I don't get it!"

"I don't either!" Eldridge Eubanks pulled in his lower lip and looked oddly at Moore. "Why should the terrorists concentrate in the Devil's Spoon instead of on Sucker Flats, where the 'H' was stored?"

"Naturally you don't understand," Camellion said coldly. "None of you do." He turned and grinned like a wolf at Rossana, who seemed to shrink perceptibly before his eyes. "Without any of you knowing about it, I told her that night —the night we had the final meeting—that, instead of landing half a mile from Sucker Flats, we were going to set down in the middle of The Devil's Spoon." He continued to stare at Rossana. "She wanted to make sure we'd get a rousing welcome. No doubt she tipped off the League the very next day, and somehow The Parrot and the other two worked quickly enough to move their troops to the Spoon. No doubt they used short-wave to get the message to the canyon."

Moore was not convinced. Neither was Eubanks.

"But we have proof that the Soviets aren't working with the League!" Eubanks' tone was as desperate as his eyes were sad. "Juanita Sojeda's hatred of the Russian brand of communism was well known. She preached Marxism, yet always warned her followers of the danger of becoming Soviet captives, like that fool Castro and his Cuba."

Camellion spread his hands. "Maybe the KGB had a thread to The Parrot or to Gomara? At this point it doesn't matter. The fact that the Russians had the thread is what counts. The KGB had to have a pipeline or Rossana wouldn't have been able to warn the League about the Spoon. The Center will get the truth out of her!"

The Death Merchant grinned again at Rossana. "Care to tell us how it was done?"

"I haven't the faintest idea of what you're talking about," she said stiffly. Coolly smoking a cigarette, she looked down at her long fingernails.

"The trap on San Juan?" Moore's voice was ominous. He continued to stand, his arms folded. "I suppose she set you up for that Russian kidnap job?"

"Why should she?" asked Eubanks, not giving the Death Merchant a chance to reply. "We can assume that she tipped off the KGB that you were an American agent, but why should they want to put the snatch on you? What information would you have that would force the KGB to take such desperate measures?"

"The Russians thought I knew the names of Polar Cold's cell members!" Camellion sounded amused as he spoke, and he looked as if he were enjoying himself as he sat down in a lounge chair not far from Rossana and crossed his legs. "You see, I told Rossana that I knew the names of all forty-six cell members—the first night I stayed at her apartment. The KGB also wanted those names."

He looked at Rossana, who was now glaring at him in quiet hatred.

Camellion continued to speak in a serene tone. "I could be wrong, but I think her original job was not only to infiltrate your net, which she accomplished, but to obtain the names of all the cell members. But don't blame yourselves. It was the fault of the Center. It was the Stateside boys who checked her out. She fooled them, too!"

Leland Moore's eyes glittered as gears of logic meshed "And the KGB couldn't grab me or El because that would put the network wise, and it would reorganize cell groups. But what made you suspect Rossana?"

The Death Merchant sighed and put his hands on the arms of the chair. "I didn't suspect her, not at first. I was only fishing, throwing out lines. I'm a natural born paranoiac After the trap on San Juan, I didn't know whether the League had set me up or if one of you was the leak. Bu when I learned that there wasn't any trap at the sugar mill, I had to cross off the League. Then there was only one conclusion to be drawn: one of you had to have told the KGB about the apartment on San Juan. The KGB in Mexico had always been careful not to become involved with League activities. The KGB knew we were after the League, and under ordinary circumstances the Russians would have stayed out of it. But the chance to obtain the Polar Cold cell names was too good to pass up. Rossana gave them the address and the trap was set."

"I'll be damned!" growled Moore in disgust.

"According to many critics of the CIA, you will be!" Camellion laughed slightly, and then once more grew serious. "It was then I began to suspect Rossana, figuring that he Russians assumed I knew the names of the cell members. But I needed proof. That proof came when the Mexican intelligence service reported to West, on the gunboat, that most of the commies had been found in the Spoon. Only Rossana could have warned the League. The Russians wanted us dead."

"How about clearing up the deal that Uncle Sam must have made with the Mexican government?" Harley Korse was subdued, his tone respectful. "Would I be wrong in saying that's why there weren't any Mexican Coast Guard vessels in the Gulf?"

"You'd be right," Camellion said and smiled. "I don't know he details. I can only tell you that the Federales and the Mexican narcotics people weren't in on it. As far as I know, only the Mexican intelligence service was in on the mutual effort of cooperation, and it didn't act until the same day we made contact with the *Chanticleer*, because of security reasons."

Leland Moore heaved a long, drawn-out sigh and sat down heavily.

"Polar Cold is finished, useless"—he jerked his head toward Rossana—"thanks to that treacherous bitch. She'll get to the States! I assure you of that! And by the time the Center is finished with her, she will have set an all-time record for talking in the history of vocal cords."

"Polar Cold can still function," the Death Merchant said, "but the network will have to be reorganized." He looked again at Rossana del Moreno, the faintest curl of a smile on his lips. "But she won't be around."

Rossana's fury and hatred boiled over, exploding with all

the sudden rage of a trapped animal fighting for its life. A kind of snarling moan rumbled low in her throat and came out between her clenched teeth. She shot out of her chair and lunged at the Death Merchant, a look of insane determination twisting her features into something that did not resemble anything human. Her hands were raised, her long nails aimed at his face.

Camellion moved with such fantastic speed that Rossana could have been standing still. There was a blur of movement. Richard's right arm shot up and his fist thudded against Rossana's chin in a short uppercut. Her eyes rolled in her head and, out cold, she sank to the rug.

"Better drug her before she wakes up," Camellion suggested to Moore and Eubanks. "You'll have less difficulty with her. Getting her to the States is your job." He yawned. "Me, I'm going to bed. Tomorrow I'll fly back to the United States. Goodnight, gentlemen."

He turned and left the study, thinking of the lie he had just told. Back to the United States? No. He would fly to Belize City in British Belize, in Central America.

Then on to Surinam, the purgatory of South America!